it's
BOBA
Time
for Pearl Li!

it's
BOBA
Time
for Pearl Li!

NICOLE CHEN

Quill Tree Books
An Imprint of HarperCollinsPublishers

Quill Tree Books is an imprint of HarperCollins Publishers.

It's Boba Time for Pearl Li!

ISBN 978-0-06-322861-0

Typography by Kathy H. Lam
23 24 25 26 27 LBC 5 4 3 2 1
First Edition

* ❉ *

For Kaia, whose bottomless well
of creativity inspires me every day.

CHAPTER

1

I DECIDED TO NAME THE hot dog Oscar. I mean, how clever is that? Oscar as in Oscar Mayer, the meat company. Get it? Hilarious, if I do say so myself. Even if hot dogs aren't exactly a common dish in the Li household.

Unfortunately, a funny name was the only good idea my brain had last night. Because after I stitched through the tail end of the yarn and tucked it into Oscar's stuffing, I popped him into my backpack so I could bring him to school. With his little beaded eyes and slightly crooked smile, my newest crochet creation was just too adorable to keep to myself.

I didn't mean to sew his smile that way. I counted the number of stitches between his eyes wrong and ended up with an even number, which made centering his smile impossible. But I liked the way his crooked smile made it look like he knew something no one else did. And that yellow stripe I stitched onto his body for mustard . . . Oscar was a true masterpiece!

Priya and Cindy, my two best friends, would love him. I *had* to take him on a field trip to Lynbrook Middle School.

What a mistake.

Fast-forward to now. The sound we'd been waiting for all day had finally rung, and just like that, sixth grade was over. Summer had officially started!

I couldn't wait to get out of the most boring computer skills class ever. I scooped up what was on the desk and grabbed my backpack to shove everything in . . .

And out tumbled Oscar.

After a few somersaults, he bumped up next to the crisp, clean white sneaker of Miss Perfect herself, Kendall Stewart.

I lunged forward. But before I could get him back to safety, Kendall had Oscar in her manicured hands.

"What's this?" She turned him around to get a better look. "Aren't we a little old to be playing with dolls, Pearl?"

My cheeks burned. But against my tan skin, I knew it wouldn't show. My mom liked to remind me that it was a good thing to not have your emotions show on your face. That way, you could hide them better. But sometimes, I wished they could do the talking for me. Maybe people wouldn't be so quick to look past me if they knew what I was really feeling.

Or if I had the guts to tell them.

I'm not playing with dolls, I wanted to shout. I'm definitely too old for that. But making them with your own two hands? That's not easy!

Did I say what I was thinking, though? Of course not. My mouth liked to stop working whenever I had to confront someone, especially someone like Kendall Stewart. She always looked like she just stepped out of a movie, shining with that energy only beautiful, confident people have. Even the plastic charms on her bracelet matched the swirly pattern of the sundress she was wearing.

"Hey, give that back!" Priya leapt to my rescue, her eyes flashing and her long hair whipping forward like a bolt of black lightning. She snatched Oscar from Kendall, shoved him back into my hands, and pulled me out of the classroom in a huff.

When we got outside, I sighed with relief and threw my arm around her.

"You're my knight in shining armor, as usual." I laughed.

She flashed me a smile as big and bright as her oversized

red sweater. "And you're my damsel in distress," she quipped back, slinging her own arm around my neck.

That was our running joke ever since we became best friends in third grade. Even then, Priya was a fierce defender of the meek. The other kids always teased me for how small I was. But it was the day that a boy called me a "ching chong with glasses" that our friendship really took off. She shoved the boy so hard into the mud that he had to find another pair of pants from the lost and found.

Then we bonded over our love of crafts when I shyly presented her with a rainbow clay lump covered with mounds of glitter as a thank-you. As we'd gotten older, I could still count on her to be my voice when it wouldn't come out on its own.

"Now that you've been rescued, let me see!" She held out her hand, flipping her hair back in that dramatic way she always did. I tossed her Oscar.

"I love it!" she cooed, turning him around. "Very pop art."

"I finally finished him last night." I pushed my glasses back up my nose. Charm bracelets weren't my thing, but a fun collection of glasses was! The last day of sixth grade deserved a little extra flair, so I had picked out my bright red cat-eyed pair this morning. "See, I even sewed on mustard with this single crochet strand."

A jingling sound approached us from behind. Priya

and I looked at each other and grinned. Without turning around, we both called out, "Hey, Cindy!"

"Aww, how adorable!" Sure enough, it was Cindy, our other best friend. The long earrings dangling below her cropped haircut and the key chain collection hanging from her backpack always announced her arrival. She was like a cat with a bell on its collar.

"Wanna know what his name is?" I paused for dramatic effect. "It's Oscar!"

Priya burst out laughing. But Cindy cocked her head and frowned. "Oscar? I don't get it."

"Oh, sorry. Oscar Mayer is this huge meat company that makes hot dogs and ham and other stuff like that in the US," I explained. Cindy was new to Sunnydale and had moved here from Hong Kong at the beginning of the school year. Sometimes these types of jokes went over her head.

Her English was perfect, though, at least to my ear. But the principal was still making her take an ESL, or English as a Second Language, class, just because she mixed and matched words in a funny way and had an accent that made her sound British sometimes.

But Cindy didn't complain. "It's an easy A," she'd say.

"Now that we're seventh graders, what should we do in our first few hours of summer vacation?" I led my two best friends down the building steps and toward the bike racks in front of the school.

Suddenly, my pocket buzzed. I pulled out my phone

Incoming text from Mom.

Uh-oh. I had a feeling I knew what the message was going to say.

I swiped at it anyway.

Congrats on finishing sixth grade! So sorry, but Dad and I have to work late today. Rain check on dinner at A&J's? I put $20 in your account. Treat yourself to delivery tonight.

My heart sank. They had to work late again? My parents had promised that they'd take me to my favorite restaurant tonight to celebrate the end of the school year. The beef noodle soup at A&J's was amazing. It had exactly the right amount of spice, with the most tender beef chunks and chewy, thick noodles. Yum.

It'd also be the first time this week I'd get to sit down and have a nice, relaxing dinner with my very busy family. Or so I had hoped.

Forget it. Like they care I'm an official seventh grader now.

I closed my eyes and pictured the sad feeling sliding

off my body and out through my arms, like I'd learned from the meditation app our teachers made us download for Life Skills class.

My phone buzzed again: *$20 has been deposited to your account.*

Ugh. Who wants to eat cold, sad delivery food by themselves in an empty house on the first day of summer vacation? Even if my older sister, Jade, happened to be home, she'd be holed up in her room tip-tapping away at her computer and ignoring me anyway.

No, thank you. I knew what I wanted to do with this consolation prize of a family dinner.

"How about a drink at Boba Time? My treat! You can get as many toppings as you want—even double scoops of pudding." I jabbed at Cindy playfully with my elbow and waggled my eyebrows at Priya.

"You know I can't say no to that!" Cindy shouted, her earrings swinging up and down. "Zǒu ba!" Cindy always slipped into Mandarin Chinese when she got excited, and I loved hearing it. It was like sharing a secret that only the two of us knew.

Cindy was right: Let's go!

It was time to kick off the summer. And the best way to do that was a visit to my favorite place in town—Boba Time.

CHAPTER
2

WE BIKED TO EASTRIDGE VILLAGE and locked up by the racks in front of the barbershop with the neon "Open" sign that always buzzed and flickered when you walked by. It was kind of a sad shop, actually. The red-white-and-blue pole was broken and no longer spinning in the cheerful way it had been when I first started coming to Boba Time.

In fact, there was nothing interesting about Eastridge Village. It was like all the other egg-colored, brown-roofed strip malls that linked together in a never-ending chain along Sunnydale's main road.

But tucked away in the corner, with its pale blue awning and shiny metal round table out front, was Boba Time. It was the best boba shop in town, hands down.

The bells hanging on the front door jangled as Priya swung it open. The smell of tea and herbs and honey immediately floated over us.

"Hello?" I called out. The shop was empty, like it was a lot these days. But cheerful Chinese pop music filled the air, and the shelves were stocked full with shiny golden jars and colorful boxes like Lego bricks, all filled with loose-leaf teas and Chinese herbs. A red Crock-Pot with tea eggs inside bubbled on the counter.

"Auntie Cha?" I called out again.

A tangled mop of jet-black hair peppered with a few gray strands and piled high in a loose bun rose from behind the counter. Auntie Cha's eyes crinkled when she recognized me, a big smile breaking across her face. She blew away escaped strands of hair and wiped her hands on the black apron tied around her waist, then came around to our side of the counter. She swept me up in a big whirlwind of a hug, her long skirt swirling around our feet.

"Pearl! Welcome!" she exclaimed in Taiwanese. "Congratulations on finishing sixth grade!"

"Xièxie, Chá āyí," I replied in Mandarin, returning her hug with a big one of my own. Auntie Cha, the owner of Boba Time, always made me laugh. The energy she gave off made the air buzz with positive vibes. Even her body flowed with soothing movement, her arms fluttering like a butterfly from the silk blouses she wore as she bustled around the shop making tea for customers.

Most Taiwanese and Chinese aunties in Sunnydale were so serious and proper and only ever wanted to talk about my grades and what my older sister, Jade, was up to. But Auntie Cha was different. She didn't care what anyone else thought and just did her thing, which was run her tea shop.

"Nǐ hǎo, Chá āyí," Cindy chimed in, also greeting her in Mandarin.

The first time we brought Cindy to Boba Time, Priya told me she was surprised to hear Cindy call Auntie Cha "āyí," or "auntie," in Chinese, too.

"I always thought Auntie Cha was your real aunt! You two seem so close," she protested when I broke into giggles.

"No, no, I call her that to be polite. It's a way for Chinese kids to show respect to adults." I laughed. "Her last name isn't Chá, either. It's Yáng. 'Chá' means 'tea' in Mandarin, and everyone calls her that."

"Ooh," Priya had replied, nodding her head. "My parents make me call their Indian friends 'Auntie' and 'Uncle,' too." Like me, Priya was born here in the States, although both her parents were from Mumbai.

Then she chewed nervously on her lower lip. "So, should I call her Auntie Cha, too? Or Mrs. Cha?"

I shrugged back. "Whatever you want. It doesn't matter so much for you because you're not Chinese."

Since then, I don't think I'd ever heard Priya call Auntie Cha anything in particular. Which was a little weird, if you asked me.

As Cindy and I greeted Auntie Cha, Priya hung back, shuffling her feet awkwardly. Then she turned around and wandered off to the other side of the store.

"You are all seventh graders now! How does it feel?" Auntie Cha continued in Mandarin. She took her place behind the counter.

I beamed. "It feels great! Now I have all summer to keep working on my amigurumi."

"And I made it through my first year of school here in Sunnydale." Cindy blew out a sigh of relief. "I could keep up with everyone after all."

"Of course you could, silly." I poked her in the ribs, making her laugh. "I told you that you had nothing to worry about."

"My parents still signed me up for extra English classes over the summer, though." Cindy shrugged. "Guess it doesn't hurt to get perfect."

"You'll probably end up with better English than me." I giggled.

"If only getting used to living here was just about language. I'm glad I've got you and Priya to show me the ropes." Cindy waved in Priya's direction.

"The three of you are such smart, thoughtful girls. I had no doubt they'd help you." Auntie Cha wiped down the counter with a washcloth. "Speaking of your amigurumi, Pearl, have you made anything new lately?"

While I rummaged through my backpack for Oscar, Cindy joined Priya at a table in the corner. Priya already had a jumble of colored pencils out and was doodling away in her sketchbook.

I handed the hot dog to Auntie Cha. She clapped her hands with delight.

"Tsiok kóo-tsui-neh!" she exclaimed, switching back to Taiwanese.

"I know, he's so cute!" I replied, sticking to Mandarin. "It took me a while to sew the meat and bun together, but I managed okay."

When it was just the two of us, Auntie Cha usually spoke in Taiwanese, and I responded in Mandarin Chinese. Most people who grow up in Taiwan learn both, like Mom and Dad. But my parents thought that it'd be more helpful for me and Jade to learn Mandarin because more people spoke it, like the billion plus people in mainland China. So they spoke to me and Jade in Mandarin and asked that we respond that way, too.

Mom and Dad still used Taiwanese with each other, though. So while I understood Taiwanese pretty well,

Mandarin flowed off my tongue faster.

Auntie Cha inspected Oscar carefully, softly stroking his stitching. "Pearl, this strand of yellow mustard is a nice touch. This looks like something you can buy in a store!"

I blushed. "Aw, you always say that. I'm not *that* good."

Auntie Cha looked at me with her eyebrows raised high. "Have you shown this one to your mom?"

"No, Mom wouldn't get it." I stroked the stitches that made Oscar's crooked smile. "She never does."

Unlike Auntie Cha, my mom wasn't thrilled about my amigurumi. She'd rather I do things like learn to code or tinker with robotics. "Are you sure you should be spending all your time crocheting?" she said once when she saw me with my yarn instead of working on my geometry homework. "There are lots of new things you could challenge yourself with, like engineering or programming. Don't you want to expand your horizons and try the things that modern girls are finally empowered to do now?"

No, not really, I wanted to tell her. I wanted to do the things I liked because I liked them. Because they made me feel good. But I'd never say that to her face. That'd mean disagreeing with her, and the idea of doing that made my heart race.

"I guess so," I had finally muttered in reply before

tucking the yarn away and getting back to complementary angles.

I wondered sometimes if telling her would hurt less than seeing the little wrinkle that always appeared between her eyes whenever she saw me crocheting.

Auntie Cha, on the other hand, loved hearing about my art. She even kept a crochet teacup that I had made for her on the cash register for all her customers to see.

"Someone at school laughed at my hot dog today." I tucked my hands into my jean pockets. "That didn't feel very good."

"Oh, Pearl." Auntie Cha sighed. "You must remember that your art is for you, not for anyone else. What other people say about it doesn't matter. It's what it means to you that matters."

Easier said than done. Of course I cared about what other people said. I mean, who wouldn't?

I turned away from the counter and called out to Priya and Cindy, who were both giggling at something on Priya's phone. "What do you two want?"

Priya shrugged her shoulders. "Just my usual, please."

I groaned. "Aw, come on. It's my treat today. And it's the start of summer vacation! Try something new, like àiyù jelly or sago balls."

Priya shook her head. "No, thanks. Black tea is good enough for me."

I rolled my eyes at her. "Priya, you have no idea what you're missing. Cindy?"

Cindy jumped up from her seat and grabbed a menu off the counter. "You don't need to ask me twice! I'm going to stuff mine with a ton of good stuff."

"Now, that's more like it!" I cheered. "Priya, you sure you don't want to try anything new?"

"Yes, I'm sure," she mumbled back, then turned around to work on her drawing.

Oh well. I did my best.

While Cindy skimmed the menu, I ordered Priya's usual unsweetened black milk tea, no boba. Cindy decided to stuff her Hong Kong–style milk tea with grass jelly, two scoops of egg pudding, and extra condensed milk. My favorite was Auntie Cha's sparkling green tea with mango, which she made from scratch by pureeing real fruit. Today felt like a day for an extra scoop of boba, and I had her throw in a healthy chunk of almond tofu for good measure.

When I took out my phone to pay, the price on the reader flashed the same amount it usually did. But we had gotten loads of extra toppings. I opened my mouth to say something. The store was empty enough.

But then I caught Auntie Cha's eye.

"Congratulations again, Pearl." She winked and squeezed me on the shoulder. She handed Oscar to me, with him lying on the palms of her hands like she was giving me something precious.

I winked back.

Munching on chewy, sweet boba in a warm, cozy place surrounded by good friends and the smell of tea and honey . . .

Now this was what celebrating the end of sixth grade was supposed to feel like.

CHAPTER
3

THE SUN WAS SETTING AS I coasted up our driveway and into the garage. The evening shadows stretched across the living room, and the house was super quiet. I knew Jade was home because I'd seen her car parked on the street. But she was probably holed up in her room like she always was, tapping away at her computer.

Jade was a junior in high school—actually, now a senior—and had made waves in Sunnydale a few months ago when she designed and developed a mobile game that sold really well in the Apple App Store. Jade was a true modern girl, as my mom would say.

I had just blown the last of my dinner money on two new balls of yarn from Uncommon Threads, the knitting store I stopped at on the way home from Boba Time.

So I had to figure something out to satisfy my grumbling belly.

Luckily, the red light on the rice cooker was still on. I grabbed a bowl and scooped in some leftover rice from the night before. Then I rummaged through the pantry looking for something—anything—to make my dinner less depressingly boring.

A plastic jar with a white lid, red label, and what looked like tan-colored cotton candy inside caught my eye. It was a jar of ròusōng.

Score.

In the Li household, you could always rely on the shredded pork topping with the consistency of cotton candy to spice up a bowl of plain rice. The way that ròusōng dissolves in your mouth like a sweet and salty cloud . . .

Yum.

After scarfing down my dinner, I checked in with Jade with a knock on her bedroom door. She was sitting in the dark with her back to the door, hunched over the glowing light of her computer, a huge set of headphones perched on top of her pixie haircut. Streams of letters in different colors flashed on her screen like in that scene from *The Matrix*, an old movie that my whole family loved.

Well, everyone in my family except for me, that is.

"Hey, I'm home."

"Have you eaten?" Jade didn't take her eyes off the screen.

"Yeah."

And that was that—a typical conversation between us sisters. Sometimes I wished Jade was more like those sisters you'd see in TV shows or movies who give you advice about boys and parents and growing up.

I left my own bedroom door open a crack like my parents always wanted us to. Then I patted down my bed, moving aside mounds of loose yarn in search of my buried laptop. I finally spotted the "LOVE" sticker that adorned the cover and pulled the computer out from under a tangle of flamingo-red thread.

That "LOVE" sticker was my absolute favorite of all the decals on my laptop. Priya bought me the sticker last summer at the Handmade Craft Fair, and it had letters of the word "love" stacked together in a square. But instead of an "O," there was a pink ball of yarn.

And yarn really was my biggest love.

I discovered amigurumi last summer when my family went to Taipei, the capital of Taiwan and where my parents grew up. We had gone to visit my grandparents and our extended family, which included six pairs of real aunts and uncles, thirteen cousins, and a never-ending stream of distantly related relatives that I couldn't even start to count, let alone name.

It was so hot that showering three times a day wasn't enough to wash off all the sweat that poured out of my body every time I stepped out of an air-conditioned building and into the muggy urban air. Despite that, the trip was a blur of amazing food, bustling night markets, and nosy relatives, all oohing and aahing over how well Jade and I spoke Mandarin.

One day, we found ourselves with a whole afternoon to ourselves, just the four of us. Mom suggested we go shopping in the Xīméndīng district of Taipei, her favorite neighborhood when she was a kid like me and Jade. After a few hours wandering the streets, we needed a cool place to rest. I spotted a café with a couple tables inside that looked comfy.

Once we stepped inside, we saw right away that it wasn't an ordinary café. The tables were workbenches, and the walls were covered in rainbow after rainbow of yarn skeins. There were more colors than I'd ever seen before in my life, all in one place.

But it wasn't the cheerful yarn display that blew my mind. Stacked on the small tables in the center of the café was an array of the cutest crocheted dolls I'd ever seen. There were sea animals, zoo animals, robots, characters from books and movies, fruits and vegetables, even desserts like donuts and cupcakes. Each and every one of them had the same charming, innocent face made from two black beads or crescent-stitched eyes and teeny-tiny V-shaped mouths.

It was like stepping into a world where even the most everyday, boring things, like a coffee cup or an apple, had personality. I fell in love immediately.

"This place is adorable!" Mom had squealed like a kid, then started gushing over a display of crocheted avocado, eggplant, and corn, all smiling brightly back at us. The owner of the café must have heard her, because he came over and told us the dolls were called amigurumi, which was a mix of two Japanese words—*ami*, meaning crocheted or knitted, and *kurumi*, meaning wrapped.

"Because Japan ruled Taiwan for a while in the early 1900s, there are a lot of Japanese influences on Taiwanese culture. That inspired me to open up this store. We also offer tea and snacks," he explained, handing us a menu and motioning us to sit at an empty table.

Then Mom's face stretched even wider when she discovered that they offered homemade pineapple cake with salted egg yolk.

"These were my absolute favorite as a kid," she explained after a waiter placed a tray full of goodies on our table. "I haven't had these in years. They aren't as common as the regular kind with only pineapple." Mom picked up a small, square-shaped cake and bit into its pale yellow, crumbly crust. Inside was a bright orange chunk of baked egg yolk surrounded by pineapple filling. "Yum. Sweet and salty. Here, try a bite."

I scrunched up my nose. "Is it like the yolk in mooncakes? Um, I'm not really a fan."

"I'll try." Jade took a bite, then made a face. "Uh, no, thanks. I prefer the normal fènglísū."

Mom and Dad both burst into laughter.

"Ah, my all-American girls," Dad chuckled. "Okay, my turn. Try this." He held up what looked like a ball of squishiness sprinkled with sawdust and nestled inside a cup-shaped wrapper. "These are traditional Taiwanese peanut môa-chî."

"Mochi? Isn't that Japanese?" I poked at one with my finger.

"Well, yes, when a lot of people see a sticky rice cake like this, they think of Japanese mochi, which is usually filled with something. But we have our own version of rice cake in Taiwan, which is softer and stickier, without anything in it and served warm." He blew gently and took a bite, the môa-chî stretching as he pulled his mouth away. A puff of peanut powder dusted onto the front collar of his blue polo shirt.

"Mmm. I used to get these all the time from the food vendors at the night market in my neighborhood." Dad sighed, chewing slowly and licking off the crumbs that coated his lips.

Now it was Jade's and my turn to burst out laughing. My parents were usually the ones telling *us* not to stuff our faces with too much sugar!

It was like we were kids that day, hanging out and snacking on sweets together while surrounded by cuteness in every corner. I drank so much tea that it took me forever to fall asleep that night.

It was worth it, though. That afternoon at the amigurumi café was the best day of the whole trip. I soaked up every second of it.

But then, when we got back from the trip, Mom started her own tech company, which had something to do with financial software. Dad quit his job and joined her a few months later to help with business development and sales. Now their company was the only thing they ever talked about.

That family trip to Taiwan felt like ages ago. Or what I called "BSU."

Before the Start-Up.

After our trip, there were still a few weeks left before school started. To keep me busy and out of her hair, Mom was more than happy to buy me a few amigurumi books in English. But no matter how many books I studied or how many YouTube videos I watched, I couldn't get the yarn to hook in the right way.

Then, a few days before the start of school, Mom and Dad were working in the living room, hunched over their laptops. I had no idea where Jade had gone off to, and Priya was still away at sleepover camp. And I hadn't met Cindy yet.

Silence covered the Li house like a thick blanket. Frustrated with my amigurumi—and my absent family—I wanted to get out and do something. Anything.

Maybe something cool and refreshing would help. Even better if it was something like the yummy desserts I'd tasted on our trip. A quick online search of "Taiwanese dessert" on my phone popped up the listing for Boba Time. The most recent ones had comments like "This place just changed its name and is now serving boba and other desserts" and "More like a traditional tea shop than a hip Asian dessert place." There was even mention of the "Owner who wouldn't stop talking about tea."

Looking closer at the listing, I was surprised to see how close Boba Time was to my house. I biked by that plaza all the time on my way home. But the shop had never stood out to me.

Now that it served boba, though . . .

I had to check it out.

When I stepped inside, the decorations, the smell, the boxes and jars of tea, the wooden furniture . . . Boba

Time looked like the tea shops my family and I had explored together in Taipei. Even the woman behind the counter was dressed like a lot of the older women I'd seen in Taipei, with her flowery blouse, jade necklace, and long, rustling skirt.

Then, when she handed me my sweetened jasmine milk green tea with tapioca balls, it was full of fresh, floral flavor—not too sweet, not too bitter. And the bouncy firmness of the boba was just right. Or, as we say in Taiwanese, the balls were perfectly "QQ."

Drink in hand, I picked a table in the back of the shop and pulled out yarn, my crochet hook, and my pattern book from my bag. But after a few failed attempts, I threw the hook down and huffed out a big sigh of annoyance.

Suddenly, I heard a soft voice say in Taiwanese, "What are you making, young lady?"

Standing in front of me, with a dish towel in hand, was the woman who had made me my drink. But we had spoken in English at the counter.

"Um, I'm trying to learn how to make amigurumi," I replied in Mandarin, pointing to the pattern book. "Āyí, how did you know I understood Taiwanese?"

She wiped her hands on her apron and pulled back the other chair at the table. "Mind if I sit?"

I shook my head and motioned for her to sit.

"You can call me Auntie Cha like everyone else," she

continued. "And after watching you for a few minutes, I had a feeling you were Taiwanese." She gestured at the tangle of yarn. "Can I see?"

I handed her my crochet hook, and she scooted her chair in close and peered intently at my pattern book.

Auntie Cha studied the basic moves of amigurumi with me for the entire afternoon, only getting up to help the customers who walked through the door. Together, we worked through the instructions in my book, laughing at how awkward our fingers twisted and turned, and celebrating with tea and snacks when I got the stitches right.

Later that night, after Auntie closed up, I kept practicing the stitches in my room, until finally . . . I finished making my very first amigurumi doll! It was a little plump yellow duck, with two beady black eyes and tiny webbed feet, crooked stitches and all.

OMG. SO ADORBS.

And I had made it myself! I'd done a ton of crafts before, like painting and drawing and sculpting models with clay. But this was the first time I used something like crochet hooks to stitch something together.

Excited, I skipped down the stairs, two at a time, and barged into Mom's office to show her my first-ever crocheted creation.

I remember how she jumped when I swung open the

door. Then she turned to me with bleary eyes, blinking at the light that shone from the hallway into the dark room.

"Look, Mom! I made my first amigurumi!" I had boasted, hands outstretched.

"Ah, that's great. Let me see." Mom took the duck and smiled. "It's cute, Pearl! Nice work."

"Thanks!" I beamed back at her. "Doesn't it look like those little key chains that that amigurumi café owner in Taipei was selling? Some of these stitches are a little uneven. With more practice, though, I bet I could make more that are just as good!"

Mom handed the duck back to me, then rubbed her eyes tiredly. "Oh, Pearl. I know how much you love making things like this. But maybe you could elevate them a bit and add something different so they're not like what's been done before."

The air in my chest suddenly whooshed out of me, like a deflated whoopee cushion.

"What do you mean?" I tried to push down the disappointment that rose into my throat.

"Try to make them your own, so you're not copying something someone else has designed and made. Add a modern twist that brings it to now, rather than having these dolls be a little . . . old-fashioned." Her eyes filled with what looked like hope. Hope that I would do something, anything, to be more modern.

Or maybe it was just the reflection from her computer screen.

Whatever it was, I got the message. Amigurumi wasn't something she thought was worth my time.

But when I looked at the cheerful face of my first-ever crochet creation, it made me so happy. It was too late to go back now. I was hooked.

Get it??

Actually, that's the oldest pun in the crocheting world.

Since that day, I'd go to Boba Time to crochet, far away from Mom's judging eyes. I've made a ton of amigurumi, playing around with different techniques and tweaking patterns I'd downloaded off the internet to add a Pearl Li touch. Turned out it was fun to personalize crochet designs, like Mom had suggested. But I didn't do it to make them more "modern" or less "old-fashioned." It was to make them more special, more me.

And even though I didn't need Auntie Cha's help anymore, she still asked me about my projects every single time I stepped into her shop.

Mom never asked me about amigurumi again.

And now it was the start of another summer. Oscar was done, and I needed a new project. I'd seen a crochet pattern for an adorable set of sushi a few days ago that I had a feeling Auntie Cha would love.

I flipped open my laptop and pulled up Craftsee, this online marketplace where you could buy and sell all sorts of fun crafts stuff. I found the sushi pattern under "My Favorites" and clicked on the download button. Then I started up Netflix and hit the play button on the Chinese TV show I'd been watching.

I wrapped one end of the yarn around two fingers on my left hand, then picked up the crochet hook with my right. I used it to loop, twist, and pull the yarn tight to make a magic ring, the first step in any amigurumi project.

Then I checked the pattern for what was next.

Loop, loop, pull it tight.

Loop, loop, pull it tight.

My hands flew into the rhythm of making stitches while my attention sunk into the story unfolding on screen. Mind and body focused on two different things, but still working in perfect sync.

Loop, loop, pull it tight.

Loop, loop, pull it tight.

Knock, knock.

Startled, my hands jerked and dropped the stitch. I blinked my eyes as they shifted from the bright screen to the darkness of the bedroom. It was later than I expected.

Mom's silhouette stood in the doorway. The light

from the hallway was bright enough that I could tell that her eyes were red and her shoulders hunched in a way that usually meant she'd been sitting at a desk for a long time. But her computer bag was still strapped across her chest. She must have had more work to do; otherwise she would have left it downstairs in the study.

"How was the last day of school?" She quickly surveyed the state of my room. When her eyes landed on my crocheting, that little wrinkle appeared on her forehead.

"Fine, nothing special." I pulled my crochet hook and yarn into my lap, as if hiding it was going to magically turn me into someone she actually approved of.

She opened up her mouth like she was about to say something, then closed it quickly. "Sorry about dinner tonight. One of the engineers found a bug that would have delayed the pilot. I had to stick around to help the team fix it. How about breakfast tomorrow at Mama Yang's Kitchen?"

Ooh, Mama Yang's Kitchen! My mouth watered thinking about their sticky rice rolls with crispy dough inside.

But I was still mad at Mom for flaking on dinner.

I feigned an "I don't care" shrug of my shoulders that hopefully hid my excitement. "Sure, I guess that'd be okay."

Mom sighed. She looked pointedly at the yarn in my lap.

"Pearl, you're going to be in seventh grade soon. It's about time you started to think more seriously about your future." She cast one last long look at the yarn and turned away.

"Good night, don't stay up too late . . ." she said as she shut the door behind her.

"Too late making your silly dolls" was what she really meant, I could tell. Her disapproval practically lingered in the air, like a cloud of ròusōng.

I flopped backward and curled around my pillow.

But my art *was* serious.

CHAPTER
4

THE MOMENT I BIT INTO one of Mama Yang's crispy, flaky yóutiáos, my annoyance from the night before melted away.

It was bustling at Mama Yang's Kitchen as usual on Saturday mornings. We'd timed our arrival to beat the morning rush, so our table was already covered in a sea of white plates stacked with green onion pancakes, plastic-wrapped rice rolls, and a pile of long, crispy yóutiáo, or fried Chinese savory donuts.

"At first, we thought it was a binding error," Mom explained, wiping her mouth with a napkin and taking a small sip of tea. "The team chased that for a while until someone figured out a junior developer had used the same name for a module as one in the Python library."

"Common mistake." Jade shook her head. "You should be programming in Unity. It's so much more scalable."

My dad dipped a piece of yóutiáo into his bowl of soy milk. "We don't need that type of graphic treatment in the app. Scalability isn't an issue yet. What we need is to get some pilot users first."

You know that phrase "It's all Greek to me"? I always think of that saying whenever my family gets into these techy conversations about coding and programming. They literally speak in a different language. I concentrated on chewing.

A waiter dumped a steaming basket of xiǎolóngbāo on our table before dashing away to serve other guests. With my chopsticks, I carefully peeled a bun off the sticky paper lining the bottom of the basket, then quickly stuck my soup spoon underneath. As juice dripped onto my waiting spoon, an image of the plump bun with a kawaii face flashed into my head. What a fun amigurumi project that'd be! I'd have to think about how to get that pinched effect up top, though.

A middle-aged man in a black fleece jacket appeared at our table. We always ran into someone we knew when we came to Mama Yang's. This place was a staple in the Sunnydale Taiwanese community. There was no way to be anonymous here.

We even ran into Kendall a few months ago. Mom

recognized her and her family from the school science fair that happened earlier that week and had dragged me over to her table to say hi, like polite Taiwanese kids do.

But being dragged over there wasn't the worst part. It was how much Mom gushed over Kendall's science fair project.

For sixth-grade biology class earlier that year, we had to make 3D cell models that would get displayed at the school science fair. Then kids would vote on which one they thought was "Best in Class." My crocheting skills weren't quite there yet, and I thought the next best thing to an amigurumi doll would be a plush one. So, for two weeks, I worked hard on designing and sewing a plush eukaryotic animal cell, complete with lacy mitochondria and a Golgi apparatus made with a silk ribbon. I stitched small buttons onto the cell body for the lysosomes, then squeezed dots of puffy paint to make the teeny-tiny ribosomes. I even sewed little lashes onto the felt eyes that I added to the cell body.

My model wasn't perfect, with a few threads poking out here and there and some stitches that zigged and zagged instead of following each other in a straight, neat line. But I still loved it. It had personality!

Apparently, I was the only one who thought that. Because, on the night of the fair, when all the parents came to see our models and the voting started, I won a humiliating total of zero votes.

Zero.

Kendall's model, on the other hand, blew the competition away. She 3D-printed the whole thing, then programmed a mobile app so that when you tapped a button, a light next to each organelle would light up. Then you could read more about the organelle on the phone screen.

Her model was so incredibly techy and cool. Meanwhile, my plush cell model kept tipping over because I didn't balance it just right when I sewed all the components together.

Mom oohed and aahed in front of Kendall's table forever that night. And she kept gushing about it at Mama Yang's Kitchen. "See, Pearl, the kind of things you could do if you learned more about technology like 3D printing or how to wire up components? Kendall, your model was amazing. I'd never seen anything like it."

Kendall had beamed under Mom's praise. "Thank you, Auntie Li. I worked really hard on it. Pearl, your felt model was . . . umm . . . cute. But I could show you how you could have made it way better and way cooler if you 3D-printed some details."

I screamed at Kendall inside my head. Cute?! That's it?! Sure, my model *was* cute. But there was more! Couldn't she see how much thought and care I'd put into picking the materials and sewing them by hand?

But then Mom nudged my shoulder. "That's a great idea, Kendall! Pearl, you can do better than cute, right?"

My heart sank like a brick tossed into a pool. I was sure both Kendall and Mom could see how red my face flushed that day. But it wasn't from being mad at Kendall for saying my model could be better and cooler.

It was because Mom had just admitted in front of other people that she wasn't proud of what I could do.

Especially if it was made with some art supplies and a needle.

Thinking about that conversation made the yóutiáo in my mouth turn into glue. Luckily, it was Mr. Huang standing in front of us today, not Kendall Stewart.

"Ah, Mr. Huang, how are you?" My dad put down his chopsticks and politely greeted him in Taiwanese. We all followed suit, chiming in with our own greetings.

"Busy these days. It's the start of summer, and we're about to start the first week of camp." Mr. Huang's hands clutched two plastic take-out bags. "I'm bringing food to the instructors now." Mr. Huang ran after-school and weekend coding classes for middle and high schoolers at different locations around town. It was in one of his classes that Jade first started working on her mobile app.

"That's great to hear." Mom gestured at me. "Hear

that, Pearl? It's not too late to sign up."

Oh no. Here we go again.

I nervously pushed my glasses up my nose. "Um, okay," I mumbled back. "I'll think about it." I eyed the half-eaten rice roll on my plate.

"Yes, come try a class, Pearl!" Mr. Huang nodded enthusiastically. "I'll even let you take your first one for free. If you're anything like your sister, you're going to love coding. Then you'll be able to enjoy a long, exciting journey through the world of technology with Code Together!"

Mom clapped her hands excitedly. "That's so generous of you, Mr. Huang," she exclaimed. "Pearl, isn't that nice? There's no reason for you not to try a class now."

Ugh. There were plenty of reasons to not take a Code Together class. But I couldn't be rude to Mr. Huang. So I nodded at him with as much enthusiasm as I could muster.

"Thank you for the offer, Mr. Huang. Like I said, I'll think about it."

He flashed me a thumbs-up, then turned toward Jade. "By the way, Jade, we'd love to have you come back this summer to give a talk about your experience with us. We're thinking of expanding and opening another location, so we'll need some help marketing. Maybe even let us take a few photos of you for our brochures? You could be the face of Code Together Academy!"

"Uh, maybe?" Jade started to squirm around in her seat, and her face turned pink. Her skin was lighter than mine, more of that porcelain whiteness that so many of the Taiwanese aunties in Sunnydale seemed to love. Although some still tsked about her freckles.

I guess Mom was right. At least my darker skin did a better job of hiding what I was feeling in awkward moments like these.

Still, I wondered why Jade was so reluctant to be the face of a real business.

Mom spoke up again. "Of course Jade would be happy to help. We owe you so much, Mr. Huang, for introducing her to programming in the first place!" Her face practically burst with pride.

"Mom!" Jade shot her a look. "Thank you for the opportunity, Mr. Huang. I'll think about it, I promise," she said, the tips of her ears still a little red.

Wow, Mom and Mr. Huang were laying it on pretty thick today. Both Jade and I had to be grateful to Mr. Huang while saying no as politely as we could.

Dad cleared his voice uncomfortably. "So, a new location for Code Together? That's great! Where are you thinking?"

"Eastridge Village. The owner of that boba tea shop in the corner is thinking of selling."

My heart skipped a beat, and I nearly choked on the rice roll I'd just snuck a bite of.

What?! Was he talking about Boba Time?

Mom glanced at me, worry replacing the excitement that was on her face a few seconds ago. "How interesting," she said carefully, her voice switching from casual small talk into information-collecting mode. I could always tell when adults are walking that fine line between gathering intel but also trying not to come across as nosy. "I had no idea that Auntie Cha was thinking about giving up the shop."

Mr. Huang's voice dropped to a whisper. "Apparently, she needs to upgrade some equipment but doesn't have the money. Business hasn't been that good since Sweet Yam Cafe opened downtown."

I'd heard about Sweet Yam Cafe, although I'd never been there. According to Cindy, it was one of the most popular dessert chains coming out of Taiwan. Apparently, they didn't only serve boba tea there. They also sold bowls of tofu pudding, sweet taro balls, grass jelly, red bean soup, even shaved ice that you could top with anything you wanted. The decorations inside were supposedly very modern and flashy, and you were given a buzzer so you could wander around nearby shops until your order was ready.

Cindy told me that lines snaked out the door no matter

the time of day. The shaved ice was especially popular. It was probably an easier dessert concept for non-Asian people to get behind than tofu pudding and grass jelly.

But there was no way a place like that could be as special and warm as Boba Time.

Mr. Huang glanced at his watch. "I should get going before the next round of classes start. Please enjoy the rest of your breakfast. I'll be in touch, Jade." He slid his way through the crowded tables and past the line of waiting customers.

I stared at his retreating back, as if that could rewind time and erase what I had just heard.

I couldn't believe it. Was Boba Time really in trouble?

CHAPTER
5

MOM AND DAD EXCHANGED GLANCES, and Jade nudged me under the table with her knee. Dad reached over and put his hand on mine.

"Are you okay, Pearl?"

This was one of those moments when I wished my voice would just say what was in my head. But what if my family thought I was being silly, caring about boba tea this much? Like caring about crochet?

"Yeah, I'm fine," I mumbled, pulling my hand away. I swallowed the rice in my mouth and took a long sip of soybean milk, avoiding their eyes.

The three of them looked at each other. Mom reached for a piece of green onion pancake with her chopsticks and placed it on my plate.

"So . . . how are you planning on refactoring your code, Jade?"

To my relief, they kept talking about whatever it was they were talking about, leaving me alone with my jumbled thoughts.

What was going on at Boba Time? Sure, the shop *was* empty a lot. But I just assumed that things would pick up again over the summer, when kids were out and about more. Although it was true, too, that Boba Time was a bit old-fashioned, with mostly older Chinese and Taiwanese customers. Priya didn't like boba, so she never went without me and never brought her other friends there. Cindy, who knew about all the latest and greatest food trends from East Asia, liked going to cooler places, where she could get popping boba or flavored drinks like black sesame matcha lattes.

You didn't see a lot of kids my age at Boba Time.

But that old-fashionedness was what I loved most. Boba Time was so intimate and safe. There, I could be whoever I was. I could geek out about Chinese movies or TV shows, speak Chinese, and listen to the music that kids in Sunnydale didn't but kids in Taiwan did.

Auntie Cha loving my amigurumi also meant I could crochet as much as I wanted to. No disappointed, judgy eyes there.

Boba Time needed to be in my life.

Like a robot on autopilot, I polished off what was left on my plate. But I couldn't eat anything else. After Dad took care of the check, I followed my family out the door and across Lakeview Street to walk the few blocks between the restaurant and our car. As I lagged behind my family, I was so preoccupied that I tripped right over the sign squatting outside the art supplies store.

Oof.

Ignoring the bruise already forming on my shin, I quickly straightened the sign back up, skimming the smudged chalk as it tottered into place. And my heart leapt into my throat.

The Handmade Craft Fair was coming to town!

Every summer, Priya and I eagerly waited for Handmade to arrive in Sunnydale. We had gone together for the past three years, although she almost missed it last summer because she was still away at camp. Luckily she got back just in time.

Priya's favorite part of Handmade was chatting with the sellers about what inspired them and their creations. I was a little shy talking to strangers like that, so I focused on looking for new techniques I could learn from the crafters who crocheted.

Handmade was one of the best things about Sunnydale summers.

I spotted Dad half a block ahead.

"Hey, Dad, wait a minute!" After he flashed me a thumbs-up, I ducked into the store and grabbed a Handmade Craft flyer from the counter. Folding it up quickly, I jammed it into my back pocket before dashing outside. Then, *boom*, ran smack into someone stepping into the store.

"Ack!" we both screamed, and a tote bag hit the floor as pieces of paper went flying.

"Pearl Li! What are you doing??"

It was Kendall Stewart.

I dropped to my knees to avoid looking her in the eyes and grabbed the small, square papers scattered across the store's entryway. I quickly piled them up in a messy stack and handed it to Kendall.

"Watch where you're going next time," she scolded as she snatched her papers from my outstretched hand with a huff.

"Sorry, Kendall," I mumbled, then escaped out the door in a flash.

Ugh. She's the worst.

What was Kendall Stewart doing at an art supply store anyway?

But as I dashed down the street to catch up with my family, I decided to let it go. I had enough things on my mind, like Boba Time closing. Trying to figure out why the Queen of Tech was about to buy art supplies wasn't worth it.

I caught up with my family, and we piled into the car to head home. As my mom steered our car past Eastridge Village, I craned my neck to catch a glance of Boba Time. Somehow, it felt like if I could see Boba Time where it was supposed to be, tucked away in its little corner, then it'd mean that it'd stay there forever.

I spotted Auntie Cha sitting at the table out front and peering at a stack of papers through her reading glasses. My heart sank.

If she was outside, it meant there weren't any customers inside. Again.

Not a good sign.

CHAPTER
6

THE MINUTE OUR GARAGE DOOR shuddered shut, my mom grabbed her laptop from the kitchen counter and closed the office door behind her. My dad pulled out his phone, probably to make business calls, and Jade grabbed a can of HeySong Sarsaparilla from the fridge before heading into her room. I followed her before ducking into mine, then pulled out my crocheting from under my bed. Maybe the rhythm of counting stitches would calm me down.

But the yarn kept tangling in ways that made no sense, and I kept losing count. I threw my crochet on the ground and flopped facedown on my bed.

The truth was, I was dying to go over to Boba Time. Maybe Mr. Huang misheard Auntie Cha? Or maybe

Auntie Cha had some other plans and said she was thinking about closing Boba Time to distract Mr. Huang?

There had to be another explanation.

But what if this was none of my business? Would it be rude if I asked Auntie Cha directly? This was adult stuff . . . not kid stuff.

After two more attempts to crochet, though, it wasn't working. I had to know what was going on. Auntie Cha would be honest with me if I asked . . . right?

I need to hear the truth. For Oscar, and all the future Oscars to come.

Before I left my room, I stopped to listen at the door. Was there any chance that one of my family members was coming to comfort me? They had heard what Mr. Huang said about Boba Time at the restaurant, too.

But it was silent in the Li household. Everyone was heads down in this house turned workplace.

Guess I'm on my own.

I found my dad in the living room and told him where I was going. Then I headed to the garage, hopped onto my bike, and made it to Eastridge Village in no time.

When I stepped into Boba Time, it wasn't empty like I thought it would be. An older couple in matching blue tracksuits sat in the corner reading different sections of the Chinese newspaper.

Whew. Auntie Cha still had customers. Mr. Huang must be wrong.

I recognized the couple as friends of Cindy's parents from Hong Kong. I greeted them with a bow of my head and a "Good morning" in the little Cantonese I knew. They smiled back.

"Are you going to Cindy's to play mahjong later, Auntie Lin and Uncle Zhang?" I asked politely, in English.

"Yes, of course. It's Saturday!" Uncle Zhang responded. Auntie Lin and Uncle Zhang came to Boba Time every Saturday morning, along with a small group of other Cantonese couples. They'd sip on tea and munch on snacks before heading to Cindy's house, where her parents hosted a weekly mahjong game in the afternoon.

From behind the counter, Auntie Cha greeted me in Taiwanese as usual.

"Pearl, gâu-tsá! Good morning." Her hair bobbed in its messy black bun as she reached for a gold jar above the sink and twisted it open. She took a quick whiff, nodded to herself, and scooped a small spoonful into a red ceramic teapot. Then she motioned me over with a wave of her hand. "Come here and smell."

Despite my mood, I couldn't stop the grin that spread across my face. Not only did a visit to Boba Time usually come with a pep talk, but you could also count on some sort of lesson on tea.

I walked over to the counter and sniffed from the open jar. Was that the slight scent of rice and barley?

"Hmm. Is it . . . white tea?"

"You're right!" Auntie Cha laughed. "I've taught you well. It's white peony and is good for your immune system. The flavor is light and delicate." She twisted the jar tight and put it back on the shelf.

"So, Pearl, have you made anything new since yesterday?"

"I'm working on something, but it's not done yet, Auntie Cha." I shuffled my feet nervously. How was I going to bring up what Mr. Huang told us this morning? And with customers here?

Mom and Dad liked to remind me and Jade about the concept of miànzi, especially before occasions when we might interact with a lot of grown-ups. "Saving face is very important to Chinese people," Mom always insisted. "You never want to put someone, especially someone older, in a position that might make them look bad in front of other people." I didn't want to embarrass Auntie Cha with questions about Boba Time when there were customers around. But I needed to know what was going on.

"I can't wait to see your next creation. Your dolls are so well made that they look like you can buy them at a store!" Auntie Cha picked up a kettle and poured some hot water into the teapot, then capped the pot to allow the tea to steep.

I had asked Auntie Cha once how she kept track of how long to steep tea, especially when she was preparing different types with different timings for multiple customers. My mom used an electric timer at home that beeped. But I'd never seen a timer at Boba Time before.

"It's all up here," Auntie Cha had replied, tapping a finger to the temple of her forehead. "After you've been making tea for as long as I have, I know when it's ready."

I secretly timed her the next time I was at Boba Time with my mom and dad. Like most of the older customers, they had ordered a pot of tea instead of boba. And true enough, right as the second hand on my watch hit three minutes, Auntie Cha picked up the ceramic pot with their green tea and started pouring.

As Auntie Lin and Uncle Zhang's tea steeped, Auntie Cha bustled about, gathering together a glass pot and some teacups and placing them on a wooden tray. She grabbed a ladle and scooped up two tea eggs from the Crock-Pot on the counter, then put them in a small bowl. Her internal clock must have rung, because she picked up the ceramic pot and poured the now-perfectly-prepared, steaming tea into a glass one.

"Give me a minute," she said to me. Then she scooted around the counter and brought everything to Auntie Lin and Uncle Zhang.

"This tea will do wonders for your aches." She placed the tray down on the table with a clink and pointed to the glass pot. "I'll bring you more when you're done with this one. As you know, tea is best when it's freshly prepared."

"At other places, the tea gets ruined and will taste bitter if the leaves sit inside a pot at your table," Auntie Cha always explains to new customers when they ask about the glass pot. "Plus, the leaves last much longer by steeping them just right, removing them, drinking the tea, and then steeping the leaves again with fresh hot water. We do it right at Boba Time," she'd then say with a proud smile.

Uncle Zhang put down his newspaper while Auntie Lin poured her husband and herself some tea.

"You know best. No one in Sunnydale knows more about good tea than you." He waved at the door. "The others will be here shortly."

"You're too kind." Auntie Cha smiled back. "I'm ready for them. It's so nice to have you all here."

Seeing two of Auntie Cha's regulars appreciate her so much made my heart ache. Where would these sweet aunties and uncles spend their Saturday mornings if Auntie Cha closed Boba Time?

I suddenly had an idea.

"You're expecting more guests, Auntie Cha. Would you like some help bringing in some supplies from the back room? You just need to show me what you need."

51

"Why, yes, thank you, Pearl. That'd be very helpful. Come with me." Auntie Cha wiped her hands on her apron and gestured to me to follow.

Once we were in the storeroom and out of earshot, I took a deep breath. I had to know. "Auntie Cha, is everything okay with Boba Time?"

She spun around to face me, her eyes growing big. "What do you mean?"

"Is there anything wrong with the shop? I heard . . ." My voice trailed off.

Auntie Cha sighed and sat down hard on an industrial-sized box of disposable cups. "Ah, háizi, this is not something to concern yourself with. Let the adults worry about business."

I swallowed down the wave of disappointment rising to the surface. She didn't trust me after all?

"Auntie Cha, I'm not a kid anymore. You said so yourself. I'm going to be in seventh grade soon."

"It's true—you are not a kid anymore. You're a smart, knowledgeable young lady." She paused and looked at me intently. "Okay. I will tell you the truth."

Although I had a feeling I wasn't going to like what I was about to hear, I couldn't help but feel a small pang of pride. Auntie Cha really did treat me like a grown-up.

She folded her hands neatly on her lap. "Boba Time is not doing well. The fridge is on its last legs, and there's a strange whirring sound coming from it. But I can't afford to buy a new one or fix this one."

"How much would it cost to fix it, Auntie?" I asked.

"About two thousand American dollars."

My heart sank. That was a lot of money.

But then she continued.

"It's not only about the fridge, though. I'm also a little tired, Pearl. I've been here in the States for the last fifteen years, working at this shop by myself. I've been thinking. This might be a sign that it's time to take a step back from the shop. There are some other . . . important things I could be taking care of."

Important things? But all Auntie Cha had in Sunnydale was Boba Time. No family, no nothing.

"Auntie Cha, don't give up on Boba Time." My mind whirled, grasping at whatever straw I could. "I can help you. Mom and Dad can help you. They know a lot about business. My sister knows a lot about selling things online, too. We could try to make enough for the fridge, then think about how to get more people to come here."

"Don't worry, Pearl. I won't give up that easily. Boba Time has been my life for the last fifteen years. I built it from my own two hands. And you, and people like Auntie Lin and Uncle Zhang, mean a lot to me." She smiled tenderly at me.

"But I must be practical, too. I don't want to buy new

equipment if the shop will need to close in six months, Pearl. That will be a waste, and I don't want to waste anything." Auntie Cha reached out and touched my hand.

"I know you care very much about the shop, Pearl. Your passion reminds me of someone very dear to me. But what will be will be."

A jingle rang through the shop signaling the arrival of more customers. She stood up and wiped down the wrinkles on her apron.

"Come, I'm needed out front." Auntie Cha gave me a sad smile and squeezed my shoulder softly. Then she pointed at a corner.

"There's a box of lids I could use your help bringing to the counter. Thank you, Pearl."

Auntie Cha turned and walked away.

Now it was my turn to sit down hard.

Things were worse than I thought. Not only was Boba Time in real trouble, but Auntie Cha seemed like she had already accepted what was going to happen. And it sounded like once that fridge broke, she was going to close her shop. Then I'd have nowhere to go for my boba.

Or more importantly, for my pep talks.

The worst thing was that there wasn't anything I could do about it.

Was there?

CHAPTER
7

AFTER MY CHAT WITH AUNTIE Cha, I biked home slowly, taking lazy loops at intersections when there were no cars around. Usually, gliding along on my bike pedals made me feel calmer, like I was flying high above whatever was bothering me. And today, I really needed to feel that way.

Mr. Huang was telling the truth. Boba Time might actually go away.

Sure, there were plenty of other boba places in Sunnydale. And I could crochet at any of them without Mom around.

But Boba Time was special.

After a few more loops, I gave up and just biked straight home. Because no matter how much I glided, I couldn't get that calm feeling I needed.

Back in my room, I flopped backward onto my bed with my hands over my eyes.

Worst day ever.

Crackle crackle.

What was that??

I reached in my back pocket and yanked out the culprit. It was the Handmade Craft Fair flyer. But for some reason, seeing it made me even sadder. Handmade Craft was all that I loved about crafts . . . the community of other makers, the skills they had spent so much time perfecting, and the idea that you could make money doing the things you loved. And make other people happy at the same time.

Somehow, with the possibility of Boba Time closing, that future felt so far away for me.

I sighed. Might as well mark my calendar now for at least one thing to look forward to this summer. I unfolded the flyer, smoothed out its edges, and pinned it to the mood board that hung over my nightstand.

Then I saw the fine print.

Interested in selling your crafts? Up to 10,000 customers come to the fair every weekend! For more information on how to sign up for a booth, visit this link.

Whoa. Ten thousand people come to the fair??

There were always plenty of booths selling crocheted items at Handmade, although most of them sold wraps or blankets or scarves or baby clothes. But I'd never seen anyone sell dolls like my amigurumi.

A strange tingle started to travel up and down my back. I opened my closet door and lugged out the big plastic tub where I stored the dolls I'd made that I hadn't given away to either Priya, Cindy, or Auntie Cha. I dumped them out so I could get a sense of how many I had.

I had a pretty big assortment of amigurumi, from robots to ice creams to bees to octopuses.

Then Auntie Cha's comments from earlier echoed in my head. *Your dolls are so well made that they look like you can buy them at a store.*

Was she onto something?

What if someone *could* buy my dolls?

Not at a store, though. What if they could buy them . . . at a Handmade Craft booth?

I picked up a crocheted unicorn and inspected it closely. My amigurumi always made me smile. Crocheting them, putting the pieces together to form a whole doll, seeing them looking back at me with their cute, charming faces . . .

Could my creations make other people smile, too?

And make the money that Auntie Cha needed to save Boba Time?

My heart started to pound. Then I remembered what my mom always said when she was deciding whether or not to start her own business: *Do the math first.*

Before she started coding her software, Mom had pored over spreadsheets on her computer for months, tweaking calculations to figure out how many customers she'd need to make sure her idea could make enough money to be a real, self-sustaining business. Dad did the same thing when he joined the company, making revenue projections and figuring out which markets to go after with his sales calls.

I could make a revenue projection for selling my amigurumi. And if the amount I could make was close to what Auntie Cha needed, then that would keep Boba Time around.

First, I counted up how many dolls I already had.

Sixty-five dolls.

Then I found my phone under a half-finished monkey and tapped on the calculator app.

It was summer, so I didn't have any homework to worry about. And Handmade Craft was still three months away. If I worked hard at it, I could probably make ten dolls a week.

10 dolls x 12 weeks = 120 dolls

Add the 65 I already had = 185 dolls. I could make more to push that number up to a nice, even 200.

That meant I could have as many as two hundred dolls to sell.

With ten thousand customers a weekend, getting two hundred customers would be a breeze.

If I sold each doll at ten dollars each, that'd be two thousand dollars total.

Which was exactly how much Auntie Cha said she'd need to repair that fridge once it broke.

It was possible.

I stopped for a moment and took a deep breath. Maybe I was getting ahead of myself. A twelve-year-old like me selling at a craft fair like Handmade Craft? Plenty of kids showed up to shop. But I'd never seen someone my age behind a booth. What did it take to reserve a booth anyway?

I needed to know more. I opened up my laptop and typed in the link printed on the flyer.

The website featured photo after photo of stunning booths filled with the most amazing handmade crafts—from jewelry to pottery to paintings to clothing to my favorite, knit and crochet goods. And the people behind their booths were all also happy and proud and confident, showing off the things they had made and hoping customers would make a purchase.

Could I become one of them?

I clicked on the button labeled *Booth Guidelines*. It looked like you could sign up for different booth sizes, and you could have one to yourself or share with someone else. Each booth came with a table and two chairs, and decorations were up to you, although the fair organizers suggested investing in a good sign with the name of your store.

Then I saw it.

Cost to reserve a booth: $150 due at sign-up.

Like a deflated balloon, my shoulders sank. Well, that was that. I didn't have that kind of money.

I closed my laptop and flopped back on my bed. Then I turned to my side and hugged my knees close. My dolls were strewn across my bedroom floor.

Anyway, Mom was probably right. My dolls weren't special enough.

Who'd buy my amigurumi anyway?

CHAPTER

8

A SOFT PING WOKE ME up after a long night of tossing and turning. I fumbled for my phone and finally found it squeezed between a tamago sushi doll and a blue octopus with seven legs. I squinted at the text through bleary eyes.

It was a group text from Priya to me and Cindy. *Morning! Wanna come over for a movie hang?*

I stretched my arms wide and yawned, trying to loosen my tight muscles. I had spent the rest of yesterday holed up in my room, trying to distract myself from worrying about Boba Time by watching Chinese TV shows on Netflix.

And crocheting, of course.

Today was a new day, though. The house was quiet

as usual, which meant no one else was up and about. Might as well go hang out with my friends, then.

But I needed a pick-me-up to shake me from my dismal mood. And I knew where to get it.

I texted Cindy and Priya back.

I'm in. But damsel had a bad day yesterday. Need a burst of boba energy.

Priya replied right away.

Knight will meet you at BT in 15.

A few seconds later, a thumbs-up from Cindy popped up on my phone screen.

I pulled myself out of bed and threw on a plain white shirt with my black jeans. To match my gloomy mood, I put on my gray-rimmed glasses with the tortoiseshell pattern. Today was not flair-worthy at all.

When I got to Boba Time, Auntie Cha was behind the counter, chitchatting with a customer and scooping up tea leaves from a large jar into a bunch of smaller ones. Priya and Cindy hadn't gotten there yet.

I joined Auntie Cha at the counter. "Excuse me, one moment," Auntie Cha said to the customer, then turned toward me. "Gâu-tsá, Pearl. What would you like this morning?"

"My favorite, please," I replied.

"Sparkling mango green tea with boba, coming right up!" Then she paused for a moment, inspecting me closely. "And I'll throw in an extra scoop for you this morning." Auntie Cha put her hand on mine and gave it a gentle squeeze. Then she went back to chatting with the other customer as she got my order ready.

How did Auntie Cha do it?? The way that she could pick up on how I was feeling without me saying a single word was amazing.

But her little gesture, although sweet, made me feel even sadder. What was I going to do without her and Boba Time?

A few minutes later, Auntie Cha wiped down the sides of the boba cup and handed it to me. I paid for it with my phone, thanked her, then turned around to go outside to wait for Priya and Cindy at our table outside.

But as I reached for the handle, the door swung open, and I froze.

Because who had just entered the store but Kendall Stewart herself.

What was *she* doing here?

I recognized the tall man in a gray sweater and dark

blue jeans standing next to Kendall as her dad from that time we ran into them at Mama Yang's Kitchen. I'd also seen Mr. Stewart's face before in newspapers and online articles. He was a tech executive at one of the biggest social media companies here in Silicon Valley.

On his arm was a tiny gray-haired woman I'd never seen before. She was chatting away in Taiwanese, hands gesturing animatedly, while Kendall's dad nodded his head.

My parents' voices echoed in my head. *Remember, always be polite, especially to elders.* I fought the urge to walk straight past and greeted them instead.

"Hi, Mr. Stewart. Hi, Kendall."

I faced the older woman and bowed slightly like my dad taught me to show respect to elders, making sure to use the more formal word for "you"—"nín" instead of "nǐ"—in my greeting before introducing myself in Mandarin.

"Nín hǎo. Wǒ jiào Lǐ Xiǎozhū."

"Ah, you are a classmate of Kendall's? And you speak Mandarin!" The woman switched to Chinese. "You were born here in the States?"

"Yes." I smiled proudly. "I understand Taiwanese, but it's easier for me to respond in Mandarin."

Mr. Stewart chimed in, also in Mandarin. "Wow, good for you! Unfortunately, my Taiwanese and Mandarin are both a little rusty. Lucky thing Māma has just moved here from Taipei to live with us now. She'll make me practice." He squeezed her shoulders affectionately.

Kendall had explained to us last year as a part of a family history assignment that her dad was half Taiwanese on his mom's side and half white on his dad's side. Apparently, Kendall's grandfather was from Texas and had met her amah when he was living in Taipei and teaching American history at the university. He even spoke Mandarin Chinese really well because he studied it before arriving in Taipei for his teaching job.

Kendall's grandma slapped his hand, teasing her son. "Āiya, living here in the US for the past twenty years is no excuse for not speaking anymore, érzi."

"Ma. It's not that bad." He feigned hurt and put on an exaggerated pouty face, sticking out his lower lip in protest.

Despite my gray mood, I couldn't help but giggle at their back-and-forth banter. Adults could be so cute sometimes.

Then she grabbed my hand tightly and gestured at Kendall. "You must teach my wàiguórén granddaughter how to speak Mandarin as well as you do. Or else she'll never know her roots."

I furrowed my eyebrows at Kendall's grandma's use of the phrase "wàiguórén." Although the term technically meant "a person from a different country," it was usually used to describe anyone who didn't look Chinese. Although I was born here in the States, not Taiwan, Chinese people probably wouldn't call me a wàiguórén. What mattered was that I "looked" Chinese.

I stole a glance at Kendall. How did she feel about being called a wàiguórén?

Kendall looked back at me with a blank face.

Then it dawned on me.

Kendall didn't understand Mandarin. Not a word.

For a split second, I almost felt bad for her. What was it like to have your own grandmother say that you didn't look Chinese? And to not be able to follow the conversations your own family was having?

Actually, I *did* know what that felt like, sort of. My family spoke in tech all the time—and I never got what they were talking about.

Suddenly, Kendall pointed at my feet with a long finger. "What's that? Yarn?"

Taken back, I looked down to where she was pointing. A balled-up tangle of pink yarn pooled at my feet. Blushing, I gathered it up quickly and stuffed it back into my jean pocket.

"Still doing crafts, Pearl?" Kendall's eyebrows wrinkled in the middle. "Come on, you could do so much cooler stuff with new technologies. Even your mom said so. Doing things by hand is so . . . imperfect. And old-school."

Ugh. Who did she think she was?? Doing things by hand was so much fun . . . and much harder than it looked! Taking the time to train your hands to move in the way they needed to in order to make awesome stuff was one of the biggest reasons I loved doing crafts. It was so satisfying.

Plus, every fingerprint, every stitch, every imperfection, were what made my creations special. Unique.

And how dare she rub my mom's pride in her to my face? Mom should have been gushing about her daughter's model, not hers.

I guess Kendall made a mistake when she walked into that art store yesterday. She obviously didn't care about crafts at all.

And just like that, I didn't feel sorry for Kendall being called a wàiguórén anymore.

Then I spotted Priya and Cindy walking across the plaza parking lot toward the shop. My backup was here.

Plus, we were at Boba Time. This was my turf.

I pushed my glasses back up my nose and jutted my chin up high. Ignoring Kendall, I turned to face her grandmother.

"I'd be happy to teach her," I responded.

Then I looked straight at Kendall and continued in Mandarin. "But only if she asks nicely."

Seeing Kendall's face glow red felt amazing.

With that, I quickly said my goodbyes and swung open the door on my way out. The bells jangled behind me like the clapping of hands.

Take that, Kendall Stewart.

I dashed across the parking lot to meet Priya and Cindy with a warm feeling of satisfaction in my stomach. It must have shown on my face because the second she spotted me, Priya furrowed her eyebrows and asked, "Hey, what's up with you? Why do you look so happy?"

Cindy had a concerned look on her face, too. "What's going on, Pearl? What happened yesterday? We were worried sick!"

"Let me get my bike and I'll explain." I led them to the bike racks and quickly unlocked mine.

Priya pointed in the direction of Boba Time. "Wait, you don't want to hang out here for a bit?"

"No, Kendall Stewart is in there."

"Kendall Stewart? What's she doing at Boba Time?" Cindy asked.

I put my finger up to my lips to shush her. "I'll tell you later. Let's get out of here." What if Kendall and her family came out of Boba Time's doors? Sure, I just did the bravest thing I'd done in a while. But I wasn't ready to do it again.

I ushered us in the direction of Priya's house, which

was a short twenty-minute walk away. Once we were safely across the parking lot, I told them about my conversation with Auntie Cha yesterday, about how she didn't have money to fix the fridge and that she said she had other important things to worry about.

"And when that fridge breaks, she might close Boba Time's doors forever," I finished, panic rising in my voice.

"Oh no, that's terrible." Cindy shook her head.

Priya bit her lip in that way she did whenever she was thinking hard. "Do you have any idea what other important things she was talking about, Pearl?"

I picked at the thread on the crocheted donuts hanging from my bike's handlebars. "No idea. It didn't feel right to ask."

"Maybe we shouldn't rush to conclusions then. Maybe there is something else more important than Boba Time that we don't know about."

I glared at her. "More important than Boba Time? Like what?"

Priya shrugged her shoulders. "I don't know, Pearl. We don't know everything about Auntie Cha and her life."

I took a slow, long breath, trying to push down the little pang of annoyance that was making its way to the surface. Did Priya not get how big of a deal it'd be if Auntie Cha closed down Boba Time? And what it would mean for my amigurumi?

"Is there anything we can do, Pearl?" Cindy asked.

"I don't know," I sighed. "Make two thousand dollars over the summer?"

Priya frowned. "Wait, I don't get it. If you just got this bad news, then why were you all bouncy a few minutes ago?"

I quickly told them about my dramatic send-off of Kendall.

"Ha, tǐngkù de!" Cindy giggled when I finished.

"Right? Not bad, huh?" I grinned at Cindy.

But Priya got all quiet again. I nudged her with my shoulder. "Hey, knight in shining armor. I thought you'd be glad that this damsel finally spoke up!"

Priya kicked at an invisible rock on the sidewalk. "I dunno, Pearl. Even though Kendall was being mean about your crafts, talking in a language someone doesn't understand isn't very nice, either." She looked back and forth between me and Cindy pointedly.

I tugged at my glasses, which suddenly felt like they were squeezing my temples tighter than usual.

"I'm not sure what you did counts as 'speaking up,'" Priya continued. "In fact, it sounds like you were being as mean as she was. Maybe meaner, because you did it in front of her family."

My heart dropped like a brick. Priya wasn't on my side with this one?

Cindy stepped to the left to avoid a trash can at the edge of someone's front yard. "What's Kendall like anyway? I've never talked to her before."

"I had English Literature with her in the fall," Priya said. "We had to do a group project with a few other kids. She seemed all right. She did her fair share, which is more than I could say for the other kids in our group."

"Well, Kendall put down my cell project in front of my mom. She thinks she's better than the rest of us because she knows how to use all this fancy technology and is a big shot around school because of her dad. It's like art isn't cool enough for her," I said, my voice a bit higher than it usually was.

"Well, what you said wasn't very cool, either," Priya said. "Especially because she didn't understand it."

Ugh.

Although Priya actually had a point. I *was* being spiteful . . . and I did embarrass Kendall in front of her grandma, who was already being a bit mean herself by calling Kendall a wàiguórén.

But me being a jerk to Kendall didn't hide the fact that Priya defended her first *and* accused me of being the meaner one. She used to stick up for me, no questions asked. That was one of the reasons I loved her.

Was that changing?

We stopped at the intersection to wait for the light to signal when it was safe for us to cross. A few awkward seconds ticked by.

Suddenly, a white Lexus pulled up to the side of the road. The passenger side window slid down, and Cindy's mom poked her head out. "Hi, girls! Weren't you going to Priya's?"

"Yes, we're on our way now," Cindy replied. "Where are you and Dad off to?"

The man in dark sunglasses and checkered polo shirt waved at us from the driver's side. "We're heading to the Great Pacific Mall in Sarasota. You left the house so quickly this morning that we didn't have a chance to tell you, Cindy. You girls want to join us?"

"Oh, I want to come! I'm out of sheet masks and want to see if they have any new ones from Korea." Cindy pulled open the back door. "Pearl? Priya? What do you think?"

I usually loved browsing all the fun goodies from the other side of the world. But the thought of Boba Time closing still gnawed at me.

"No." I sighed. "I'm not in the mood. I've got my bike anyway." I wiggled the handlebars, making the donut amigurumi that hung from them jingle.

Priya glanced at me, and her face softened. "I'll stay

here, too. But thanks for asking, Cindy."

My heart leapt for a quick beat. Was my knight in shining armor back?

Cindy hopped into her parents' car, then waved good-bye out of the open window. "Text you guys later!" she called out as they pulled away.

The light turned green, and Priya's eyes met mine. "You still want to come over and watch a movie?"

I hesitated. Priya didn't seem to get how serious this Boba Time situation was. Would hanging out with her now help me feel better about it?

But maybe she decided to stay because of me. And the crochet donuts hanging from my bike's handlebars made my seed of an amigurumi idea grow slightly bigger.

Priya did love Handmade Craft. And my amigurumi. She'd tell me what she thought of me selling my dolls there.

"Sure, let's do it. Plus, I want to ask you about an idea I have. It has to do with Handmade."

"Color me intrigued!" Her black hair whipped backward, and a bright smile broke across her face.

I grinned. This was the optimistic, supportive Priya I loved.

With her help, maybe there was a real chance I could save Boba Time.

CHAPTER
9

I LOVED GOING OVER TO Priya's. Walking inside was like stepping into an amazing forest of color and patterns and life. Her dad was a painter, and her mom was a professor of South Asian art at the local college.

Their house was way cooler than mine, with art scattered in every room. And statues. And tapestries. And more art.

My house? We only had a few crooked pictures hanging on the otherwise-blank white walls. Super sterile. Super boring. Nothing creative ever happened there.

Except my amigurumi, of course.

When we walked into the kitchen, Mr. Gupta was inspecting a huge painting laid out on their kitchen table.

"Hello, Pearl. How are you?" He stroked his beard with one hand. In the other one, he cupped a steaming mug of masala chai.

"Hello, Mr. Gupta. I'm good, thank you."

"How are your parents? Have they launched their product yet?" He sipped from his cup.

"They're fine, and a bit busy. The pilot launch is in a few weeks. Thank you for asking." *Remember, always be polite to adults.*

"Programming, how fascinating. It's like creating something out of thin air with ones and zeros." He waved at the air with a flourish, like he was holding a paintbrush.

"Oh, Baba, don't be so dramatic." Priya giggled.

They were from the same family all right.

Mr. Gupta blew at the steam wafting up from his mug. "Pearl, remind me what their product is?"

"Um," I fumbled. I actually didn't know. "It's something that's supposed to help companies keep track of their sales, I think."

"That sounds promising. I sure hope their system is better than mine, which is mostly me scribbling down buyers' information on scraps of papers!" Mr. Gupta chuckled. "Then they end up all over the place in my studio, covered with dots of paint and smudges of color. Speaking of color . . ." He turned toward Priya, who was putting some cookies on a plate. "How do you like those new soft pastels, beta?"

"They're amazing!" Priya exclaimed. "What a difference to have artist-quality pastels. The colors are so much more intense."

"Definitely. Good materials make it easier to make good art," Mr. Gupta agreed.

"I'm still trying to get the blending technique right, though." Priya rubbed her right index finger against the back of her left hand, like she was smudging color together. "I want a soft transition effect, but I just can't get there."

"It'll take some practice. Layering can get you a similar effect to blending. I can show you later how I do it."

The conversations between Priya and her artist dad, compared to those between me and my techy mom, were like night and day. I'd give an arm and a leg to be able to geek out with my family about yarn weights and hook sizes.

Priya didn't know how lucky she was to have such creative parents.

"Thanks, Baba! Okay, let's go, Pearl." She grabbed two bottles of coconut water from the fridge, and together we headed to the basement. Or, more accurately, Priya's art studio.

When Priya and I were nine years old, we saw a show

on TV with this fuzzy-haired man who'd teach people how to paint these amazing landscapes. Bob Ross was his name, I think. We got obsessed over his calm voice and the soft way he dabbed paint onto the canvas.

After seeing the show, Priya announced to her parents that she was going to be an artist, too, and that she was going to take over the basement so she could work there. Her studio quickly became one of our favorite places to hang out. We'd spent hours playing with different art mediums without having to worry about getting things dirty.

Today, charcoal sketches were taped all around the walls, and two colorful drawings lay against the easels. A thin layer of powder dusted everything in sight, probably from those pastels Priya had been experimenting with.

I sank into her super-plush, paint-splattered bean-bag and swatted at the dust that poofed up. Priya settled onto the rug in front of me, tucking her feet under her crossed legs.

"Okay, Pearl, what's your idea about Handmade Craft?" she asked.

"Well, I was thinking . . ." My heart started to pound. Was I really going to say it out loud?

Priya looked at me eagerly, patiently. Sitting in my best friend's art studio, surrounded by the things both of us loved to do . . . I felt a small glimmer of hope.

Maybe this idea could become real.

"I was thinking . . ." I started saying slowly. "You know how Auntie Cha needs money for the fridge that's about to break?"

Priya nodded. "And that she might close the shop for those other important things? Yeah."

I bit my lip. "Let's imagine that those things got taken care of, and that the only thing she needs to keep Boba Time open is the money to fix the fridge. What if I could help her with that by selling my amigurumi at Handmade?"

Priya's face lit up in a flash. "Wow! Selling at the fair to help Boba Time . . . That's a great idea! People would totally buy your dolls."

"You think so?" Priya's words made me feel a thousand times lighter already.

"Absolutely! Your dolls are so fun and quirky and well made. I see plenty of amigurumi on Craftsee, and most of them aren't half as good as yours! If people buy those, then they'll buy yours, too."

I still wasn't sure, though.

"What if no one wants to buy something made by a twelve-year-old? Or worse, if they laughed at me for doing crafts like crochet in the first place? Like Kendall did." I picked at the seams of Priya's beanbag.

Priya huffed in exasperation. "Come on, you can't let people like that bring your art down. Plus, Kendall's just one person. Everyone else loves your dolls."

Not my mom, though, I wanted to say. Did you forget, Priya? Not everyone has artsy parents like yours who love and support everything their kids do.

A little bubble of annoyance started to rise to the surface.

But I did my best to swallow it down. I needed Priya if I was going to pull this off.

And it was a huge relief to hear her say my idea wasn't totally off-the-wall. Even though what she said stung sometimes, I knew Priya never held back what she thought.

If she said I could do it, then she meant it.

But a big obstacle still stood in my way.

I sighed. "There's a problem, though. If I want a booth at Handmade, I have to pay a hundred and fifty dollars for it."

Priya's mouth dropped open. "A hundred and fifty dollars? That's so much! There's no way a kid could afford that on their own."

"I know. So how am I going to get a booth, then? There's not enough time for me to save up for it." I flopped back into her beanbag chair.

"And I just splurged on that fancy box of pastels."

Priya stared off into space. "Wouldn't it be cool if kids had their own craft fair where we didn't have to pay so much? We could sell anything we wanted and not worry about what adults think."

"Yeah, how cool would that be!" I agreed. "But Handmade is my only option right now. With ten thousand customers expected to come through that weekend, a booth might be the only way I can make enough to help Boba Time."

"Ten thousand customers? Wow. You're going to sell a ton!" Priya clapped her hands excitedly.

"How am I going to get a hundred and fifty dollars, though?"

Priya grimaced. "Could you ask your parents?"

Sigh. There she went again, forgetting how much my mom didn't like me doing amigurumi.

She still wasn't getting how hard it was for me to share crafts with my family of techies. Sometimes I wished she'd admit how easy it was for her to be an artist, coming from a family of art lovers.

"I can't ask them, Priya, you know that. They'd never go for it." I punched the beanbag in frustration.

"Are you sure, Pearl? I'm sure they'd understand if they knew how much it meant to you," Priya insisted.

"I'm sure. Just drop it, okay?" My tone was as sharp as a razor blade.

An awkward silence hung in the air. Priya shifted her weight around uncomfortably.

I sighed and started fiddling with my phone. Maybe finding a fun new crochet pattern would help me deal with this Priya weirdness and spark some ideas. That always worked before.

I tapped on the Craftsee logo on the home screen and started scrolling. Hmm, a chubby bee? Too easy. That was one of the first things I ever made. An octopus? I'd made that one, too, although it took a while to crochet and stitch on all eight legs. A robot? Been there, done that. And I'd learned how to do an invisible color change with that project, which is how you change yarn colors seamlessly between stitches. I crocheted a blue heart right into its gray body with that technique. I'd seen other robots with a heart sewn on after the doll was complete, but none with a heart as a part of the actual pattern.

Suddenly, a flash of inspiration hit me.

Like in that game, *Tetris*, all the blocks in my brain fell into place, and row after row of bricks disappeared, one after the other, like a path suddenly opened up for the idea that just popped into my head.

"Priya. What if I opened a Craftsee shop?"

Her eyes widened.

"That could be my pilot test for the craft fair!" I

leapt up. "I could put my dolls online. If people buy my designs on Craftsee, it'd mean people at the craft fair might buy them, too! I could make enough money to pay for the booth, and maybe even some extra for booth decorations."

"Oh my gosh, you could totally pull it off, Pearl!" Priya tossed her phone on the beanbag chair in her excitement. "Your work is perfect for the Craftsee crowd!"

Plus, a great part of this plan was that I could stay anonymous. No one would know it was me running the shop: not my parents, not Kendall, no one at school . . . Basically no one who thought a twelve-year-old shouldn't be playing with dolls or wasting time making them.

Although I'd still have to deal with all that if I actually got a booth at Handmade Craft. Eep!

But one step at a time.

Even better than being anonymous was that if no one bought anything, if I totally failed, only my friends would know. Then I could pretend nothing happened and go back to crocheting for fun.

Though that'd also mean the end of Boba Time.

I shook my head as if to erase that thought out of the realm of possibility.

Priya crouched next to me, and we skimmed the Craftsee app together on my phone. It didn't look that hard to set up a shop. You needed to pick a shop name, take photos of the things you wanted to sell, write some descriptions, and add bank information so people could pay you for what they wanted to buy.

"Do you have a way to collect the money?" Priya pointed at the screen with a worried look on her face. "And to pay Craftsee for what they charge you to sell? That part might be tricky."

"Well, I have that bank account that Mom and Dad put my allowance in. And money for things like takeout or food delivery. They never check it."

For once, it was a good thing Mom and Dad were so busy these days.

"You'll need a shop name, too. Ooh, this will be so fun!" Priya grabbed a notepad and started writing furiously. "How about Amigurumi by Pearl? Or Pearl's Creations?"

"Maybe something about crochet? So people know what the shop's about?" I replied. "I don't know if lots of people know what amigurumi means."

"Pearl's Crochet Creations?" Priya chewed on the end of her pen. "That's a mouthful, though."

"How about Kawaii Crochets?" I suggested. "'Kawaii' means cute in Japanese, and people use it to describe the amigurumi style all the time. And the word 'amigurumi' is Japanese, too. We Taiwanese people have a lot of history with Japan, so using that word in my shop name could work."

"Perfect!" Priya beamed. "Kawaii Crochets it is!"

A ball of hope started to form in my belly. But then . . .

"Uh-oh. Pearl, look at this." Priya pointed to the lower half of the screen.

Craftsee's Terms of Use require all shop owners to be at least 18 years of age. Individuals under the age of 18 are considered minors on Craftsee and are not permitted to open their own shop.

Just like that, the ball of hope unraveled. I was definitely not eighteen years old.

"Wait, Pearl. There's more." Priya kept reading out loud:

However, minors under 18 are permitted to operate a Craftsee shop if they have the explicit permission of their parent or legal guardian. The shop must be created by the parent or legal guardian. Once the shop is opened and approved, minors are permitted to operate it under the direct supervision of the aforementioned adult.

Priya grabbed my hand. "There's still a chance! According to this, you can have a store. All you need is for your mom or dad to register an account and let you run it. No problem!"

The annoyance that I'd been trying to keep down bounced right back up. *Again, Priya, with my parents??*

But the hope on her face made me pause for a second. Was there a chance I could be wrong about this?

Maybe, just maybe, my mom would say yes to the idea of something as simple as running a Craftsee shop. I could talk about it as a way to learn more about running an online business, like she and Dad—and Jade—were doing. It wasn't in person like it'd be with Handmade Craft, which meant I'd be taking a much smaller risk. I could shut down the Craftsee shop if no one bought anything, instead of watching thousands of people walk by my booth and not spend a penny.

Plus, selling my dolls this way wasn't only about me. This was also about Boba Time and Auntie Cha.

There was something really important on the line.

But even if Mom said yes to Craftsee, she might still say no to Handmade. Both needed to happen if I had any chance of saving Boba Time.

One step at a time, I told myself. I'd cross that bridge if, by some miracle, I actually got there.

I took a deep breath. "No promises, Priya. But I'll think about asking my parents about the Craftsee store."

Priya cheered and gave me a hug. "Woo-hoo! Let's toast to it!" She handed me a bottle of fresh, cold coconut water. We twisted the tops off and clinked the bottles together.

"To the future Kawaii Crochets shop, run by Pearl Li herself!"

I grinned at Priya's words.

Run by Pearl Li. That had a nice ring to it.

CHAPTER
10

AFTER WE WATCHED A MOVIE in Priya's studio, I decided to bike the long route home, through the park, instead of past the library. The summer air was so fresh and energizing, and I needed to seriously consider asking my mom to sign up for the Craftsee store. I'd promised Priya.

With every breath I took, every press of a bike pedal, asking my mom about the Craftsee shop started to feel more and more real. She talked about business all the time, even BSU. And she was thrilled when Jade started making money from her mobile game downloads.

Dad would probably like my idea. I bet he'd want me to learn how to sell things. That's his jam.

But Mom called the shots in our family. She was the

one I needed to convince first.

An uphill slope in the road forced me to pedal harder, quickening my breath. If my dolls sold well on Craft-see, maybe Mom would be excited about me selling at Handmade Craft, too. That was what a pilot was for—to test the market for real customers. Mom was about to do the same for her own business and put something out there to see if people liked it.

The road leveled out and started a gentle descent. I took my feet off the pedals to let myself glide, and the crocheted donuts dangling from my handlebars jingled as they knocked against each other in the breeze. I had crocheted them a few months ago and experimented with sewing beads on top of the "frosting" for sprinkles. I even added a little bell inside each one. They came out pretty cute, if I do say so myself!

Seeing my amigurumi reminded me how much I loved crocheting—and how much my mom didn't. But if people paid money for my art, then my mom would see that my hobby was something worth doing. And it'd be the ultimate proof to show her that I had real skills and real talent.

Then maybe I could get her face to shine with pride the way it did when Mr. Huang asked Jade to be the Code Together Academy spokesperson.

Okay. I'll do it. I'll ask. She couldn't possibly shoot my

business idea down . . . Could she?

I guided my bike home and parked it in the garage before walking inside the house. I could see light shining through the crack under the door to Mom's study.

She was home.

I had to do this.

For Boba Time.

I took a deep, cleansing breath, in through the nose and out through the mouth. Here goes nothing.

I knocked softly.

"Come in."

I pushed the door open. The click-clacking of computer keys continued without skipping a beat.

"How's the business going?" I said to Mom's back.

"Fine." Mom's eyes didn't budge from the screen.

I took a deep breath to steady my nerves. Go for it, Pearl! I shouted in my head.

"Mom, I have a business idea I wanted to talk to you about."

The click-clacking stopped. Mom swiveled the desk chair around to face me. She inspected me closely.

"A business idea? Okay, what is it?"

"I want to sell some of my amigurumi on Craftsee."

"Your amigurumi . . . Oh, you mean your dolls?"

I nodded.

"Hmm, okay. Why?"

Good question.

The answers ping-ponged around in my head like those bouncy balls I used to get at birthday parties when I was a kid. To prove to her that my passion wasn't only a cute hobby I did to pass the time, but something that was really important to me. To prove to the Kendall Stewarts of the world that things made by hand could be as appreciated and cool as things made with machines and mechanics.

And the most important reason—to hold on to the one place where I could be whoever I wanted to be.

But I couldn't say all that out loud. Because saying how I felt made those feelings real.

Then what if I failed?

I picked the safest reason.

"I want to help Auntie Cha with Boba Time. I want to make enough money so she can replace her fridge and keep the business going."

Mom's eyebrows shot up. "So what Mr. Huang told us at Mama Yang's is true? Auntie Cha might have to close Boba Time?"

I nodded, tears springing to my eyes.

"Oh, Pearl. I'm so sorry to hear that. I know how much you love that place." Mom held out her arms, inviting me in.

I sank into this rare moment of her undivided attention, trying to ignore the butterflies in my stomach.

"It's so hard being a business owner, especially a solo one." Mom tsked, shaking her head. "Poor Auntie Cha. Did you know that she gave me some helpful advice when I first started my company?"

"What did she tell you?"

"She told me that when things got rough with the business, I should try to remember and hold on to why I loved the work that I did."

Despite my nerves, I couldn't help but crack a small smile. That sounded like Auntie Cha, all right.

I straightened my shoulders and steeled my resolve. "I think I can help Auntie Cha by selling my amigurumi. I want to start by trying to sell some online, on Craftsee. Just a handful in a pilot, like what you and Dad are doing. All I need is for you to help me set up the Craftsee account."

Mom leaned back in her chair and rubbed her eyes. "Hmm, I'm not sure that's a good idea. Running an online business takes a lot of time and energy."

"Mom, I can do it. Lots of people sell crochet dolls on Craftsee already."

"Even more reason to not do it. That sounds like a saturated market. You'll need what's called a differentiator. What is it about your dolls that make them so different and special that people can't buy them from anyone but you?"

And just like that, she switched from normal Mom to tech-founder Mom, analyzing the situation in that super-careful way she always did now. I almost turned around to leave.

But then I thought of Oscar and the details I'd put on him to make him special. Mom had said it before, that it'd be good to make my crochet designs a little different, so I'm not copying other people. And I'd been doing that, like with Oscar's crooked smile, the yellow stripe of mustard.

This was important. This could be the fate of Boba Time. I couldn't back down this time.

"My designs are good, Mom. Priya and Cindy love them. Auntie Cha loves them." I pulled Oscar out of my pocket. "I made this last week. I can show you the other things I've crocheted."

Mom held out her hand, and I gave her Oscar. "Those are your friends. I'm your mom. Of course we're going to say nice things about them. It's completely different with strangers who have no personal connection to you."

A knot of tension started to tangle in my stomach.

Mom inspected Oscar closely. "This little guy is quite cute, Pearl." She smiled. "It's like those dolls in that café in Taipei."

The knot loosened a tiny bit.

She remembered.

"You're going to have to sell a lot of these to help Auntie Cha, though. I'm not sure it's a good idea to open yourself up to the world this way." She looked back at me with furrowed eyebrows.

But why? Was she saying I shouldn't do it because she thought my dolls weren't good enough? Or because she was afraid my feelings were going to get hurt if people didn't buy any of my dolls?

It had to be the first thing. How could running a business hurt someone's feelings anyway?

My cheeks started to flush. But this time, my voice found itself.

"You let Jade start a business," I protested. "What's so different about me starting one?"

"She was selling a mobile app, Pearl. People around here love that kind of thing. And distribution is so easy. People only have to click a button and they get the product on their phones right away. It's different when you have to handle inventory, shipping, complicated things like that. I don't know how all that works. I'd have no way to help you navigate those logistics."

Oscar sat on my outstretched hand, his expression full of hope. But mine was slipping away.

"I think it's great that you want to help." Mom reached

out and patted my arm. "But businesses come and go. That's the harsh reality of being a business owner." She paused. "Especially a woman business owner."

None of this made any sense to me. Mom's business was run by a woman and doing fine. It wasn't going anywhere.

I knew what was holding Mom back from letting me do this. It wasn't about distribution or the harsh reality of business or being a woman business owner.

Mom didn't believe in me.

I snatched Oscar back from her.

"Fine. I'll think of something else."

I turned and started stomping away.

"Wait, but, Pearl . . ."

I didn't want to hear anything else about my amigurumi. So I kept going.

Alone in my bedroom, I fumed.

Silly me for thinking Mom might get on board with this Craftsee idea! She never appreciated my crocheting. And she never got that I could be as resourceful as Jade, even if I did things a little differently. Wasn't that what made each of us unique?

She thought I was a little girl who couldn't do important things on my own. Not the seventh grader I was going to be in a few short months.

But Auntie Cha believed in me. And in my amigurumi.

Forget getting permission. I could do this myself.

I had to do it myself.

Ignoring my banging heart, I flipped open my laptop and loaded up the Craftsee website. I clicked on the *Continue Shop Setup* button and tapped through all the steps needed to complete my shop details.

When the *Please verify you are at least 18 years old* message popped up, I glared at it. I dragged the cursor over and clicked to check off the box with a flourish.

Submit.

A few seconds later, a message popped up on screen.

Congratulations! Kawaii Crochets is now live. Happy selling!

I'd done it.

Now it was up to me, Oscar, and my amigurumi to prove Mom wrong.

And to save Boba Time.

CHAPTER
11

A WEEK LATER, I PACED back and forth in front of Boba Time. Priya and Cindy sat at the metal table, staring at me with worried eyes.

"What am I going to do? It's been a week, and no one's bought anything!"

After I launched my Craftsee shop, I texted Cindy and Priya right away to share the news. Cindy wrote back with a string of heart-eyed smiley faces and party popper emojis, and Priya favorited my shop from her own Craftsee account.

I also told them that I opened the shop without my mom's okay.

Mom wasn't for it, but I launched anyway. I'll keep it open long enough to make what I need for Handmade, then I'll shut it down, I typed. *Promise.*

Priya texted me back with a clenched teeth emoji and nothing else. I guess she got why I had to do it.

But I had a feeling I'd hear more from her about this.

Whatever. I had no choice.

And now Priya and Cindy have had to put up with my constant worrying for a week, because Kawaii Crochets was not doing well. No one had bought a single one of my dolls.

Not good.

Not good at all.

Cindy raised her hand like she was in school. "What dolls did you put up for sale, Pearl? Maybe you should try selling some new ones? Like that sloth you made last month. Someone will definitely buy that one!"

"I put up the sloth, along with a bunch of different ones to see what people might like." I pulled out my phone and showed her the photos I had uploaded onto Craftsee. "See, I have some animals, a unicorn, a cupcake, an ice cream cone, even a few robots."

The idea of putting Oscar up for sale had crossed my mind when I was choosing which dolls to sell. But I couldn't bring myself to do it. He was a part of me now. I wanted him around, like a good luck charm.

Oscar was chilling out in my pocket now. I touched him quickly to make sure, though. He still had a habit of tumbling out for some fresh air.

But he hadn't brought me good luck yet. I threw my phone on the table in frustration. "What doesn't make sense is that no one is seeing my products at all. It'd be one thing if people were seeing my dolls but didn't want to buy them. But it's another thing that no one is even looking at them."

"How do you know that?" Priya asked.

"Look here." I tapped on the Craftsee Seller app on my phone. A bunch of numbers loaded up on-screen.

"Craftsee doesn't just tell you when someone bought something. It also gives you all sorts of numbers about how your shop is doing. Like here . . . every time someone looks at one of your product listings, Craftsee counts that as a 'view' and puts it in this column," I explained.

"Wow, that's pretty cool." Cindy nodded her head approvingly.

"Yeah, it should be. But look at these zeros." I jabbed at the screen. "My listings have no views at all. It's like they don't exist."

"Maybe there's something wrong with one of your settings?" Priya suggested.

"I've checked my shop settings a million times. Everything looks right." I sighed. "I'm not great with numbers, but I studied that setup guide like it was fifth-period algebra. I don't see anything wrong."

I flopped onto one of the chairs and fiddled with the straw of my Yakult green tea with grass jelly and boba. Ever since I learned about Boba Time's problems, I'd been trying to spend as much of my allowance there as I could. But what Priya, Cindy and I could pay for was pennies compared to how much Auntie Cha really needed.

Kawaii Crochets needed to start generating business now. But my Craftsee pilot was cratering, and I only had two months left before Handmade Craft came to town. Maybe I wasn't cut out to run a business after all.

A tan Prius pulled up in the front of the store and shuddered to a quiet stop. I recognized the fuzzy purple dice dangling from the rearview mirror right away. It was Jade.

Although my nerves had total control of my body right now, a small smile still managed to escape my lips. I'd noticed more Boba Time cups at home lately, and I had a feeling that my family had had the same idea as me and my friends. We were all having a little more tea and boba than we normally would, hoping to boost Auntie Cha's sales by even a tiny bit.

Seeing my family try to help Auntie Cha made me feel pretty good inside. Even if I was still giving Mom the cold shoulder for not helping me with the Craftsee shop.

Jade stepped out of the car wearing her "Girls Who Code Write the Future" T-shirt. She nodded at the three of us before disappearing inside.

Then it occurred to me. Jade sold her mobile game in the Apple App Store, and there were a ton of other apps on it, too. How did she make hers stand out?

She must have done something right because everyone at school had heard about her app and downloaded it when it first came out. I bet she could help me figure out what was going on.

Could I let her in on my secret? Jade never said much about my dolls, although I didn't think she disapproved like Mom did.

But Jade did know a lot about the rules of the internet. She might figure out that I lied and was pretending to be eighteen so I could run the Craftsee shop without Mom and Dad's permission.

No. I couldn't risk Jade finding out and telling my parents. But maybe I could get some ideas from her on how to get my products seen if I asked in a roundabout way.

When Jade emerged from Boba Time a few minutes later with a taro slush in her hand, I jumped up from my seat.

"Hey, Jade, you heading home?"

"Yep."

"Can I catch a ride?"

"Isn't that your bike over there?" Jade pointed to the barbershop with the blinking sign. I winced. My bike was pretty easy to spot in a crowd. Not only was it bright purple, but it also had those two donuts hanging from the handlebars.

"Um, it has a flat. I'll walk over later to bring it home," I lied.

Priya and Cindy exchanged glances. I prayed they wouldn't blow my cover.

"Okay, sure." Jade shrugged and gestured me in.

I waved a quick goodbye to Priya and Cindy and hopped in. Jade's car was super neat and clean as usual, although I had to move a box of tangled cords and green-and-black motherboards from the floor of the passenger seat to the back so I could stretch out my legs.

"How's the app selling?" I asked as she started up the car. On the dashboard, two bobbleheads of Neo and Trinity from the *Matrix* movies wiggled their heads at me as Jade backed the car out of the parking spot.

She was *such* a techie.

"Pretty good. I'm working on upgrades now to resolve some performance issues. It's kind of boring, though." She peeked over her shoulder as she steered the car out of the parking lot and guided it into traffic.

"Performance issues? What does that mean?"

"It's like maintenance, back-end stuff. Things most people won't notice but are critical to keep the app running well so it doesn't crash or load too slow."

I grimaced. This was all more tech talk that I didn't understand. But what was important was that Jade had a business with a product that people knew about and wanted. Mine was barely off the ground and already tanking. I needed to figure out how to get it going in the first place.

"You know, I've always wondered . . . There are so many other apps in the App Store. How do you make sure people see yours?" I tried to use the most genuinely curious yet innocent tone I could.

"Well, getting your product seen depends on how people search for it. Like what words they put in the search bar when they're looking to buy something. Those words are called keywords. My app is a memory game, so keywords like 'mobile game' or 'memory game' are ones that I use."

Ah, so keywords were . . . the key! (Another pun!)

The car slowed to silence at a stoplight. I pretended to gaze intently at the family crossing the road in front of us. "So where do you put these keywords?"

"I write them into my product description. Some sites have a section where you can add a list of keywords to the product listing so you aren't taking up space in your description. Those are helpful to use."

That was it! I'd checked my store settings a ton but hadn't checked how my individual products were being displayed. Maybe I was missing that section somewhere.

I bounced my right leg impatiently. Now that I had a potential answer to my problem, all I wanted to do was to get to a computer, pronto.

"All of this is called SEO, or search engine optimization," Jade continued. She glanced at my shaking foot. "Why are you so curious about SEO all of a sudden, Pearl?"

Uh-oh. I willed my leg to stop twitching.

"Oh, nothing." I laughed nervously. "Just curious about how my sister's app was doing, that's all."

Luckily, we arrived home at that exact moment. Jade pulled the car into her usual spot on the street and turned the engine off. I yanked open the door and darted away, hoping to avoid more questions.

"Thanks for the ride, Jade!" I beat her to the front door and leapt up the stairs to my room, two steps at a time. Flipping open my laptop, I pulled up my Craftsee shop and clicked on a product listing, then scrolled down quickly.

There it was.

A whole section where you could enter product keywords. And mine were all blank.

I spent the next hour typing in words like "amigurumi doll," "crochet doll," or "crocheted bee" into each product description. After I entered the last one, I clicked the *Save* button.

Whew.

I closed the laptop softly. Crossing my fingers, I looked up at the ceiling and sent a silent, desperate wish into the world.

Please let this work.

CHAPTER
12

THE FIRST THING I DID when I woke up the next morning was grab my phone and check my Craftsee account. Not that I hadn't checked every five minutes before I fell asleep.

My robot had seventeen views! The ice cream cone had twenty-four views! My unicorn had thirty-one!

Then something on the Craftsee Seller dashboard caught my eye. Next to the numbers that showed me how many people had seen each product listing was a column labeled *Shop Visits*. I tapped on the column description to read more about it:

This number represents how many people have visited your Craftsee shop.

Since I started my Craftsec shop a week ago, there had always been a *1* in that column from when Priya checked out my shop when I first launched it. But now there was a nice, fat *8*.

Eight is a lucky number in Chinese culture. The way you say it in Cantonese, "fā," sounds like the word for "fortune and prosperity."

This was a good sign! This meant eight people actually went into my shop page and looked around at what I had to offer. My Handmade Craft pilot test had made it past its first hiccup!

Now all I needed was someone to like what they saw enough to pay money for it.

In other words, a real sale.

I bounced out of bed, threw together an outfit, and ran downstairs. Jade sat at the kitchen table, hunched over a bowl of cereal and scrolling through her phone. Mom was frying something on the stove while Dad washed dishes, putting the clean ones into the dishwasher to dry.

I couldn't help but give Jade a big hug for the words of advice she didn't know she gave me.

"Hey. What's going on?" Jade squirmed in her seat.

"Zǎo'ān, Jade! Zǎo'ān, Mom and Dad!" I chirped my "good mornings," ignoring her question.

"Ah, speaking to me again, Pearl?" Mom said in a

half-joking, half-serious tone.

Oops. I forgot I was still giving her the silent treatment for not helping me with the Craftsee store. I paused, trying to decide what the right next move was.

Then Mom slid a fried egg onto a plate, dribbled soy sauce over it, and pushed it over to me, smiling.

Mom used to make me and Jade fried eggs every morning for breakfast before school. She always fried them perfectly, with the edges crispy and the yolk still runny when you poked through the top with your chopsticks. Then that drizzle of soy sauce mixed with the yolk made for a salty, creamy, filling breakfast that'd start each morning off just right.

But ever since she started her business, she'd been too busy to make us hot breakfast in the mornings. She and Dad had to take early calls with investors or teams working in different time zones. Jade and I had to make do with cereal or toast now.

Smelling the egg made me feel so warm inside. And it was a real treat to have everyone together in the kitchen at the same time.

Like BSU.

Fine. Time to let the silent treatment end. I was already a step closer to proving her wrong anyway.

"Thanks, Mom. Hand me some chopsticks, would you, Jade?"

Jade threw me a look. But instead of saying anything about our awkward sister-to-sister hug, she pulled out a pair of chopsticks from the drawer behind her and handed them to me.

"What are you up to today, Pearl?" Mom cracked open another egg, and it sizzled and popped as it hit the pan's steaming surface.

"I'm supposed to meet Cindy and Priya at Sweet Yam Cafe in an hour," I told her, my mouth full. "We thought we'd go check out the competition."

Seeing my family together suddenly sparked an idea.

"Hey, why don't we all go? Every time we drive by, one of us points it out. Let's get some Taiwanese dessert like when we were in Taipei last summer!" I leapt up from my chair.

Jade looked up from her phone. "Yeah, I could swing that. Do you think they'll have huāshēngtāng? The sweet peanut soup from that one place was to die for."

"Oh, yeah!" I rubbed my belly. "From that food stand at the Shìlín Night Market, right? It had that extra kick of ginger. Sooo yummy!"

But then Mom spoke. "Aw, that's a nice idea, Pearl. Your dad and I need to go to the office for a long meeting in a few minutes, though. Our pilot launches in a few days, and we can't stop."

"We need to figure out how to get more businesses

to try our new software," Dad added, closing the dishwasher and wiping his hands on a dish towel. "I haven't been able to find the right people to be beta testers, so we need a new outreach strategy. Sorry, Pearl."

My eyes met Jade's, and she shrugged her shoulders at me with an "Oh well" look on her face. I sat back down slowly. "Yeah, okay. It was a bad idea."

"How about a ride at least?" Mom said. "Sweet Yam is on the way to the office."

Another consolation prize. My parents sure were getting good at offering them.

I wanted to say no, but a ride wasn't a bad idea. Sweet Yam usually had lines out the door. If I got there early, I could save my friends a bunch of time.

Plus, I didn't mind waiting. I could start on a new pattern for an adorable crochet koala I had found the night before.

"Yeah, okay," I mumbled, scarfing down the rest of the soy sauce fried egg. "I'll go to get my stuff."

I texted Cindy and Priya on the ride over to Sweet Yam to let them know I was already on my way. They promised to come as quickly as they could. Cindy checked in with her dad, and he agreed to give me a ride home afterward.

After waving goodbye to Mom and Dad, I joined the

line, where a mix of customers stood outside, chattering away or peering at their phones. I was surprised to see that there weren't only Chinese people here. It was actually a pretty diverse crowd, with young and old, Asian and non-Asian customers all waiting or already seated and slurping desserts from big black bowls.

I wondered if Boba Time would ever attract a line like this. It would be amazing, because it'd mean a lot of new business for Auntie Cha. But the mix of people here, from so many different backgrounds . . .

Boba Time was *so* Taiwanese. I loved it that way. Stepping inside it made me feel special, like I was in on a secret that only us Taiwanese people knew. From the types of tea to how it was served to the tea eggs to the different toppings you could put inside your drink—they weren't something anyone knew about. You had to be in the know.

But Sweet Yam was Taiwanese, too. In fact, the name was a fun wink to the island itself, which people say is shaped like a yam. And the café had a ton of customers. How was it doing that?

I decided to put on my detective hat to see if I could figure out what Sweet Yam was doing right. Maybe Boba Time could learn something from a popular place like this and use some of their—what did Mom and Dad always call them?—best practices.

I couldn't learn anything until I set foot inside the shop, though. And I was still stuck in line outside.

I pulled out my crochet hook and yarn so I could start making something new while I waited.

First, I tapped my phone to see the pattern for the koala and read the first line:

Rnd 1: start 5 sc into a magic ring [5 sts]

To start this pattern, I needed to stitch five single chains into a magic ring.

Easy-peasy. It only took me a minute to do that.

Next up:

Rnd 2: 2 sc in all 5 sts [10 sts].

For the second round, I needed to crochet two single chains into each of the five I had just made. I counted carefully after I finished.

Yep, that's a total of ten single crochet stitches.

I slowly worked my way through the pattern, checking my phone every few minutes for the next instructions while inching my feet forward in line.

Stitch by stitch, step by step, closer to the front door of Sweet Yam Cafe.

"Boo!"

"Argh!" I screamed, accidentally dropping my crochet.

"Ha-ha, it's us, silly you!" Cindy and Priya collapsed into a fit of giggles. The other customers in line twittered about to see where the shriek of terror came from.

My cheeks flushed red as I picked up my crochet from the ground and dusted it off.

"You guys are the worst!" I rolled my eyes as I straightened my crooked glasses. But I couldn't hold back the smile that broke out onto my face. "Why do you always do that when I'm crocheting?"

"We love seeing how deep into it you get, Pearl." Priya tossed her hair over her shoulder in merriment. "Besides, we figured you needed a little cheer-me-up given how Kawaii Crochets is doing."

"Oh, it's getting better!" I showed them my Craftsee stats. "Jade gave me some hints on how to fix what was going on with the shop, and it's working!"

"Woo-hoo!" Cindy cheered. She swept her bangs from her eyes and tucked her hair behind her ears. Her teardrop earrings dangled around her face.

Now that my friends were here, the line seemed to move a little faster. A few minutes later, we escaped the bright summer sun and finally stepped inside the air-conditioned restaurant.

Behind the roped line that coiled around to the counter, big digital screens flashed crisp, clear, mouthwatering photos of the different dishes—from bowls of black grass jelly topped with red bean and taro balls to shaved ice stacked high with fresh fruit, condensed milk, and scoops of ice cream. On the walls were more close-up photos showing off the food.

The tables and chairs were all made from the same tan, stylish wood and stacked with brightly colored cushions that invited you to take a seat. Like at Boba Time, Chinese pop music streamed from the ceiling. But you could barely hear it over the voices of happy customers and the sounds of spoons clinking against ceramic bowls. Employees wearing hats and aprons with the Sweet Yam Cafe logo bustled around. Some cleared tables of empty bowls, spoons, and trays, while others scooped toppings onto heaps of shaved ice behind glass partitions. Through the open window between the counter and kitchen were even more employees, also sporting the same black hat but wearing white aprons instead.

Wow. This place was nothing like Boba Time.

I wasn't sure if that was a good thing or a bad thing.

CHAPTER
13

THERE WERE SO MANY CHOICES on the menu that it was hard to decide what to get. Getting boba felt like betraying Boba Time, so I settled for a hot bowl of dòuhuā, or tofu pudding, topped with red bean, taro balls, sweet potato chunks, and peanuts. While the sweet peanut soup that Jade discovered in Taipei *was* amazing, it was the silky softness of tofu pudding that I fell in love with during that trip.

Cindy had no trouble deciding. Priya took a little longer, though, because she made Cindy and me explain every topping to her, like the taste and texture of the sweet beans or what grass jelly was. I could sense the growing impatience of the line behind me, which made me a little nervous. Finally, Priya ended up with mango shaved ice with mango ice cream and condensed milk drizzled on top.

After all that explaining we had to do, Priya still went with the least adventurous choice. Sigh. Maybe I needed to stop trying to get her to fall in love with this kind of stuff.

We grabbed a table in the shopping center's outdoor plaza to enjoy our desserts. The tofu pudding was smooth and creamy with the perfect amount of sweetness. I could taste the soybean, and the red beans were cooked perfectly with a little crunch.

Even Priya's mango ice looked mouthwateringly amazing, with real chunks of mango threatening to fall over the sides of her bowl.

Sweet Yam Cafe's desserts were pretty impressive, I had to admit.

Priya, Cindy, and I didn't say a word as we scarfed down our yummy desserts.

Suddenly, I heard a rustle behind me.

"What are you guys eating?" Kendall's voice rang out.

We twisted around to see Kendall Stewart with two of her friends, Nora Thomas and Andrea Vasquez, standing next to her. Nora's golden hair was pulled back in a tight ponytail, showing off her hoop earrings and bare, pale shoulders. Andrea had on high-waisted black jeans with a striped crop top and a retro jean jacket that glittered from the rhinestones stitched on it.

Meanwhile, Kendall's glossy brown hair hung like a shimmering waterfall down her back, and she wore a short green-and-white romper with wooden sandals and big, brightly colored earrings. Her bracelet dangled from her wrist as usual, although I noticed that the little plastic charms were different today. One was even shaped like her earrings.

I wondered if Kendall made all her jewelry on that fancy 3D printer she had at home. Mom would love Kendall's modern designs way more than my amigurumi, that's for sure.

Even the phone clutched in Andrea's hand shone with its iridescent cover and an impressive, fancy-looking lens add-on clipped to the phone's camera. She probably used it to snap the amazing photos that the three of them posted on their social media accounts all the time.

I flushed and nervously straightened my gray hoodie and pushed my glasses up my nose. The only thing I put any thought into when I got dressed this morning was picking my red glasses. They were like the ones Ali Wong wore on her first Netflix stand-up special. I usually picked out these glasses when I was feeling really good, like how I felt this morning after my Craftsee numbers went up.

But not anymore. I couldn't find a shred of that

morning energy. The boldness I had felt when I ran into Kendall with her family a few days ago was gone, too.

We weren't at Boba Time anymore.

Cindy spoke up. "These are Taiwanese desserts from Sweet Yam Cafe." She waved her spoon in the direction of the restaurant. "It's super yummy. You should try it sometime. You'd probably like the shaved ice." She pointed at Priya's bowl of mango goodness.

"I don't eat anything with processed sugar." Nora waved her smoothie at us. "I'm more the all-natural type. This has chia seeds and wheatgrass."

I wanted to tell her that our desserts had a lot of natural ingredients, too, like tofu and grass jelly and beans. Priya's dish was chock-full of fresh mango pieces, like you'd find in a smoothie.

But I bit my tongue.

Kendall pointed at my bowl, tilting her head slightly. "Is that taro?"

"Uh, yeah, it's taro balls," I replied.

"My grandma puts taro into a porridge she makes for me for breakfast every morning. I'd never had it before she came. She cooks really well." She tucked some hair behind her ear and leaned forward slightly to inspect the rest of my dessert. "What's that? Sweet potato?"

Did I detect a note of curiosity in Kendall Stewart's voice? And maybe tenderness? She talked about her grandma in an almost-loving way, which I didn't expect. When I saw them at Boba Time, it looked like they couldn't even hold a conversation with each other.

Andrea wrinkled her nose. "It looks so weird. Are those beans in your dessert?"

And what's wrong with that? I wanted to retort back.

Suddenly, Kendall jumped in. "Don't say that, Andrea. It's not weird, just different from what you're used to. My amah made us some sweet red bean soup a few days ago, and it was so yummy."

Huh. Kendall defending beans in a dessert was a surprise.

"You're right, Kendall. These are red azuki beans. Pearl's has tofu pudding and sweet potato, and mine has àiyù and grass jelly. You've never had it?" Cindy blinked innocently at Andrea.

I grinned. Cindy was like a duck in the rain. Everything seemed to roll off her back in a breezy, cheerful way. She could talk to anybody, no matter how they spoke to her.

"Uh, no. We don't have that kind of thing at our house." Andrea glanced at Kendall, who stared at her with a warning look on her face. "But it looks . . . interesting." She sipped on her drink with a pout.

Kendall cleared her throat. "Well, we gotta go." She pointed at a group of kids in front of the Apple Store on the other side of the plaza. I recognized them as more kids from our school—all those super-cool, popular ones, of course.

Her eyes lingered on our food for a split second longer before she ushered her friends away. "See you guys later."

The three of us exchanged glances across the table.

That was weird.

"Kendall's part Taiwanese, isn't she?" Cindy slurped down another spoonful of her grass jelly.

"Yeah, her grandma is from there, and her dad is half Taiwanese, half white. Her mom is white, too, with her family origins going way back in Europe somewhere," I replied. "Her Taiwanese grandma moved in with them a few months ago."

"How funny that Kendall has just discovered taro, then. My dad makes me pork and taro porridge whenever I'm sick. It's the best thing ever."

"Yeah, it's kind of strange," I agreed. "How can you grow up part Taiwanese and never have taro?"

"Hey, you've never had banana cream pie before and you've lived in the US all your life! That doesn't make you less American." Priya threw a crumpled napkin at me, laughing.

I stuck my tongue out at her and threw it back. She ducked in time to avoid getting hit. "Ha, yeah, that's true. Bananas in a pie—who would have thought?" I shook my head in disbelief.

We had all watched a cooking show together a few weeks ago, and one of the contestants baked a banana cream pie, something I'd never heard of before. One of the judges even made a joke about it being as "American as apple pie," and it blew my mind.

"Right. So you can be American even though you don't know what banana cream pie is. And Kendall can be Taiwanese but never had taro. Or any other kind of food." Priya looked at me with a knowing look on her face, like she was a teacher scolding a student.

Or scolding her best friend.

I squirmed around in my seat. "Um, yeah, that's true." *But you didn't have to talk to me like I'm some little kid.*

"Well, I love taro, and I'd love to try banana cream pie someday," Cindy chimed in. "I'd heard about some of those American desserts before but haven't tried many of them. Maybe now that I'm here . . ."

Then she pointed her spoon at me. "By the way, speaking of fun shows, my cousin who lives in Shanghai was telling me about a new movie from China that's supposed to be super cute. Wanna watch it together on Netflix? Maybe after my tutoring class tomorrow?"

"Absolutely!" I exclaimed. Cindy always had the best suggestions for new Chinese shows or movies to watch.

Priya put down her own spoon. "Um . . . maybe we can watch this new movie together?"

I glanced at Cindy. "Uh, yeah, sure," I responded reluctantly.

Although Netflix had English subtitles on a ton of shows from all around the world, I liked to watch Chinese movies and shows without them. It pushed me to really pay attention to the Chinese, and I always picked up new words and phrases when I watched shows that way. With English subtitles on, my brain would automatically read them, and I would find myself not listening very closely to the spoken Chinese.

I hoped Priya would forget about it. The last time we turned on the English subtitles for her, she spent half the time on her phone anyway. Then she'd ask us what had just happened, and we had to keep pausing to explain.

No, thank you. I didn't need another reminder that Priya wasn't interested in the stuff that I was these days.

"Fine, never mind," Priya mumbled, picking up her spoon again and jabbing at the melting shaved ice heap in her bowl. "You two go do your thing."

I couldn't hold back an eye roll. But Cindy glanced between Priya and me with a worried look on her face.

By the time we'd finished our huge bowls of tofu pudding, shaved ice, and grass jelly, it was almost lunchtime. Priya had to head home for a painting class and Cindy's dad had arrived to take us home. I hopped into the car, and Cindy and I chatted about TV shows and movies all the way back to my place.

It was so natural and easy with Cindy. Why were things so hard with Priya lately?

Then, as the car pulled up in front of my house, my pocket buzzed.

After saying my polite thank-yous and waving good-bye, I glanced at it as I walked up our driveway.

Notification from Craftsee.

I froze.

I swiped at the message.

Congratulations! You've made your first sale.

My jaw dropped. It finally happened.

Someone bought one of my amigurumi.

CHAPTER
14

I STARED AT THE MESSAGE, not daring to trust my eyes.

But, yes, it was true, clear as day. A second notification flashed on screen: *$10 has been deposited into your account.*

I couldn't believe it. Someone actually liked my amigurumi enough to pay me ten dollars to own it forever. Wow. This meant my art was worth something to someone who wasn't me. Or my friends.

Mom was wrong. Opening my art to the world *was* a great idea.

I wanted to jump up and down and dance. But I was still standing in plain view of anyone who might look out the window. I shoved my phone back into my pocket and ran up the driveway and into the house.

I had an order waiting. For a real customer.

Once I got to the safety of my room, I skimmed through the order details. The amigurumi that sold was the robot with the heart, one of my favorites. Craftsee also sent me the mailing address of the customer and instructions on how to get a shipping label ready.

Shipping? Uh-oh. I hadn't thought about how to ship my dolls.

Though now that I thought about it, Mom did mention that shipping might be a tricky step. Oops.

I clicked on the *Calculate Shipping Costs* button. The next screen asked for a bunch of information, like was I shipping my product in a box or envelope, what the width and length of the final package were, how much it weighed, and the zip codes of where the package was coming from and then going to.

I remembered seeing some padded envelopes in the basement from that time Dad needed to mail something to potential investors. We also had a kitchen scale that could measure the weight of the final package.

I had a plan! But before opening my bedroom door, I put my ear to it to see if I could hear anyone wandering around the house.

It was quiet as usual. Everyone was busy doing their own thing.

Good.

Just in case, though, I stuck the robot in my pocket.

The padded envelopes were right where I thought they'd be, next to the empty milk bottles we set aside to recycle. There was a whole stack of them, so I took a few extra for the sales I hoped were coming.

I slid the robot inside of one and headed into the kitchen. I found the kitchen scale in a bottom drawer, then weighed the entire package and jotted down the number that flashed on the scale onto a Post-it. Back in my room, I found the mailing address of the customer, typed in the other details Craftsee asked for, and clicked on the *Calculate* button.

The number it spit out: $3.

Ugh. That was more than I expected. Shipping was going to cost almost a third of the ten-dollar doll I was selling!

For the next step, the website presented two more buttons. One was labeled *Charge to Buyer*, and the other had *Pay for Shipping*. It looked like I could pass the three-dollar shipping cost to the customer if I wanted to.

But that seemed like a lot of money on top of what the customer had already paid for. I bit my lip, thinking. It was probably better if I took care of shipping; I didn't want to lose my first sale because of three dollars! It also might look more generous if the seller took care of this fee. Maybe I could raise the price of my other dolls to cover for this added expense later.

With a sigh, I clicked on the *Pay for Shipping* button.

Next step: *Print Label*.

The only printer at home was in Mom's study. I had to make sure she wasn't in there.

I tiptoed down the stairs and peeked into her study. Empty. The coast was clear—for now.

I ran to my room, clicked on *Print*, and sprinted back to the study. The printer whirred and beeped, warming up as I tapped my foot.

Come on, come on.

When it finally finished, I grabbed the shipping label and spun around to leave.

"Pearl, what are you doing here?"

Mom stood in the doorway. I stuck the paper behind my back.

Think fast, Pearl.

"Um, I needed to print the Handmade Craft flyer," I lied. "I wanted to show it to Priya and Cindy."

"Ah, Handmade Craft is coming again? When?" Mom walked to her desk with a glass of water in her hand. I adjusted my position so she couldn't see what was printed on the paper hidden behind my back. She settled into her desk chair.

"The third weekend of August." I shifted my weight from leg to leg.

"I know how much you like going to the fair. Maybe I'll come with you this year. Our pilot will be launched by then. It'd be nice to spend some time together, don't you think?" She looked at me with eager eyes.

"Um, sure, we can talk about it later," I responded half-heartedly. "I gotta go, Mom."

I slowly backed my way out the study door, then spun around and made my break for it.

Back in my room, I sighed a breath of relief. My Craft-see secret was still safe.

Although lying to Mom again didn't feel great.

At least my first order was finally ready for shipping! But there was one last thing I wanted to do.

I had read on a craft blog that customers liked how personal small businesses could be, especially compared to big brands that treated customers the same. So I wanted to include a handwritten thank-you note in all of my orders.

I picked out the nicest stationery I had, a light blue pattern with cute little bears on it that I got at a stationery store in Taiwan last year. It was very kawaii, which made it perfect to represent the Kawaii Crochets brand. I wrote a short note thanking the customer for buying my robot and hoping they liked it. Then I signed my name with a flourish, folded it in half, and slid it into the package. I sealed the padded envelope shut, taped on the shipping label, and stuffed the package into my backpack.

"I'm going to step out for a minute," I called out as I headed out the door.

I practically skipped to the mailbox on our street.

This was it! My first sale ever.

But as I stood in front of the mailbox with the package in my hand, something held me back. This was the first time I was giving away one of my amigurumi to someone I didn't know. To a complete stranger. Were they going to take good care of it?

I took a deep breath and looked around. Nobody.

"Goodbye, little robot," I whispered. "You'll be okay. I hope you enjoy your new home, and I hope you make your new owner happy."

I pulled open the mailbox handle and slid the package in. It thumped softly as it landed safely inside.

Just like that, my first sale was complete.

This was easier than I thought it'd be. I'd have a real booth at Handmade Craft in no time.

CHAPTER
15

THE NEXT FEW DAYS WERE both exciting and stressful for Kawaii Crochets. After seeing how much shipping was with that first sale, I decided to raise the cost of each doll from ten to fifteen dollars. Plus, Craftsee took 5 percent of every sale I made as a transaction fee. That meant that on top of me paying three dollars for shipping, I had to pay Craftsee fifty cents. By raising the price of my dolls, I could make a profit of about eleven or twelve dollars on each, rather than the measly six dollars and fifty cents I made from the robot.

Some of my dolls were smaller than others, which meant some were going to cost a little less to ship because of the weight difference. I decided to charge the same for each doll, though, to make it simpler on customers.

But what if that fifteen-dollar price tag was too expensive? Was that going to turn away buyers?

I checked my phone every other minute that day. Even my parents, who were usually way more glued to their phones than I was, noticed how nervous I was. At dinner that night, which was leftover food from lunch at their office, Mom made me turn my phone off until bedtime.

That night was agony.

But when I finally got my phone back, the wait was worth it.

I'd made another sale!

A huge weight lifted off my shoulders after seeing that next order. My first sale wasn't just luck. Kawaii Crochets was starting to work.

Then, over the next week, another five of my dolls found new, happy owners. I'd sold a grand total of seven dolls!

All these sales brought my profit total to a little over seventy-five dollars. I was halfway to the $150 I needed to pay for a Handmade Craft booth! I was getting so close.

To keep track of how Kawaii Crochets was doing, I wrote down my sales in my notebook:

Kawaii Crochets Sales

	Item	Revenue	Expenses		Sent?	Profit	Total Profit
			Shipping Fee	Craftsee Transaction Fee (5% of sales)			
1	Robot	$10	$3.00	$0.50	✓	$6.50	$6.50
2	Cow	$15	$2.00	$0.75	✓	$12.25	$18.75
3	Donut	$15	$2.50	$0.75	✓	$11.75	$30.50
4	Avocado	$15	$3.00	$0.75	✓	$11.25	$41.75
5	Octopus	$15	$2.50	$0.75	✓	$11.75	$53.50
6	Unicorn	$15	$3.00	$0.75	✓	$11.25	$64.75
7	Honeybee	$15	$3.00	$0.75	✓	$11.25	$76.00

This morning, after sending off a crochet unicorn and honeybee to their new homes, I stopped by Boba Time to celebrate with a drink.

I'd been there for about half an hour when Auntie Cha stopped by my table. "Pearl, can you manage the shop for a few minutes while I go to the back to take care of some things?"

I nodded. It was fun to pretend I was the owner of the shop, greeting customers and ringing up orders like an adult.

With my yarn and crochet hook in hand, I settled on

the stool behind the counter. Auntie Cha disappeared to the back.

A few minutes later, her voice traveled to the front room. She talked on the phone a lot these days, although I could never make out what she was talking about or who she was talking to.

I hoped with all my heart that she wasn't talking to Mr. Huang about giving up Boba Time for his new Code Together Academy location.

Hang in there, Auntie Cha! I wanted to say every time I noticed her wringing her hands. *I got this. I have a plan!*

Luckily, the fridge was still in one piece, humming away loudly in its corner. But that whirring sound *was* starting to sound more and more like a crashing helicopter every day.

I'd decided not to tell Auntie Cha about Kawaii Crochets—for now. Not that she'd think it was a bad idea; I was sure she would be proud of me for putting my work out there.

But what if I failed? I didn't want her to get excited in case I couldn't raise the money. That was still a real possibility.

My Craftsee shop was only a pilot anyway. The real deal was selling at Handmade Craft. It was better to hold on to any news, good or bad, until I was sure this was going to work.

I swiped open my phone to find the pattern I was working on.

A notification flashed on the screen.

New customer review on Craftsee.

Oh, yay!

Something fun and surprising from making real sales was that customers were starting to leave reviews on my Craftsee page. They were all so nice, with people leaving comments like, *So sweet!* or *Fast shipping*, or *The doll is adorable! My granddaughter loves it!*

I tapped on the notification right away, excited for a little ego boost.

But this review was different.

Terrible product! The octopus I ordered arrived with two of its legs unraveled and the end of the yarn poking out. Not as advertised. Don't buy from this shop!

My jaw dropped. What on earth? I never would have sent a bad amigurumi on purpose. Something must have happened during shipping.

And this customer was so mean! Whoever it was went straight to posting this horrible review for everyone to see without giving me a chance to fix it first.

This was a problem. If other buyers saw this bad review, they might not trust me and then not buy anything.

How was I going to fix this?

Suddenly, the chime of bells filled the air. A new customer had entered Boba Time.

I tried to shake the bad review out of my mind so I could focus on Boba Time. I forced a smile onto my face.

"Hello, welcome to Boba Time. How can I help you?"

I didn't recognize this customer. He looked like a college student, with a San Francisco Giants baseball hat on his rumpled hair and a gray hooded sweatshirt on top of black jeans. Tapping his foot, he peered at the menu I slid to him.

"I'll take a green tea boba. Do you have agave syrup?"

I shook my head.

"Then no sweetness. And no ice."

I started to put the drink together like I'd done many times before. My head whirled with the mean words of the review echoing in my head like a bad song from the radio.

Terrible. Not as advertised. Don't buy from this shop.

I grabbed the pitcher of pre-brewed green tea that Auntie Cha kept in the fridge and topped off the drink with a scoop of boba, a few ice cubes, and a dollop of honey, which Auntie Cha usually uses to sweeten her drinks. I handed the customer his drink and typed in the amount he owed into the cash register.

He took a sip and made a face. "Wait, did you add

something sweet to this? I told you, no sweetness!" He swirled the drink with the straw, making the ice cubes clink together.

"And I said no ice cubes. What is this?"

Argh. My head was so distracted I completely blanked on his request for no sweetness, no ice cubes.

"I'm so sorry!" I grabbed the tea back from him. "I'll make you another one."

"That's right that you'll make me a new one, little girl. What is a kid like you doing managing this store anyway?" He shook his finger at me.

I stood, rooted to the spot in shock. No one had ever been rude to me like that before.

What was this man talking about? He didn't know me! I wasn't a little girl—I even had my own business. And it was making real money!

Usually, my voice escaped me in moments like these. But something inside me cracked. How dare he say that to me here, in my beloved Boba Time?

I opened my mouth to yell back.

But then Auntie Cha dashed in, wiping her hands on her apron.

"Sir, sir, I'm so sorry! I asked Pearl to tend to customers while I did a task out back." She spoke quickly, in English. "Let me fix it. I'll make you a new tea and give you a coupon for a free drink the next time you come."

He huffed at her. "You shouldn't be so irresponsible and leave a kid out here. What if something bad happened?"

I couldn't believe this man's attitude! And for a grown-up like him to speak that way to Auntie Cha? Where was his sense of respect??

But Auntie Cha didn't say anything. She made him another drink, but without honey and ice cubes this time. Then, not only did she give him a coupon like she said she would, but Auntie Cha also gifted him a free box of her signature green tea blend!

I scowled in the corner but did my best to stay out of her way.

Finally, the bells jangled behind him as he left. The second the door closed softly shut, I turned to Auntie Cha.

What had just happened?

CHAPTER 16

"WHY WERE YOU SO NICE to that man?" I exploded. "He was awful! And he said such mean things about me and you and Boba Time!" I paced back and forth. "No one should talk to anyone that way."

Auntie Cha sighed, wiping her brow with the apron. "Sometimes, it's not worth arguing, especially when a customer is angry." She continued in Taiwanese. "Yes, he was rude. But this is my shop, and I want happiness here. If you stay positive and respond with kindness, then the only way they can respond is to do the same."

"But what he said . . . That wasn't fair, Auntie Cha."

"Well, did you make a mistake, Pearl? Did he get what he wanted?"

I couldn't deny that she was right. I did make a

mistake. Although it was that crummy review's fault, not mine.

"A confrontation with a customer isn't about who's right or who's wrong. What's important is to walk away from a hard conversation knowing you were the best person you could be in that situation. And that they walk away willing to give your store another chance." Auntie Cha wiped the counter and poured some green tea into a small cup. She scooped in some boba and handed it to me with a smile.

"Don't worry. Mistakes happen. I'm glad to see you were willing to stand up for yourself. Just think about why you're doing it. It's different when you're representing a business."

Huh. I hadn't thought about that before. I always wanted to be like those people in movies or TV shows who could say that perfect zinger in response to a mean comment. They'd land the comeback and then walk away with flair, leaving the offender behind, speechless and groveling.

But maybe Auntie Cha was right. Business was different. You needed people to come and buy from your shop over and over again. Was there anything to gain from being mean back to a mean customer?

I reread the bad review on Kawaii Crochets with Auntie Cha's words in my ear. Kawaii Crochets was my store. I had the power to keep it a positive place. And be a good, responsible shop owner.

What just happened gave me an idea on how I could right this amigurumi wrong.

When I got home a few hours later, Jade and Dad were chatting in the living room. I waved a quick hello, then bounded up the stairs and flipped open my laptop. I pulled up the bad customer review and clicked on the *Reply* button.

Reading those harsh words still hurt. But Auntie Cha's words echoed in my head: *What's important is to walk away from a hard conversation knowing you were the best person you could be . . .*

I could be the bigger, kinder person here.

I took a deep breath and started typing:

I'm so sorry that happened. I'd never trick you on purpose. Can I make it better by sending you a new doll for free? You can pick any one in my shop. Or I can make you a brand-new octopus. Please let me know, and thank you for the review so I can fix the problem.

It wasn't easy to click the send button. But I did. Typing "thank you" was especially hard, because, to be honest, I wasn't feeling very thankful that such horrible words were out in the world for everyone to see. Plus, sending the customer an extra doll, free of charge, meant I would have one less to sell.

But I swallowed it down.

I had to. Boba Time needed me to be a good, responsible business owner.

Like Auntie Cha.

Now all I could do was wait for the customer to respond.

A distraction would be super helpful right now. I wandered back downstairs and joined Dad and Jade in the living room. Cups of tea steamed on the coffee table, although one mug was empty. I helped myself to a handful of guāzǐ from the bowl that balanced between my dad and sister on the couch. I popped one of the watermelon seeds in my mouth and cracked open the shell with my back teeth as I settled into an armchair.

"I don't know, Dad. I don't want that type of publicity," Jade was saying. "Can't I keep working on the app and not be the face of anything?"

Dad nodded at me but kept talking to Jade. "It might be fun. You'd get a photo shoot out of it, maybe even some pictures you could use to advertise your app." He pointed at the smiling teenagers on the Code Together Academy pamphlet he held in his hand. They looked like they came straight from some stock photography website.

In other words, corny and boring.

I guess Mr. Huang had followed through on asking Jade to help Code Together Academy with marketing. I could see why he'd be excited about having a real student like Jade on the cover.

But Jade didn't seem that excited about the idea.

I cracked open another watermelon shell and pulled out the seed with my fingers. Tossing a handful of empty hulls into a bowl on the coffee table, I chimed in. "Wow, Mr. Huang was serious about you being the Code Together spokesperson? That's so cool! You'd be in the ads and everything."

"But I don't want to be in ads." Jade sighed.

Mom walked in carrying a kettle and her tea timer. She poured some hot water into the teapot sitting on the table and placed the kettle onto a coaster. Then she set the timer and settled into the armchair opposite of mine.

"Jade, we're not going to force you to do anything you don't want to do. But you're an important figure in the case for inspiring more girls to explore technical fields. Think about how many girls will look up to you and follow in your footsteps. You know how big the gender gap is between men and women engineers in the Valley," Mom said.

Jade ran her hands through her short hair. "I know, I

know. But I'm not sure I want to be a role model."

"Well, I think you can be more grateful to Mr. Huang for supporting you all this time. It's only a few pictures, isn't it?" Mom pushed harder.

A small flicker of jealousy flashed through my body. If Jade became the Code Together spokesperson, then she'd forever cement her position as my parents' favorite kid.

I wouldn't have a fighting chance.

Plus, it wasn't fair that Mom and Dad were both ganging up on Jade.

Time to change the subject.

"Hey, Mom, Dad, how's it going with the pilot?" I hadn't talked to them in a few days about how their work was going because of how busy I'd been with Kawaii Crochets. But I knew they launched the pilot of their software two days ago.

Jade threw me a grateful look.

"It's going smoothly so far, although it's still early," Dad replied. "So far, all the customers who are beta-testing it for the next few weeks have been set up with the software and are using it."

"I still think we need to find a few sole proprietors selling physical goods, though," Mom said. "There's no one like that testing our product yet."

"A sole proprietor? What's that?" I asked.

"It's one person running a business on their own," Dad replied. "That type of business owner has different needs than a business with a team where they can divide and conquer tasks, with several people managing finances and using our product. A sole proprietor does everything—making the product and selling it and keeping track of sales."

The tea timer beeped, and Mom removed the strainer from the pot and put it on a small plate. Then she poured tea into the empty mug. "Pretty much all our testers right now are selling digital products or have others managing fulfillment for them. I'm a little worried that our product doesn't do enough to help sole proprietors manage complicated tasks like packaging and shipping."

Mom clearly has some weird chip on her shoulder about businesses selling physical products. She didn't want me to sell my dolls because she thought that part would be too hard for me. But now she needed more businesses who did exactly that to help her with hers. What gives?

Craftsee actually made that part pretty easy with whatever formula they used to calculate shipping. In fact, their entire online system also made stuff like taking orders and managing payments a breeze, although they did take a percentage of my sales in exchange.

Dad helped himself to a handful of guāzǐ. "I'll keep working on that, I promise. The big moment will be when we have all the feedback at the end of the month. Hopefully there won't be major changes to make before the big product launch."

I thought about how it took me a little while to figure out how to get people to see my Craftsee listings.

"How are you going to make sure people know about your product when it gets out there? Will you use SEO, too?" I asked.

Jade laughed. "Wow, Pearl! You were listening when I was talking about that the other day, weren't you?"

Dad looked surprised. "Good question, Pearl. I hired a SEO agency to help us with our online marketing. They'll manage all of that."

I grinned. Finally, I had something to add to my family's conversation.

Mom leaned forward, her eyes sparkling. "Pearl! Does this mean you're interested in learning more about SEO and how the internet works?"

Oh no.

"It was just a question," I mumbled, biting down hard on another seed.

"If you want to know more about how SEO and search engines and websites work, Code Together has weekend classes, I think." Mom looked at Jade for confirmation, like Jade was already the expert on everything Code Together.

Jade tucked her hair behind her ear. "Uh, yeah, maybe, I'm not sure."

Geez, thanks for helping me out here, sis. I shot her a glare.

"Mom! I'm not going to take Code Together classes," I said. "Plus, this has nothing to do with coding. It's about running a business, isn't it?"

"What do you think makes SEO work? What do you think is figuring out how to pick those keywords and which businesses to show? It's algorithms and code. You can't learn about business these days without learning about technology, too," Mom insisted.

Dad cleared his throat. "Okay, everyone, let's take this down a notch." His eyes bounced between me and Mom.

Mom ignored him. "Maybe learning a bit more about how the internet works will inspire some stronger business ideas, Pearl."

"Business ideas?" Jade looked at me with furrowed eyebrows. "You had one?"

I sure did . . . and it's working! I wanted to shout. If only they knew—that'd shut down this whole conversation in an instant.

But what if Kawaii Crochets never got another sale

after that bad review? It was too early to tell my family about my shop now.

Plus, there was my little white lie about being eighteen years old.

I did the only thing I could think of—escape. Quickly.

I stood up from the armchair, my hands full of empty watermelon seed shells. I tossed them into the bowl on the table.

"Geez, all I wanted was to have a chat with my family. Does it always have to turn into a conversation about me not being techy?" I growled. I stomped back upstairs.

Mom was like a broken record. I'd show her that I didn't need any of that technology stuff to make my business successful.

Just my amigurumi.

I spent the next few hours in my room, avoiding Mom and crocheting and watching Netflix. Then, right as I finished making an amigurumi carrot, with cute loops of green yarn, my phone buzzed.

Craftsee message received by customer.

I sat up straight from my lounging position in bed. Heart thumping, I swiped at it.

Yes, a replacement would help. Thank you for responding so quickly. I appreciate your good service.

I breathed a sigh of relief. Crisis averted. I had a solution to the bad review problem.

And more importantly, a satisfied customer.

This didn't mean the bad review was going away. Craftsee wouldn't let me delete it. Plus, I was losing money on this. But if other people see this conversation, then they'd see that I was doing my best to make them happy. They'd see that I was willing to put good customer service ahead of profit. They'd see that Kawaii Crochets was a good store, with good products.

And a good shop owner. Maybe I did have what it took to make Kawaii Crochets a real thing.

It was run by Pearl Li herself after all.

CHAPTER
17

"HERE YOU GO. THANKS FOR coming to Uncommon Threads."

The cashier handed me a paper bag with the three new skeins of yarn I'd picked. My win yesterday deserved a little celebration, so earlier this morning, I decided to bike downtown to Uncommon Threads to pick up some new colors I'd been eyeing.

Today, I was taking home smoky quartz, jelly green, and ripe peach.

I mean, who wouldn't want a peach amigurumi made with ripe peach yarn?

It was a nice, pleasant summer morning in Sunnydale, so I decided to take the long way home through the park.

Strolling couples, kids on scooters, and yapping dogs greeted each other on the walking paths of Rinconada Park. As I coasted along, I spotted some familiar figures up ahead, sitting on a picnic blanket by the side of the path.

It was Kendall Stewart and her Taiwanese grandmother.

My first instinct was to keep biking and pretend I didn't see them. But I couldn't ignore my parents' voices in my head: *Always be polite, especially to elders you know.*

With a sigh, I hopped off my bike and leaned it against a tree. Small pieces of patterned paper were scattered across the picnic blanket where Kendall and her grandma sat. They each held something in their hands, and their fingers moved quickly, like fluttering butterflies.

They were folding origami.

What was the Queen of Tech doing with origami??

Kendall glanced up as I approached. She bowed her head and scrunched her shoulders upward, like she was embarrassed to be caught doing something she didn't want to be seen doing. "Pearl! What are you doing here?"

Her skin was light enough that I could see her face flush.

I didn't want to admit that I was following my

parents' rules like an obedient little kid. So I ignored her and turned to her grandma instead.

"Nín hǎo, nǎinai."

"Ah, nǐ hǎo." She flashed me a big smile. "Look, I am doing origami with my granddaughter. Doesn't she pick it up fast?" She held an intricate paper fox on her palm.

"Wow, that's very nice!" I inspected it closely. It wasn't like any origami I'd ever seen before. Orange paper had been folded into the shape of a fox, and white paper peeked through the face to create plump cheeks. Even its orange tail had a white tip and was curled snugly around its body.

Having made a lot of crafts, I could tell it was exceptionally good handicraft skill. "You made that, Kendall?" The words escaped me before I could stop myself.

Kendall looked surprised at my reaction.

"Yeah, it's something I do with my grandma." She met my eyes and then quickly looked away.

"Kendall's been doing origami with me ever since I moved here. She's been teaching me English, and I've been teaching her origami. And look how good she's gotten!" Kendall's grandma beamed proudly, patting Kendall tenderly on her arm.

Kendall smiled back, then glanced back at me, her cheeks turning pink again. "Um, Pearl, do you mind telling me what she's saying?"

I nodded. It was the least I could do after how mean I was to her the last time I ran into her at Boba Time.

Thinking about that incident made me remember how Priya was harsh to me, too. Ouch.

I quickly translated for Kendall. "Your grandma was telling me how you two do origami together and how much she enjoys it."

"Thanks."

Kendall folded down a corner of the piece of paper in her hand, then looked at her grandma with raised eyebrows. Her grandma shook her head and guided Kendall's fingers to fold in the other direction.

I suddenly felt a pang of jealousy seeing them enjoy origami together. It was like whenever I saw Priya and her dad connecting over their art. What would I give for my own mom to care about my crafts the same way?

Kendall's grandma flipped her paper around and used her fingernails to make a strong crease. "What about you, young lady? Are there any crafts that you like to make?"

My face flushed. I shot a sideways glance to Kendall. Was she going to make another mean comment about my "imperfect" plush cell model or my "doll" that I was too old to be playing with . . . or the strands of yarn that seemed to follow me everywhere?

Instead, she kept folding.

Oh, right. She didn't know what her grandma was asking.

Still, this was not the time to bring up my amigurumi. I didn't want to hear about 3D printing again.

Although Kendall *was* doing handicrafts herself now. And she seemed to be enjoying it.

Just in case, though . . .

"No, I don't do that many crafts," I lied.

And with that, it was time to leave. "Enjoy the afternoon, năinai," I said in Mandarin, backing away slowly. I walked back to my bike and hopped on.

Who would have ever thought that Kendall Stewart would be making something as intricate and delicate as origami with her own two hands? And with her grandma, too?

Maybe there was more to her than I thought.

Ever since I took care of the bad review, sales from Kawaii Crochets kept coming in! I was getting so close to the $150 I needed for the booth fee. But with only a month and a half left before Handmade Craft and me without a real spot to sell yet, I was starting to worry.

Time was running out.

Then, on Saturday night, I was crocheting in my room and watching another Chinese series on Netflix when my phone rang.

I tapped on the green button, doing my best to keep the crochet hook and string of yarn in my hands in the right position. Cindy's chirpy voice chimed through the air.

"Pearl! I have good news for you!"

"Oh, yeah? What's going on?" I finished up the last stitch in that round with a final slip stitch and fastened off.

"You know how my parents play mahjong every Saturday with their mahjong group?"

"Sure, I remember. What about them?" I shrugged.

"They want to buy your dolls! When I got back home from my English class, Auntie Lin saw the cat on my backpack, and she gushed over it for, like, ever! Turns out she had a pet cat like it when she lived in Hong Kong. She asked me where I got it. She wants one, too."

"Really?" I sat up straight, clutching my yarn. "That's amazing!"

"Wait, there's more." Cindy's voice was breathless. "When I showed her your Craftsee account, she said she wanted the duck, too. And then another auntie grabbed my phone from Auntie Lin, and she wants the ice cream one! Pearl . . ." Cindy paused. ". . . Five of the aunties want your dolls!"

I couldn't believe it. I did the math in my head. Five more dolls at fifteen dollars each would be a whooping seventy-five dollars with no shipping or transaction fee, which would bring me well past my $150 goal! That was enough for the Handmade booth!

Then Cindy's words sunk in.

"Wait, you showed them my store on Craftsee? Do they know it's mine?" A wave of panic overcame me, and my heart started to pound. I wasn't ready for people to know this was my store! What if they told someone or said something about it to my mom? She couldn't find out—not yet.

"Oh, no, I didn't tell them whose shop it was," Cindy reassured me.

Whew.

"Cindy, that is amazing. I can't believe they liked my work!"

"I knew you could do it, Pearl!"

"Okay, I'll bring you the dolls they want. Can you ask the aunties to bring you cash to pay for them?"

"Absolutely. Congrats, Pearl." Although I couldn't see her, I could hear her earrings jingle, which probably meant Cindy was jumping up and down in excitement.

I had the best friends.

And pretty soon, I'd have a booth at Handmade Craft, too.

Kawaii Crochets was going big-time.

CHAPTER
18

A WEEK LATER, ALL THE aunties had paid Cindy for the dolls they wanted. After Cindy called me with the news, we agreed to meet at Boba Time to make the exchange. I texted Priya to join us.

We needed to celebrate with boba tea, of course!

Priya was locking up her bike when I cruised into the parking lot. She squealed and tackled me in a big hug before I had a chance to hop off my bike.

"You did it!" she hooted.

I grinned back, trying not to fall. "I'm not all there yet! There's still a lot to do."

"But you're going to have a booth at Handmade. No other twelve-year-old has ever done that before!"

It did feel pretty amazing.

"I know. I can't believe I'm doing this!"

"You're going to set an example for others now. Maybe I'll even sell my own drawings next year. Wouldn't that be amazing?" Priya bounced up and down in excitement.

"That would be amazing, for sure," I replied. "But first, I have to pull this off." I grimaced at the thought of standing behind a booth and talking to strangers about buying my amiguruimi.

"Aw, you'll be fine. I'll help you! I can, right?" Priya smoothed down the flyaway strands of her rumpled, bike-helmet hair with both hands. "It'd be so fun to be on the other side of a booth and chat with customers about your amazing dolls."

Priya would be an absolute natural behind a Handmade Craft Fair booth. We always spent hours at Handmade because she'd talk to pretty much every single booth vendor, asking questions about their creative process and what inspired them to make the things they sold. Having her by my side to charm customers into buying something would be so comforting and fun.

"Of course, silly knight! I'm counting on you to be there." I threw my arm around her shoulder. "I can't do this without you."

Brrring brrring.

"And Cindy, of course." We both turned around and

sure enough, there was Cindy, pedaling toward us with her silver bike and ringing the little bell on her handlebars. She took her helmet off and blew her bangs out of her face before giving me a big hug of her own.

"Congratulations, Pearl! I have your money right here. You did it!" She hopped off her bike and slung her backpack forward, patting it enthusiastically.

I grinned back. "Thanks to you! Let's go celebrate with some boba first."

After we said our hellos to Auntie Cha and got our drinks, we settled in at our usual outdoor table.

"It's cool that you're selling so many at once." Priya leaned back in her chair, twirling her straw. "Handmade is going to be like that. Groups of people buying stuff together."

"I sure hope so." I took a long sip of my winter melon lemon tea with lychee jelly, then reached behind my chair for the bag full of the aunties' amigurumi dolls. "Here you go!" I handed it to Cindy. "Signed, sealed, and delivered."

"Thanks, Pearl. And for you . . ." Cindy rummaged through her backpack and pulled out a thick red envelope with shiny gold lettering on it.

"Ha, what's this about?" I giggled.

Priya looked confused. "Isn't that a Chinese New Year envelope?"

"Yes, that's a hóngbāo. Adults usually put money in these red envelopes for kids to welcome in the new year," I replied. "What are you up to, Cindy?"

"This money isn't regular money, Pearl. This is money that will welcome even more fortune and prosperity," Cindy insisted, almost indignantly. "We have to give this moment the respect it deserves."

She held out the envelope with her two hands. "Gōng xǐ fācái . . ."

". . . hóngbāo ná lái!" I finished, taking the envelope with my own two hands and laughing out loud.

Wow. It felt so good to see my hard work paying off. I was *so* close to Handmade Craft now.

Priya leaned back in her chair and crossed her arms. "You're doing it again," she mumbled.

I lowered my hands slowly. "What's wrong, Priya?"

Priya's eyes darted between me and Cindy, then she shook her head. "It's just . . . when you two speak in Chinese, I don't know what you're talking about."

Cindy furrowed her eyebrows. "Oh, I'm so sorry. Sometimes it slips out."

"Yeah," I agreed. "But it's not a big deal. . . . We weren't saying anything important. It's only a funny expression we say at Chinese New Year, when we wish each other good fortune and then tell the other person to hand the red envelope over."

Cindy leaned toward Priya, eagerly grasping her hand. "We'll be more careful next time. We're sorry."

Priya's face softened. "It's no big deal," she said softly, staring at her hands.

"Right. Sorry," I muttered. Although I still didn't see why it bugged Priya so much. Did Priya have to understand *everything* Cindy and I talked about?

Plus, she didn't seem interested in the other things Cindy and I liked. So what was wrong with us saying a few Chinese things here and there?

"Okay, let's do it my way now." Priya tossed her hair back and sat up straight. She raised her black tea drink high in the air with a big smile. "To Pearl Li and Kawaii Crochets."

"To Boba Time," Cindy added.

The three of us clinked our drinks together.

"And to Team Kawaii." I grinned at my best friends.

Good thing I had such great business partners by my side. I couldn't have gotten this far without them.

Later that night, back at home, I filled in all the sign-up forms for my Handmade Craft booth from my laptop. What Priya had said about being the first twelve-year-old to have a booth made me wonder if there was a minimum age to be a Handmade seller, so I checked the fine print on the forms three times. But there was no place I had to tell them how old I was or check a box saying I was at least eighteen.

Whew. I didn't have to repeat my Craftsee lie.

My heart still thumped hard against my chest when I clicked on the *Confirm Application* button, though.

It was finally happening.

The next few days were agony. What if they rejected my application for some reason? Or if there weren't any booths left to claim?

Then, on Wednesday morning, I was scarfing down cereal in the kitchen when I checked my email again.

A message with the subject line, *A Note from Handmade Craft*, appeared on the top of the screen.

My spoon clattered to the floor as I grabbed my phone with two hands:

Congratulations! A booth has been reserved for Kawaii Crochets at the Handmade Craft Fair coming to Sunnydale, California.

It was official.

I was going to be a vendor at the Handmade Craft Fair.

I dashed upstairs and immediately swapped out the glasses I was wearing for my special red pair.

I also couldn't resist a celebratory dance. In the privacy of my room, I threw Oscar up in the air and twirled like an ice-skater before catching him on his way down.

That wasn't enough to get all my joy out! So I leapt onto the bed, tossed Oscar higher and higher, and jumped up and down like a little kid.

I mean, I had no choice. Kawaii Crochets deserved it.

Breathless, I finally flopped onto my bed and screamed into my pillow. It was happening!

Suddenly, Mom's voice called out from her office downstairs. "Pearl! Everything okay up there? It sounds like the ceiling is about to come crashing down!"

Oops.

I tried to slow down my breath and speak as normally as I could. "Yeah, everything's fine!"

Silence. "All right." Her door creaked shut again.

Whew. That was close. I took a few more deep breaths and gathered myself together.

Okay, focus, Pearl. Now what?

Included in the email was a checklist of things to do to get ready for the fair:

Inventory. Decide how many products you will bring to each day of the fair. We suggest you bring a little more than you hope to sell. Don't forget to prepare price tags for your items. We recommend you offer a variety of products across a range of price points.

Booth decorations. You will be provided with a folding table and two chairs. We recommend you bring a sign with the name of your booth, something to cover the provided table, and a way to display the items you plan to sell.

Business cards. Include your shop name, contact information, and a link to your website or Craftsee store. Many people will buy products online after meeting you at the fair.

Wow. There was a lot to do. And I only had about a month to get ready.

It's okay. I can do this.

First things first. Inventory.

My Craftsee shop was a pilot test for Handmade Craft. I should see what sold well on Craftsee, then make sure I had plenty of those types of dolls to sell at Handmade.

I flipped open my notebook to the page where I'd been keeping track of my sales:

Kawaii Crochets Sales

	Item	Revenue	Expenses		Sent	Net Profit	Total Profit
			Shipping Fee	Craftsee Transaction Fee (5% of sales)			
1	Robot	$10	$3.00	$0.50	✓	$6.50	$6.50
2	Cow	$15	$2.00	$0.75	✓	$12.25	$18.75
3	Donut	$15	$2.50	$0.75	✓	$11.75	$30.50
4	Avocado	$15	$3.00	$0.75	✓	$11.25	$41.75
5	Octopus	$15	$2.50	$0.75	✓	$11.75	$53.50
6	Unicorn	$15	$3.00	$0.75	✓	$11.25	$64.75
7	Honeybee	$15	$3.00	$0.75	✓	$11.25	$76.00
8	Jellyfish (replacement for Octopus)	($15)	$3.00	$0.75	✓	($18.75)	$57.25
9	Pink Cupcake	$15	$2.75	$0.75	✓	$11.50	$68.75
10	Ice Cream	$15	$3.00	$0.75	✓	$11.25	$80.00
11	Cat	$15	$0.00	0	✓	$15.00	$95.00
12	Duck	$15	$0.00	0	✓	$15.00	$110.00
13	Robot	$15	$0.00	0	✓	$15.00	$125.00
14	Purple Cupcake	$15	$0.00	0	✓	$15.00	$140.00
15	Pineapple	$15	$0.00	0	✓	$15.00	$155.00

Okay, so what could I learn from this to help me get ready for Phase 2 of Operation Save Boba Time?

The robot was the first thing I sold, and a second customer ordered one, too. Six of the fifteen dolls were some kind of food. No one bought any of my people dolls, or the sloth, which was Cindy's favorite.

Then I looked at all the customer emails I'd gotten to see if there was anything I could learn from them. Eight of them had mentioned that my dolls were gifts for their kids or grandkids.

Hmm. Based on what sold and didn't sell on Craftsee, I should make sure I had plenty of food-themed dolls and robots to sell. Also, designs that a little kid might like.

I pulled out my box of amigurumi from my closet and dumped them all onto the bedroom floor. I sorted the amigurumi into piles by theme and did a quick count. I'd need to make more food ones, for sure. And more robots.

The Handmade Craft organizers suggested having products at a range of prices, with some more expensive and some more affordable.

My dolls had sold well at fifteen dollars each, so I could probably keep that price tag. But what affordable, less-than-fifteen-dollar product could I sell?

A bunch of smaller dolls rolled around at my feet. I

picked up two of them and inspected them closely. I had made them when I was first learning how to crochet. They were basically little balls that could be turned into different animals, like a frog or panda or lion, by adding eyes or ears. I'd also added a chain and key ring to make a few of them into key chains.

When I first realized that I'd have to pay for shipping, it didn't make sense to put these key chains up for sale on Craftsee. They would probably need to be priced at about five dollars because they were small. And then, if it cost a dollar or two to ship, it'd still only mean a three- to four-dollar profit on each key chain.

Definitely not worth it.

But I wouldn't have to pay for shipping at Handmade. And five-dollar key chains would be pretty affordable for shoppers. Plus, I could make a bunch more really fast.

I had an inventory plan! It was a lot I needed to crochet to add to my stock of product, but I could do it.

Next up was to figure out booth decorations. How was I going to turn an online Craftsee shop into a real booth that could display all my amigurumi dolls *and* catch the eyes of over ten thousand customers?

Time to call in Team Kawaii.

CHAPTER
19

A FEW HOURS LATER, THE three of us met at Second Closet, Sunnydale's biggest secondhand store, to look for booth decorations together.

It was Priya's idea to come here when I called her for help.

"We'll find lots of fun stuff at Second Closet. My dad comes here all the time for random supplies, and my mom's found some special South Indian antiques here, too," Priya explained. "Your amigurumi have such big personalities that your booth design needs to have the same quirky vibe. I bet things will be cheaper there, too."

I'd never been inside Second Closet before. But I figured Priya would know what she was talking about.

Especially if it was a place the entire Gupta family liked going to.

Then, when we stepped inside the store, my jaw dropped open. The place was packed wall to wall with the most random mix of knickknacks I'd ever seen. An assortment of kites hung from the ceiling along with hand-painted signs pointing out different sections of the store, from arts and crafts to media to office to garden to kitchen. Bins of empty egg cartons, metal tins, and plastic lids overflowed in front of the cash register, and brightly colored stools and chairs dotted the space between aisles and aisles of picture frames, desk lamps, wooden crates, and discarded trophies.

There was even a stack of old wooden wagon wheels propped up to the side of the entrance.

Team Kawaii grinned at each other.

It was treasure-hunting time!

The first aisle we walked down boasted a huge assortment of dusty vintage signs and posters.

"How about something like this?" Cindy held up a wooden sign with "Welcome" painted in curly pink letters with flowers and vines swirling around.

I shook my head. "Too floral. I want something charming, with personality. We're going for the kawaii look, remember?"

"How about this one?" Priya pointed at a poster with

"Reach for the sky" printed on it, and a plump cartoon cat flying through the air with a rainbow trailing behind it.

"Closer! Snap a pic." She held out her phone and took a picture of the poster and its price tag.

"I can't believe you're going to be hosting a booth at the fair! How many people did you say are going to come?" Cindy's voice drifted over from the next aisle.

I pulled out the crumpled to-do list from my jeans pocket, although I already knew the number by heart. But maybe I'd get used to the ridiculously high number if I saw it enough times.

"Ten thousand customers."

Nope. My heart still raced.

I was going to need a lot of boba to keep my courage up.

On Craftsee, no one knew who I was. I had listed my shop owner's name as Pearl, no last name, nor initial. For the shop owner's picture, I put in a picture of Oscar instead of a picture of myself.

Handmade Craft was much scarier because I would be actually standing behind a booth, which meant people would know that I made all these dolls.

I got the chills thinking about it. And not in a good way.

"Hey, over here!" Priya waved us over from two aisles away.

She pulled at a set of pastel blue suitcases nestled between a stack of silk ruffled pillows and a set of dusty golf clubs. "You could open these up and use them like a display for your dolls. It could be way more fun than a boring stand or shelf."

"Oh, how cool!" I dashed over. She popped open one of the suitcases to reveal red-and-white-striped lining inside.

Priya really did have the best ideas.

"Have you decided on your colors yet?" Cindy's voice floated up above somewhere close by.

"Not sure yet," I called back. "Maybe something pastel? Like baby blue or cotton-candy pink?"

"Come check out this tablecloth"

I found Cindy three aisles over holding up a patterned mint-and-pink tablecloth. "It's not blue, but the green and pink are cute together. And look at these suns! They've got those big kawaii eyes and tiny mouths, like your dolls."

"Love it!"

We wandered the store for over an hour. In the photo section, I got the idea to use these silver tabletop stands to clip price tags or product labels. Priya was on creative fire and came up with another fun idea to use real food containers, like fruit baskets or colanders, to put my food dolls inside.

With each find, Priya snapped a photo of the product and its price tag. I couldn't buy these decorations now. I still had to figure out how to get them from the store to my house and where to hide them.

But at least I could get an idea of what everything might cost.

After an hour, we had our final list of decorations ready. While Priya read off the prices from her phone, Cindy entered them into the calculator app on hers.

I crossed my fingers that the total would be low. After I paid the Handmade booth fee, I had forgotten to shut down my Craftsee shop, like I had told Priya I would. A few more sales came in, which meant I had about fifty dollars in my Craftsee account.

For now, my Craftsee shop was on "vacation" mode. I had to save the rest of my inventory for Handmade . . . but I didn't want to get rid of everything on Craftsee yet.

Maybe there was a chance I could keep selling after saving Boba Time.

"All right, here's the total!" Cindy tapped her phone with a flourish.

Her face dropped. She flipped the phone around so we could see.

$124.32.

My heart sank. I didn't have that much.

Turns out, to make money, you need money. I needed

money to book the booth. Then I needed even more money to sell at the booth.

And there wasn't enough time to wait for more Craft-see sales to come in.

Now what?

CHAPTER
20

PRIYA AND CINDY TRIED TO cheer me up by taking me to Boba Time. But when we stepped inside the shop, who was standing at the counter but Kendall Stewart herself.

Again.

Next to her, staring at the menus in their hands with confused looks on their faces, were Nora Thomas and Andrea Vasquez.

What were they doing here??

At the sound of the bells clinking against the front door, all three of them turned around. A relieved look fell across Auntie Cha's face.

"Hi, girls!" she called out in Mandarin. "Look, some of your classmates are here."

Kendall waved us over. "Funny seeing you here again, Pearl. Do you come here a lot?"

"It's her favorite place in Sunnydale," Priya chimed in, walking over to stand by my side. She seemed to stretch herself a bit taller, like she was getting ready to defend me. I felt my heart swell a tiny bit. There was my knight in shining armor, like from before.

Kendall looked around the shop. "Yeah, this is a super-nice café. My grandma loved the tea that she got last time, so my dad asked me if I could come get some more for her. He's been busy with his job, so I told him I'd do it."

"What's he working on anyway?" Nora piped up. "Give us the inside scoop on what's coming!"

All the kids at Lynbrook Middle School knew that Kendall's dad led the team that worked on the newest features for one of the most popular social media app companies in Silicon Valley. He—and, by extension, Kendall—was a big deal around here.

Kendall shuffled her feet and stared down at them. "Come on, you know I don't know anything. He doesn't share those details with me. He's not allowed to share them with anyone."

"Holding out on us again!" Andrea nudged Kendall with a roll of her eyes.

"No, I really have no idea." The tiniest of wrinkles

appeared between her eyes. "Even when I try to learn about the newest tech, he never says if any of it has to do with what his team is working on."

Hmm, that was a surprise. I assumed that Kendall knew all the ins and outs of the new technologies her dad was working on, and that her insider knowledge was why she turned her nose up at anything that wasn't as "state-of-the-art."

I guess she didn't know any more than the rest of us did.

I was also surprised to hear that Kendall tried to learn about new technology as a way to connect with her dad. I had tried to do the same, with the whole SEO thing, although Mom took it in a direction I wasn't expecting.

Sounds like Kendall and I both had some work to do to keep up with our techy families.

Auntie Cha spoke up in English. "Pearl, these girls aren't sure what to order. Maybe you can help them with the menu."

Nora waved the menu in her hand. "Yeah, sorry, but I'm not sure what these things mean. It's all . . . different." She threw a glance at Kendall, who smiled back at her encouragingly.

I took the menu from her and skimmed it. One side was in English, and the other was in traditional Chinese characters. On the English side, there were just a few short phrases explaining the different tea bases and toppings you could combine to customize your boba tea.

I knew Boba Time so well that I hadn't looked at a menu in ages. It *did* look awfully confusing.

"Hmm, well, why don't I suggest something?" I asked. "My favorite is the sparkling mango green tea with boba."

"Oh, I love mango," Andrea said. "But boba's a bit heavy. Anything . . . lighter?"

"You could try àiyù jelly instead," Cindy suggested. "It's like a fruity, lemon-y Jell-O. It's made from a special type of fig that grows in Taiwan."

Andrea nodded. "That sounds good. I'll try that."

"I don't like to have sugary things," Nora proclaimed with a toss of her head, ponytail swinging. "Anything here for me?"

Priya piped up. "I don't like sweet things, either. You could get a nice chilled tea, no sugar. The black tea blend here is kind of special."

I bit my lip, thinking. I remembered that Nora had a wheatgrass smoothie when we ran into her at Sweet Yam Cafe.

"You might like grass jelly. It's made from a mint-like plant and has an herbal flavor. And it's not that sweet."

"I add a little ginger to give it a special taste. It is good for the skin, too." Auntie Cha said proudly.

Nora touched her porcelain-smooth face. "Yeah, I guess I'll try that."

"And I'll try the taro slush with boba," Kendall said.

Cindy laughed. "You sure like taro, don't you?"

Kendall smiled back, tucking her hair behind her ears. "I guess I do!"

Cindy, Priya, and I sat at a table to wait for our turn to order while the other three girls chatted by the counter. After Auntie Cha prepared their drinks, she handed Kendall a jar of tea for her grandma, then rang up their orders on the cash register. Kendall pulled out a wallet from her purse to pay; then the girls grabbed their drinks and took a sip. They nodded at each other approvingly. Andrea pulled out her phone and snapped a selfie of them posing with their Boba Time drinks.

A car honked, and Nora and Andrea headed outside while Kendall stopped by our table.

"Thanks for the recommendations, Pearl. You sure seem to know a lot about Taiwanese stuff," Kendall said.

"I guess," I managed to reply, pushing my glasses up my nose. "My family went to Taiwan last summer, and I learned a lot then."

"Well, this is all new for me. Until my grandma moved in with us, I didn't have much of a reason to get to know this side of myself. To tell you the truth, it can be a bit overwhelming at times," Kendall confessed, playing with her straw. "But I'm learning . . . slowly."

The car honked again. Through Boba Time's glass doors, I could see Andrea standing next to a silver Tesla with the door open, motioning at Kendall.

"Thanks again for your help with the menu, Pearl. These drinks are yummy." Kendall took a sip of her taro slush, then turned to leave. "See you three around," she called out. I watched through the shopwindows as Kendall and her friends piled into the car, Boba Time cups in hand.

The disappointment from leaving Second Closet empty-handed earlier this morning still weighed on me. And it was a bit unsettling to see Kendall and her friends here at Boba Time, which was *my* special spot.

It was even weirder to get a glimpse into Kendall's world. She was only now starting to learn about her Taiwanese side? And was all this new tech she talked about her way of trying to connect with her dad?

It was a little hard to figure out. Who *was* Kendall Stewart anyway?

Whatever had just happened, though, I did feel a little bit better.

Because despite everything, we had just helped score Boba Time some new customers.

CHAPTER
21

TEAM KAWAII HUNG OUT A bit longer at Boba Time before we each headed home. I had a lot of crocheting to do to hit my inventory goals.

When I stepped into the house, Mom, Dad, and Jade were all gathered together in the kitchen.

"Hi, Pearl! We were about to call you," Mom said from behind the kitchen counter. "Dad and I have been working so hard lately that we thought it'd be nice to take a break and go watch a movie together. You in?"

"I'm going, too." Jade took a canned drink from the fridge. "I'm going cross-eyed trying to figure out how to make a new feature work on my app. I need a break."

My heart leapt at the chance to do something—anything—with my family. It'd been a week since I had stormed off after Mom insisted I take classes at Code Together Academy. But one of the unspoken rules of the Li household was to avoid any touchy topics for as long as we could, so things had gone back to relative calm in our house.

Our energy still felt a little weird, though. A family hangout would wipe that last trace of awkwardness away.

Then a bright yellow Post-it with the words "Handmade Craft" caught my eye. It was stuck neatly on the calendar that my parents kept pinned up on the kitchen wall.

Oh no. Mom was serious about coming to Handmade with me. How was I going to manage that??

Plus, there were only a few weeks left until the fair. And my amigurumi wasn't going to make itself. I still had *so much* to do.

"Um, I wish I could, but I need to stay and talk to Priya about something," I lied.

"You sure, Pearl? It's not like you to give up a chance to do things together." Mom looked concerned.

"Yeah, I know," I mumbled. "But I promised."

Please, please, please let it go.

Mom looked at me for a long second. "All right. We'll miss you." She gave my hair a quick tousle, then got up from her seat. "I'm a little hungry. I'm going to bring some stuff to munch on to the theater." She started rummaging through our cabinets for snacks.

"I'll get my coat." Jade turned and headed upstairs.

Dad got up, too. "There's some stuff in the car I'm going to unload before we head out," he told Mom. "Let's meet out there in a few. See you later, Pearl." He waved as he shut the door to the garage behind him.

I sighed. What a bummer that I had to crochet. This was the first time since I started making amigurumi that it felt like a pain.

It was even worse that I was about to miss out on a family moment, with all three of them taking a rare break from their work.

Then I remembered Kendall talking about what her dad and his team and whatever work they did. Like her, I didn't really know much about Mom's business.

But I could change that. Maybe Mom and I could be more like Priya and her dad, who shared everything.

"Hey, Mom?"

"Yeah?" She poked her head out of the pantry, her hands clutching a box of green onion soda crackers.

"Before you leave, do you mind if I ask . . . what does your product actually do?"

"What do you mean, Pearl? You know the gist, don't you?"

"Yeah, I know it is supposed to help small businesses

with their finances. But how does it do that?"

Mom shoved the crackers into her bag and joined me again at the kitchen island. "What I'd like to do is help small businesses. Sometimes they have trouble keeping track of all the sales they've made and who's bought what and from where. Right now, there is software for that, but it's hard to use if you aren't trained in accounting. I'm making something that's cheaper and more user-friendly, something that anyone can easily use."

"How do these small businesses manage their finances now?" I wondered out loud.

"Right now, they have to pay a lot for systems with features they probably don't need or figure out how to use the complicated tools that exist. Or just write it all down. Sometimes they end up with papers and receipts and invoices all over their desks."

A bell rang in my head, tickling my memory. I'd heard someone say those exact words before. But who . . . ?

"You mean like Mr. Gupta, Priya's dad? He sells his paintings at galleries and online. He says it's hard for him to keep track of everything he sells."

Mom stared at me, eyes widening. "Yes, exactly like Mr. Gupta. Hmm, I hadn't thought of that angle. But it's true that artists like Ravi Gupta are a type of business owner. Sole proprietors, to be exact." She tapped her cheek with her finger. "I wonder if he'd be interested in being a beta tester for our product."

Jade popped her head into the kitchen. "Mom, we better get going." She pointed at her Apple Watch. "Movie's going to start soon."

"Well, I hope my explanation of the business makes sense, Pearl. I appreciate you asking," Mom said, smiling as she hoisted her bag over her shoulder. "I'm always happy to tell you more another time."

Then she and Jade headed into the garage, and I watched from the kitchen window as Dad backed out our Subaru and drove away.

When the car turned the last corner, then disappeared into the evening, I swallowed down the lump of disappointment stuck in my throat.

It did feel good to know a little more about what my mom and dad spent all their time doing, and it was exciting to hear that it was something that could help artists like Mr. Gupta. I was also glad they were taking a break. . . . They had been working so hard.

I wished I could hang out with them now.

But even though I really wanted to go to the movies with my family, I couldn't slow down. Kawaii Crochets needed me to stay home and work. Boba Time needed me, too. I had made the right decision.

Deep down, though, I wished that it wasn't one I had to make.

With my whole family out of the house, I settled into my room and pulled out my supply of yarn. But seeing the rainbow of bright colors didn't cheer me up like it usually did. I called Priya and Cindy, hoping one of them could help me pass the time. But Priya didn't answer and Cindy had to finish her summer tutoring homework. I turned on Netflix, but my heart wasn't into the show I'd been watching. I clicked on the stop button with a sigh.

At least I could count on Oscar. I pulled him out of my pocket and stroked him gently. Propping him up on my nightstand, I smiled back at his crooked grin.

With Oscar as my only company, I forced myself to make more amigurumi. According to my inventory plan, robots were a good place to start.

Off to work.

Rnd 1: 4 sc into a magic ring [4 sts]

Rnd 2: 3 sc in all 4 sts [12 sts]

A few hours later, the garage door rumbled open. My family was back. I had finished making one robot and was just starting on a second one.

I ran downstairs to join Mom, Dad, and Jade.

"How was the movie?" I asked as Mom walked into the house, peeling off her jacket.

"It was great! Twist ending, though, so I can't say too much." She winked at Dad, who was shuffling his feet into slippers, and Jade, who was already rummaging through the fridge for a snack. "Can you believe what happened at the end?"

The three of them burst into laughter. There they go again, talking about something I didn't understand.

But this time, it was my fault for not joining them.

I mumbled my "good nights" and trudged back up to my room. Seeing my new robot didn't cheer me up like the sight of my amigurumi usually did.

Although I'd made some progress on my Handmade Craft inventory, making something I'd already made before was a little boring. I wasn't a creative artist anymore, testing my skills and trying out new techniques.

I was a factory, churning out as many products as I could.

CHAPTER
22

A FEW DAYS LATER, I walked into Boba Time with my notebook in hand and my head clear and ready for a chat with Auntie Cha. With all my hard work getting ready for Handmade, I figured it was also time to start thinking about how to get more customers into Boba Time. The money I was hoping to make was going to be just enough to fix the fridge. The next step was, as my mom would say, to "figure out a long-term, sustainable business plan" for Boba Time.

Ever since going to Sweet Yam Cafe a couple of weeks ago, I'd been mulling over some ideas that I wanted to share with Auntie Cha.

"Zăo'ān, Auntie Cha! It's Pearl!" The bells jangled behind me. As usual, the scent of tea and honey welcomed me. A small group of aunties chatted away in the corner, and a pair of college-aged girls with a stack of textbooks on their table tapped away on laptops.

Auntie Cha was nowhere to be seen. But I could make out the smell of star anise and licorice in the air. Auntie Cha must be making a new batch of tea eggs.

"Gâu-tsá, Pearl!" a muffled voice responded from the back. "I'm coming!"

She emerged a minute later, blowing her hair out of her eyes and wiping her hands on her apron. Her long black shirt flowed behind her, leaving behind a small cloud of dust. "Sorry, I was clearing out some space in the back. What can I get you today, young lady?"

"Actually, I wanted to talk to you about some ideas I had about Boba Time." I motioned for her to take a seat at one of the tables. "Do you mind?"

"Sure! I'm always happy to talk to you. But let me check on the customers first." She spoke quietly to the ladies, then made her way to the college students. When she was satisfied that they had what they needed, Auntie Cha settled in next to me.

"I went to Sweet Yam Cafe a few weeks ago. Have you been?" I asked.

She shook her head.

"They do some interesting things there that you could

do here, too." I pulled out my phone to show her some photos I'd taken when I was there with Cindy and Priya.

"See, their whole menu is in pictures, and they show all the ingredients and where they come from and how they're made. When those girls were over yesterday, they had a hard time figuring out what to get because the menu was only in words. Maybe you could make menus with more visuals for people who don't know much about your teas and toppings. Sweet Yam Cafe also had really nice printed posters that show off the food. You could design some, too, and hang them up." I showed her some sketches of menu and poster designs I'd drawn inside my notebook.

Auntie Cha listened, nodding her head as I continued.

"Another idea is to make sure people know how natural and healthy everything is here. Andrea liked the fruity tea with àiyù jelly because of how light it was, and Nora liked the grass jelly and how it's good for your skin. Also, remember that rude customer who came in?"

"Yes, of course." Auntie Cha gave me a sympathetic look. "He was quite mean to you."

"It's okay." I smiled back at her. "I learned my lesson. Anyway, he asked for agave syrup. Do you know what that is?"

She shook her head.

"I didn't, either, so I checked it up on the internet. Apparently it's a more natural sweetener than regular white sugar."

"Interesting." Auntie Cha pointed at the ingredients behind the counter. "Most of the things I sell here *are* natural. I make my own purees with fruit from the market and add honey instead of regular sugar. None of that artificial, flavored powder here!"

"Exactly! I think you could do more to make sure new customers know how amazing and fresh your toppings are. You could explain that in the menus or have a list of special drinks and toppings that are especially good for you."

I took a breath and looked at Auntie Cha with eager eyes. "Well, what do you think?"

But she didn't react right away. A thoughtful expression had settled onto her face.

My heart thumped, and my hands started to get clammy. Oh no. Were my ideas terrible?

"You have such a big heart, Pearl," she finally said, leaning forward to touch my hand. "It's an honor that you care about Boba Time so much. These are wonderful ideas."

Whew. I sat back in my chair with a sigh of relief.

"But it's time I told you a story."

Uh-oh. Prickles started to travel up my spine.

Auntie Cha looked down at her hands. "Pearl, when I came here fifteen years ago to make a living, I left something important behind in Taiwan." She sighed. "No, not something, but someone."

Auntie Cha's eyes filled with tears, and she took a deep breath. Then she looked straight into my eyes.

"I left my daughter behind."

My jaw dropped. "Auntie Cha, you have a daughter?"

"I do. She was your age when I left. She had just turned twelve." Auntie Cha dabbed at her eyes with the corner of her apron. "Oh, Pearl, I remember how hard she cried when I left. But I had to. I knew nothing about this country, and I thought I could do more for her if I came alone to run the shop."

"But then . . . who took care of your daughter after you left?" My heart pounded. Auntie Cha wouldn't have left her own daughter all by herself . . . would she?

"My older sister was married and had two kids. I left my daughter with her." Auntie Cha fiddled with the pocket of her apron. "I was a young mother with no husband, and I was scared. When I heard that a family friend was looking for someone to take over a shop lease in Sunnydale, I jumped at the chance to move to America. I'd always wanted to open a tea shop, but there were so many in Taipei. A tea shop in a US city like Sunnydale felt like a special opportunity.

"But what about my daughter? I discussed it with my sister and brother-in-law, and we thought it was better for her to stay in Taipei, surrounded by family and friends. Making her come to a country where both of us would be completely alone didn't seem wise. My plan was to come here, start Boba Time, and then send for her to join me.

"Then one year turned to two, two turned into five, five into ten. Boba Time started to do well after the first few rocky years. Every month, I sent money back to my sister so my daughter could go to the best schools and have the best tutors. The best of everything. But it wasn't enough. My daughter wanted me. She was sad and angry that I left her. For a business." Auntie Cha put her head in her hands and sniffed.

My heart ached for Auntie Cha and her daughter. I could see why Auntie Cha would feel bad about making a twelve-year-old leave her friends to move to a completely new country. Although Cindy had me and Priya, she still texted her friends and family back in Hong Kong almost every day. I knew how much she missed them.

But I imagined how much worse it must have felt to be left behind by your own mother. And to feel like she chose her career over you.

Actually, I didn't need to imagine it. I knew exactly how she felt.

"Do you talk to your daughter now?" I asked.

"I do. Luckily, my sister is a patient and caring mother to both her own children and my daughter. Little by little, my daughter grew to trust her more and more. She now loves my sister like a mom. So she is still surrounded by love, and we talk often on the phone. She graduated college a few years ago and has a great job. She got married a year ago and is about to have a baby. I'm going to be an amah!" Auntie Cha smiled proudly.

"That's so great! You're going to be an amazing grandmother." I beamed back at her. Then I paused.

"But, Auntie Cha, what does all this have to do with Boba Time? And my ideas?"

She sighed. "Every few years, I manage to save enough money to go back to Taiwan. Our time together during those trips makes me so happy. But I cannot stay with her for long because Boba Time needs me. There is no one else who can keep it running. And even though it's not as much as before, I still send the money the shop makes back to Taiwan. With the baby coming, the money will be even more helpful.

"For now, Boba Time is surviving. But I will need to make a big decision soon."

I forced my voice to speak. "What kind of decision?"

Auntie Cha looked around Boba Time, taking in every corner with a sad look on her face. The group of aunties suddenly burst into laughter, all chuckling over some inside joke. The two girls must have finished their studies and were now sharing a set of headphones. They moved their shoulders together, snapping their fingers at a music video flashing on one of their laptop screens.

"I built this shop with my two hands," Auntie Cha continued, her voice quiet. "My hopes and dreams live here. And I've made so many friends because of it. Sunnydale is my home. Like Taipei was.

"I don't want to give up Boba Time. But Taipei calls to me, too. Every night, I ask myself . . . when that fridge finally breaks, do I fight for Boba Time's future with new ideas like yours? Do I keep helping my family from here?"

She took a deep breath.

"Or do I give up Boba Time and move back to Taiwan to be with my daughter and grandchild?"

I couldn't believe what I was hearing.

Auntie Cha wasn't only thinking about giving up Boba Time. She was thinking about leaving Sunnydale.

Forever.

My body felt the way it did right after getting off a roller coaster. A mix of feelings jumbled inside me. I felt sorry for the guilt Auntie Cha had in her heart and for how much she had been missing her daughter. And sad for the daughter who missed her mom for so long.

But what if the one adult who truly understood me, who truly saw me—and my amigurumi—went away? The thought left me breathless and my legs weak.

Whatever I was feeling, one thing was clear. This wasn't just about losing Boba Time.

I was about to lose Auntie Cha, too.

CHAPTER 23

AFTER LEAVING BOBA TIME, I called Cindy and Priya in a panic. They agreed to meet me at Priya's, stat.

But when I got to Priya's home, seeing it filled with the art that she and her family shared didn't calm me down like it usually did. It did the opposite. Seeing how close her family was around their shared passion reminded me of how little of that I had in my own life.

Cindy and Priya were lounging on the floor cushions when I got to the art studio. They sat up straight when I walked in, though, and looked at me with concerned faces.

"Zěnmele?" Cindy asked. "What's wrong, Pearl?"

Taking a deep breath, I told them what Auntie Cha had told me, about leaving her daughter back in Taipei many years ago to start Boba Time. And about Auntie Cha wanting to go back to Taiwan now.

"So when the fridge breaks and Auntie Cha doesn't have the money to fix it, she'll close Boba Time and leave Sunnydale forever. I have to make Handmade Craft work, or Auntie Cha will leave, too!" I finished, desperation rising in my voice.

Cindy scooted over and put her arm around me, squeezing me gently. "I'm so sorry, Pearl. It'll work, you'll see. Your dolls are awesome. How will anyone resist?"

But Priya stayed where she was, her lips puckered. "But what about Auntie Cha's daughter? Family is so important. She probably misses her mom a lot," she said softly.

I wiped my nose with the sleeve of my shirt. "I know. She's about to have a baby, too."

My chest tightened at the idea of Auntie Cha's real daughter in Taipei without her mom for so long.

Or was it from panic at the idea of being alone here in Sunnydale, without the one adult who got me and got my art?

I couldn't tell.

"That's kind of a beautiful thing, isn't it?" Priya leaned forward. "Auntie Cha is going to be a grandma!"

Even though it wasn't what I was hoping to hear, I

couldn't deny that Priya was right. Auntie Cha was going to be an amazing amah.

But I needed her, too. Here in Sunnydale.

"Well, Auntie Cha can always go to visit," I insisted. "Or have her daughter come here. Boba Time is her business; it's her shop. That's gotta mean something important, too." I could hear my voice get higher with desperation.

Plus, her daughter wasn't really alone. She had a husband and friends and the mom she grew up with, Auntie Cha's sister. That was more than enough family, wasn't it?

Pearl, you have to focus on what's most important right now.

You need to get to the Handmade Craft Fair.

I tried to ignore what Priya had said. Because the biggest problem of all still needed solving.

I turned toward Cindy and directed my thoughts at her, avoiding Priya's eyes.

"I've thought it through, and I'm going to be fine on inventory if I keep crocheting." I got up and started pacing back and forth. "If I can't get money for decorations, I could make do with a white tablecloth. But Mom wants to come with me to Handmade this year. How am I going to sell stuff at the fair if I go as a customer? And do it in a way that she doesn't find out about Kawaii Crochets?"

Cindy looked back at me with a blank face, while

Priya shook her head. "See, Pearl . . . if you had gotten permission from your mom to start Kawaii Crochets on Craftsee, this wouldn't be a problem."

Ugh. I knew Priya would eventually throw that in my face. I just knew it.

"That's not helpful, Priya," I replied through clenched teeth. "Can we focus on how I can sell my amigurumi at Handmade without my mom knowing?"

"Fine," she mumbled back, looking away.

What was up with her? Geez.

I threw out a wild idea. "Maybe I could hire someone to stand at the booth and pretend to be me?"

"No way. You can't do that. That'd cost a ton! Plus, you're the artist. You have to be there to represent your work." Priya shook her head, her long black hair whipping back and forth.

"Or I figure out a way to make her think it changed dates to the weekend after. Then she won't come when the fair actually happens."

Cindy frowned. "That'd be a tough one to pull off. There are posters all over town with the actual dates."

I swallowed down the lump rising in my throat. "Help me, please, Team Kawaii," I begged. "I have to make this work."

I turned to Priya desperately. She was being so righteous that I felt like screaming into a pillow. But her ideas were usually amazing.

And I needed a really good one right now.

"Come on, Priya. Help me save Boba Time. For my art. You know how important that is . . . to both of us," I pleaded. "Be my knight in shining armor."

Priya tucked her hair behind her ears. "I do have an idea to make Handmade happen for you. But I don't think you're going to like it."

I leaned in close. "What?"

"I really think you need to come clean with your mom. You need to tell her about Kawaii Crochets. And what you want to do at the fair."

I sucked in my breath and stopped pacing. No way.

Staring at Priya in disbelief, I groaned. "I can't believe you're suggesting that again. You know I can't do that!"

She stood her ground. "Pearl, your dolls are great because you're great at what you do. And because you love amigurumi. I'm sure your mom will let you sell there if you tell her how much it means to you. And she'll help you, too. She knows a lot about business and raising money, doesn't she?"

"I can't tell her yet," I insisted. "Not until I have more proof that my amigurumi is good enough."

"Isn't your love of crocheting enough? My parents know how much I love art, and that's why they support me. Give your mom a chance. She'll get it."

I spun around.

Enough with Priya's endless optimism and all her talk of supportive parents. She just didn't get it how our families were totally different.

And no amount of me pushing back was going to get her to understand.

So I exploded instead.

"Priya, get off my back about talking to my mom!" I shouted, louder than I'd ever spoken to anyone before. "Why do you think everyone's got parents like yours? It's so easy for you. . . . Your parents love the same things you do. Why can't you see how hard it is for me, with parents who don't? Why can't you be on my side, no questions asked?"

Priya's face flushed red.

But I wasn't done. For the first time in my life, my voice was finally saying exactly what was in my head.

"You keep pointing out times I'm wrong and other people are right. Why are you always defending everyone else? Why aren't you defending me anymore? You defend Kendall, you defend Auntie Cha's daughter, you defend Auntie Cha . . . you're even defending my mom! What about me and what I need? What about standing up for that?" I glared at Priya from the middle of her studio. "Geez, Priya! It's like you don't get me anymore! You never try anything new, like at Boba Time or at Sweet

Yam Cafe, even when I tell you how good it is. You don't pay attention when we watch Chinese shows, and then you complain when Cindy and I talk Chinese with each other. What is up with that? What is your problem??"

I threw my arms out wide in frustration, my heart beating a mile a minute. "Why are you such a bad friend??"

Priya gaped at me and my outburst.

But she was never one to take harsh words lying down. Even if they came from her best friend.

She leapt up, eyes blazing. "You're right, Pearl. I *am* defending other people. Because you're the one being selfish. And inconsiderate of other people's feelings. You're only thinking about what you want and what's best for you. What about other people, the people you say you love? What about what's best for them? Maybe Auntie Cha should leave to be with her family!

"And you're right—I don't get you. I don't get why you're working so hard to prove your amigurumi to other people. Just own it, Pearl! Who cares what other people think? You hide behind a vague name on Craftsee and want to get some stranger to stand behind *your* booth and sell *your* art?? You're missing the whole point! Art is about taking a stand for what you believe in, about doing what you love! How can you be a real artist when you can't even talk to your mom about it?"

"Don't fight, please! We can figure something out together," Cindy pleaded, her eyes bouncing between the two of us.

But it was too late. The thread holding us back for so long had finally been cut.

Priya ignored Cindy and pointed her finger at me angrily. "You're the one with the problem. Why are you so scared all the time?"

This time, it was my face that burned red.

I couldn't believe it. It was like Priya saw deep into my heart, at the thing that'd been holding me back, then decided to viciously pull it out into the open to expose to the world.

How dare she.

I steeled my resolve for one last zinger. "I'm not scared." I glared at Priya. "And I don't have a problem. I just need a better knight."

With that, I grabbed my things and stormed out of her house.

Forget Priya and her ideas. I didn't need her.

I'd figure this out myself.

Back at home, I stomped through the house and slammed my bedroom door shut.

My best friend didn't get what was going on.

She didn't see how important Boba Time was to me.

She didn't see how important my art was to me.

She didn't see how important Handmade was to me.

And how could she possibly think that my mom would be okay with me selling my amigurumi at Handmade Craft?? Had she been listening to me at all?

Mom didn't want me selling on something anonymous like Craftsee. Handmade Craft would be out of the question, for sure.

Selling at Handmade would mean her younger daughter was still playing with dolls. And not doing useful things like designing and programming mobile apps like her other, way-more-successful daughter.

No way would Mom be okay with Handmade Craft. Anyone who thought she would be didn't know anything about her.

Or about me.

I was sick of Priya and how her perfectly artsy family accepted her as she was. Why didn't she get how lucky she was? And how unlucky I was to have parents who wanted me to be someone I'm not?

It was so unfair.

I had to go through with Handmade and without my mom knowing. The whole point of being there, aside from saving Boba Time, was to prove to her that my passion was serious and real. To show her how crocheting stuffed animals could be as worthwhile as programming an app. Priya had nothing to prove.

But I did.

I flopped onto my bed, stared at the ceiling, and took a deep breath.

Focus, Pearl. Handmade.

But my head kept going back to what my best friend and I had just said to each other. Priya and I had never fought before. And I'd never confronted anyone like that before.

Is this what it was like to finally say what you're thinking out loud?

Like you'd swallowed a thousand rocks?

A ping from my phone interrupted my muddled thoughts.

It was Cindy. *Well, that was horrible. Call me if you wanna talk?*

Ugh. I felt so bad that Cindy was there for Priya and my big fight. But I knew she'd get what I meant. She had tough parents, too. They were constantly signing her up for extra tutoring classes.

"Hey," I sighed into the phone.

"Hey," Cindy replied softly. "How are you doing?"

"I'm so annoyed!" I couldn't hold back. "Priya doesn't get it! Can you believe that she thinks I should tell my mom what I want to do? Who does she think she is?"

There was a long pause. So long that I thought the

connection had dropped. But I could still hear Cindy breathing on the other end.

"Cindy?"

"It's not a bad idea, Pearl," she finally responded. "To talk to your parents."

I couldn't believe what I was hearing.

Cindy continued. "Selling at Handmade is a big deal! Ten thousand people? That's so many! Maybe your mom can even help you sell at the booth."

The idea of my mom helping me run Kawaii Crochets almost made me laugh. Because it was totally impossible.

"After you left, Priya got really upset. She even told me that she's been feeling left out lately, like when you and I talk in Chinese and about stuff like boba and Chinese TV shows or movies. You two have been best friends for so long. I don't think it's easy for her to share you with me. Especially when she doesn't know much about the stuff you and I like."

Cindy's words made me pause. Was that why Priya had been acting weird these days? Because of me and Cindy?

"I haven't been leaving her out on purpose, though," I said. "It's a pain to have to explain everything to her. It's not like she cares about the things we do anyway." That was so obvious, with her boring black tea, that super "safe" mango shaved ice, and not paying attention during the movie we had watched together.

"Well, even if we don't do it on purpose, it makes her feel bad. So we should be careful about including her, Pearl," Cindy replied.

"But, Cindy, haven't you noticed how Priya keeps pointing out times when I'm wrong, or that she's so quick to defend other people? She never did that before. And that has nothing to do with you and me," I insisted.

"Actually, I like that about Priya. She's super considerate of other people and where they might be coming from," Cindy confessed. "Maybe *how* Priya points out those things could be better. But a lot of times, she's right, I think."

I bit my lip. It was true that Priya had always been a defender of people. That was how we got to be friends in the first place. We didn't know each other very well back when we were only eight years old.

But she still stood up for me.

When it came to my amigurumi and my mom, though, Priya had it way off.

"Well, she may have good points sometimes. But Priya still doesn't get why going to Handmade is so important. Mom hates my amigurumi. That's why I need Auntie Cha," I vented. "And Boba Time."

"Oh, Pearl," Cindy said softly into the phone. "Is

Auntie Cha really the only adult you think will ever care for your work? Is Boba Time really the only place where you can crochet?"

I felt tears spring to my eyes. I'd been wishing all this time that Auntie Cha wasn't the only one.

But the adult whose approval I wanted the most wasn't interested in my amigurumi at all.

Cindy paused for a long second. "Priya might be right. Maybe you need to let Auntie Cha go, Pearl. For her sake. And yours. Maybe you need to love your art on your own, no matter what other people think. Like your mom."

At her words, my heart dropped to the floor like a ball of yarn falling from my hands, then rolling far, far away.

Cindy, too? She also wanted me to give up on Boba Time? And on Auntie Cha?

I could feel my chest burn. Was what I wanted so out there, so unreasonable? Couldn't I have a safe place, too, like Priya had with her art studio, where I could work in peace? Couldn't I have a chance to show off my work and have people gush over it and tell me how proud and amazed they were of what I could do, like at Handmade?

I wasn't getting that from Mom. I needed to get it from somewhere.

And not a single one of my best friends understood that.

"No," I said to Cindy, my voice rising again. "Boba Time is my safe place, and it needs to stay here in Sunnydale. And I need to get to Handmade so people who love crafts can see what I can do. If Priya doesn't get that, then I don't need her."

"You, too, Cindy," I continued, my voice wavering. "I thought you'd understand. But obviously you don't."

Before she could reply, I tapped the red button on my phone. I didn't need someone else to explain myself to.

Just like that, Team Kawaii was done.

CHAPTER
24

THE NEXT MORNING, I WOKE up to swollen eyes, a growling stomach, and an empty heart.

Last night was awful. I tossed and turned for hours without sleeping a single wink. No matter how hard I tried to keep my tears back, my brain kept playing our terrible fight over and over and over again, on looping repeat, like never-ending echoes bouncing around in a huge black cave. It was the first time in our five years as best friends that Priya and I had ever yelled at each other. It was also the first time I'd ever hung up on anyone, let alone a sweet, kind friend like Cindy.

Then, when I finally managed to open my groggy, puffy eyes in the morning, the sight of my amigurumi scattered around my room made me even angrier, even sadder. This thing I loved was causing me so many problems. How'd I get myself into this mess in the first place?

And I still had no idea how to solve the "Mom at Handmade" problem. Everything was falling apart.

I buried myself under the covers and tried to block it all out. Eventually, though, I couldn't ignore my grumbling stomach. So I dragged myself out of bed and headed to the kitchen in search of food.

But there was no rice in the rice cooker and no soy sauce fried egg waiting for me today.

Of course there wasn't anything to eat. Who in this family would bother making sure I was fed?

At least there was a package of dried fish snacks on the counter. I helped myself to a handful of the long, thin strips.

What a terrible breakfast.

Like everything else going on in my life.

As I chewed on the salty snack, I racked my brain, trying to think of a solution to the Handmade problem.

But my head kept going back to the fight. Was Handmade even possible without Team Kawaii by my side?

I had no choice, though. I wasn't going to apologize. Cindy and Priya were the ones insisting that I risk everything by telling my mom.

If I did that, then what if all I've accomplished up to now was wasted?

Unless I was the one being stubborn . . . ? And self-ish . . . ?

I took a deep breath and willed myself to concentrate on the most important problem at hand. My head was too mixed up to process the other stuff.

Okay, so I needed to figure out how to go to the fair, but without Mom tagging along. Convincing her not to come was going to be hard.

But if she thought I wasn't going anymore, she wouldn't go, either. Could I come up with something else that weekend that she thought I'd be going to instead of Handmade Craft? It'd have to be something that'd cover up the fact I was going to be out of the house for two days. It'd also have to be something that she wouldn't be able to do with me.

My shuffling feet brought me to the empty living room. I flopped down onto the couch, where a Code Together Academy pamphlet lay on the coffee table. It was still there from when Dad and Mom tried to convince Jade to be their spokesperson a few weeks ago.

Seeing the Code Together pamphlet made a new wave of anger rush up to the surface. It represented all that my mom cared about and wanted me to be, and all that I didn't care about and wasn't.

I picked it up and flung it across the room.

What I would give for Mom to be as excited about

me spending a whole weekend at Handmade as she was about me spending a whole weekend learning how to code. She never let up about wanting me to take a coding class. And at this point, there was no way I'd waste a whole summer weekend in front of a computer.

I wouldn't give her the satisfaction.

But wait . . .

A whole weekend?

An idea started to take shape inside my gray, grumpy head.

I scrambled to where the pamphlet had hit the wall and then slid back behind the sofa. I lay flat on the floor, stomach down, reaching as far as I could for the crumpled brochure. After sitting back up and sweeping off the dust bunnies on my shirt and arms, I flipped to the page in the pamphlet with the dates and times of all their classes.

A weekend class was scheduled on the same days as Handmade Craft.

What if I told my mom that I wanted to go to a weekend class at Code Together? It'd be the perfect cover. She'd be so thrilled that I was finally showing an interest in coding that she wouldn't even think to question my decision.

Mr. Huang had offered to let me take a class for free last month when we were at Mama Yang's Kitchen. So my fib wouldn't cost my parents any money.

Then, when I came back from the weekend with all the money I made from Handmade, she'd be so impressed that she wouldn't care that I lied about the class. She'll see that I did it for the right reasons.

Could it work? What would Priya and Cindy think of my idea?

I fumbled around in my pockets for my phone so I could send them a text.

Then the memory of yesterday's fight flooded into my head.

Team Kawaii was no more. I was on my own.

Here come the waterworks again.

Suddenly, a footstep creaked above my head. I blinked back my tears, wiped my nose quickly with the back of my hand, and pulled myself off the floor. I threw the pamphlet back onto the living room table and headed upstairs.

But when I walked into my room, a dark blob came into view.

"Ahhh!" I screamed.

"It's only me, Pearl!"

It was Jade, perched on my bedspread, dressed in all black.

I gasped, clutching my chest. "Jade! You nearly gave me a heart attack!"

"Sorry about that." Jade held Oscar in her hands, whom I had left on my nightstand. "Well, this one is cute."

"His name is Oscar," I panted. "So . . . what's up?"

"Nice name." Jade put Oscar back in his place. Then she leaned forward, inspecting me closely. "Are you okay? You look a little puffy."

I rubbed my hands on my face self-consciously. "Yeah, I'm fine," I lied.

Jade furrowed her eyebrows. "Okay . . . if you say so."

"What do you want, Jade?" Seeing my soft, comfy bed spread made me ache to slide back in and hide under its safety.

"I was thinking about going out to Sheng Kee Bakery for breakfast. Wanna come?"

I paused. Although wallowing in self-pity was my plan for the rest of the morning, the idea of a hot dog cheese bun did make my stomach growl. That sad handful of fish snacks didn't cut it at all.

"Sure, I'm in," I agreed.

I could wallow in self-pity later . . .

But with a full stomach.

CHAPTER
25

AFTER I MADE A QUICK stop to the bathroom to splash some cold water on my face, we strapped ourselves into Jade's Prius, and she steered the car in the direction of Sheng Kee, the Taiwanese bakery that my family had been going to for years. They sold a whole bunch of baked goods there, from red bean buns to milk toast to my favorite, hot dog cheese buns. My parents also ordered our birthday cakes from Sheng Kee every year. Their fresh taro cake was to die for, with the most decadent taro cream layered between light and fluffy vanilla sponge. Yum.

The smell of flour, butter, and sugar greeted us as we stepped inside the bakery. The buns were displayed in plastic bins, and we each grabbed a tray and a pair of plastic tongs. We picked out the ones we wanted; then the server wrapped them up at the cash register and handed us each a white wax-paper bag.

"Why don't we have a bun or two here before heading home?" Jade suggested.

"Sure, I can do that." I pointed to a table in the back. The metal chairs squeaked as they scraped against the floor.

"So, Mom asked me if I wanted to go to Handmade Craft with you two in a few weeks." She peeled the paper backing off the red bean bun she fished out of her bag. "Something about a girls' day since we've been so busy this summer."

Uh-oh. My fake Code Together plan wouldn't work if Jade came, too.

I opened my mouth to downplay the whole thing, when . . .

"I didn't know much about the fair, so I went to their website to see what kind of shops would be selling there. I noticed a cute amigurumi one called Kawaii Crochets." She raised her eyebrows. "Sound familiar?"

My heart thumped.

"Uh, what do you mean?" I stared hard at my bun.

"Well, there wasn't much on the actual Handmade site about the shop. But there was a Craftsee link. After I clicked on it, I thought it was interesting that the owner is from Sunnydale, is named Pearl, and has a crochet hot dog doll just like yours as their profile pic."

Busted.

I sighed, then told Jade about all I'd been up to, starting with my Craftsee shop and now with the Handmade Craft Fair.

I kept my idea about the Code Together class to myself, though. I wasn't sure if I'd go through with it. And if I did, maybe it was better for Jade to not know. For her sake.

She tore off a piece of bun and popped it in her mouth, then licked her fingers. "I get why you want to help Auntie Cha and Boba Time. That's super sweet of you. And your amigurumi dolls are really cute, at least the ones I've seen. But why are you keeping all of this a secret?"

I chewed slowly. "Mom's never appreciated my crocheting. She thinks it's too old-fashioned and girly and that no one will buy anything."

"So what? Don't you like doing it? Isn't that enough?"

Jade sounded like Priya and Cindy.

"Yeah, but it'd be nice if she was into it. I'm twelve, Jade. Maybe I shouldn't be obsessed with things like cute crochet hot dogs and donuts and stuffed animals." My face started to flush, thinking about how badly I'd done at the science fair, and how not a single kid had voted for my plush cell model.

Jade snorted. "Puh-lease." She ran her hands through her pixie haircut. "If I had a nickel every time someone told me what a teenage girl should be doing . . ."

"Mom wants me to be like you, a programmer. She won't take me seriously as an artist. Plus, I did ask her to help me with the Craftsee account."

"Oh, yeah? What'd she say?" Jade pulled apart another piece of her bun.

"She said no. She said it'd be too hard for me because I'd be selling physical products, rather than something someone could just download with the click of a button."

"Well, how are you doing so far? And how much do you expect to make at Handmade?" Jade asked.

I told her my numbers.

"Hey, that's not bad at all. You have a fair chance. You've thought this through."

A small flame of pride flicked in my stomach. It felt good to be talking about what I was doing with someone who knew a thing or two about business.

"Well, the fact that you started a business with your mobile app made me think I could do it, too. And you did help me out when I first started doing this," I confessed. "Do you remember me asking you about how you sold your app on the Apple App Store?"

Jade's eyebrows shot up. "Yeah, that day in my car.

What was that about?"

"I needed to figure out why no one was looking at my Craftsee listings. You gave me some good advice, although you didn't know it at the time."

"Ha, I'm glad I could help. You seem well on your way to hitting your goal."

"I'm not there yet. I need to throw Mom off of Handmade and figure out how to pay for booth decorations. And the fair is coming up fast!" I scrunched up the remaining paper from my hot dog cheese bun. "This is a lot harder than I thought."

"Tell me about it." Jade chuckled. "And there's a whole new set of pressures that comes if your business does well."

"What do you mean?"

Jade shifted her weight on the chair. "It's this whole being Code Together's poster-child thing. Mom's laying it on pretty thick."

"Yeah, I hear you." I snorted, happy to have something to connect with my sister on. But I felt kind of bad for all the pressure she was getting.

Although the idea of being a poster child sounded pretty good to me.

"Jade," I asked. "Why aren't you into being the spokesperson for Code Together? Isn't it a good thing for people to know what a talented programmer you are?"

She shrugged and took a long sip of her drink. "Honestly, I don't want the attention. It's a lot of extra work to live up to other people's expectations. And that's not why I started making the app in the first place anyway. I was doing it for me, because it was a fun challenge."

"But attention means people care about what you're doing," I said. "It means they're interested."

"Sure, it can feel good to get some attention and validation." Jade shrugged. "It's when people start to expect me to do things in a certain way that's hard. It's not easy to separate what I want from what other people want."

"Well, having people care too much sounds way better than having people not care at all. Mom and Dad don't care that I crochet cute cuddly animals, that's for sure." I sighed.

"I don't know if it's that they don't care," Jade said. "Maybe they don't understand it."

I grimaced. "Well, it'd be nice if they tried to understand it a little bit. At least if people end up buying my stuff at Handmade, Mom will see that I'm not the only one in the world who cares about crochet. And crafts."

Jade looked at me for a long while. "Be careful what you wish for, Pearl. When you start to rely on how other people react to your work instead of creating just to make yourself happy, it changes things. Especially when you turn something you love to do into a business. It becomes a whole new game you have to play."

I wasn't totally sure I knew what she meant by that. Although I remembered what it felt like when my family all went to the movies together and I had to stay home to crochet. Making amigurumi I hoped to sell to other people *was* starting to feel more and more like a chore by the day. If it was totally up to me, I would rather pick designs that I could challenge myself and my skills with.

Jade crumpled up the empty paper wrapper from her bun and tossed it onto the table.

"You know what, Pearl?" she said, wiping her hands off with a napkin. "I'll give you the money you need for your booth decorations."

"You will?" I looked at her, surprised. "Why?"

Jade shrugged. "I might not know much about the world of arts and crafts. But I care about you and what you're trying to do. I had no idea you were so passionate about . . . what did you call it? Amigurumi? I thought it was just something fun you liked to do while you watched all those Chinese shows on your laptop."

Eesh, that stung a little. Guess she hadn't been taking me and my amigurumi that seriously, either.

But I could see her side of it. I did always have some TV show or movie playing at the same time I crocheted.

What mattered now, though, was that she got how serious I was about my art. Not only that, she was willing to give me money for my craft.

Jade said she cared about me, too. That was a surprise to hear.

But it felt good.

"Thanks, Jade." I smiled. "It'd be awesome to have your help."

"Plus, any new business venture needs capital to pay for start-up costs. Without it, it's super hard," she said.

Tell me about it.

Jade stuck out her right hand and grinned. "Okay, it's settled, then. I'm Kawaii Crochets's first investor. Let's shake on it."

I grabbed her hand with mine and pumped it up and down a few times.

"Now we're more than just sisters. We are official business partners," Jade declared, laughing out loud.

I beamed back at her. It felt great to have someone on my side again.

Now Kawaii Crochets's booth could look as amazing as I wanted it to be! I bet Jade would even be willing to drive me back to Second Closet to grab the decorations that Team Kawaii picked out together a few days ago.

Team Kawaii. Thinking about Priya and Cindy made my heart ache. It was so much fun rummaging through so many fun goodies and designing my booth with my two best friends. They've kind of been my business partners in this whole thing, too.

I never would have known about Second Closet if it weren't for Priya and how artistic and creative she was . . .

And she knew about that place because of her family. Was I wrong for being so jealous?

I shook my head to push my best friend out of my head. Now wasn't the time.

Jade leaned back in her chair and crossed her arms over her chest. "Now that I've taken up some risk in your business, I do have one condition. Actually two."

Uh-oh. I should have known there'd be a catch. Mom and Dad always complained about the "demands of their investors."

"Okay, what are they?" I crossed my arms, too.

"Consider telling Mom about your plans. I knew you liked making crochet, but I didn't know how much it meant to you. Or how much Boba Time means to you right now, for that matter. Mom might not, either."

I groaned inside. Her, too? Why didn't anyone get that there was no way I could change Mom's mind?

But all Jade said was to think about it. For the booth decorations money, I could do that.

I nodded reluctantly.

"Also, you might want to check in with Auntie Cha. Have you told her how much Boba Time means to you?

Or how much she means to you? If she knew how much you cared, maybe that'd get her to be a little more pro-active in figuring out a way she can keep the shop *and* have more quality time with her daughter." Jade tapped her lips with her finger, thinking. "More practically, sometimes adults don't want help from kids, you know? Especially when it comes to money. She might not accept what you want to give her, even if you offer it."

Uh-oh. Jade had a point. When Auntie Cha told me about Boba Time's financial problems, she seemed almost resigned to whatever was going to happen. I didn't get the sense she was fighting that hard for Boba Time.

Maybe if she saw how hard I was working to keep her here, she'd see how important it was to keep Boba Time running. And accept the money I'd give her.

As for Jade's suggestion to tell Auntie Cha how much both her and Boba Time meant to me, thinking about it made my heart beat faster. For me to say all that so openly, so freely . . .

I wasn't sure I could.

Jade uncrossed her arms and rested her elbows on the table. "Also, how are you going to keep Mom away from Handmade? She seemed pretty excited about going with you when she talked to me about it."

"I'll figure something out," I lied. Although I already

had a plan, it wasn't a great one, because it meant lying again to my mom.

But maybe I had to go through with it. With every day I had left before Handmade, the more my goal felt within reach.

And I was a big step closer now, thanks to my new business partner.

CHAPTER
26

ON THE RIDE HOME, JADE'S comment about Auntie Cha not accepting my help kept repeating itself over and over in my head. Maybe it was worth checking in with her, just in case.

And I didn't need to tell Auntie Cha everything, including why I was doing all of this.

Or say out loud what was really at stake.

Because what if I failed?

At my request, Jade dropped me off at Boba Time before heading home. Auntie Cha was sitting with a customer at a long table, a row of teacups in front of them. "Here, try this one. It's roasted oolong from the mountains of Alishan in Taiwan," she said to the woman, handing her a teacup with both hands. The woman held the cup up to her nose, sniffed it, and then took a sip. She nodded approvingly.

This tea tasting could take a while. So I sat in my usual spot and pulled out my crochet hook and yarn. Got to keep working on my inventory, one tedious stitch at a time.

I was getting real close to hitting my lifetime quota of crocheting the same amigurumi robot over and over again—and the patience that went along with it.

The customer finally left a few minutes later with a bag full of tea.

"Hi, Pearl." Auntie Cha wiped down my already-sparkling-clean table with a damp dish towel. "How is the crocheting going? What are you making today?"

I showed her my half-finished robot.

"Hmm, haven't you made this one before?"

"Yes, I have. Actually . . . I wanted to talk to you about this robot. And what I'm doing with it."

"Oh?" She looked at me curiously.

I wasn't sure where to start.

"Um, how's the fridge, by the way?"

She pointed to it as it rattled in the corner. "It's hanging in there."

"And how's your daughter?"

Auntie Cha burst into a huge grin. "Look, she sent me this picture!" She pulled out her phone, tapped at it a few times, and then turned it around to show me a photo. A young woman with eyes like Auntie Cha's grinned at the camera. Tied up in a high ponytail, instead of a messy bun, was the same luxurious jet-black hair. The woman stood in front of a table full of dishes, like at a banquet, and all around her were a bunch of friends. On one hand, her fingers flashed a *V*.

A flash of envy shot through me. This was the person that Auntie Cha would leave Sunnydale for. Her daughter seemed happy. Did she really need Auntie Cha? She'd managed for so many years without her. She even had a bunch of friends by her side.

Not me. No Priya, no Cindy. I'd checked my phone a bunch that day, my heart leaping every time I saw a new notification, hoping it was one of them, reaching out to apologize or to talk.

But nothing.

Then, in the picture that Auntie Cha was still holding out in front of my face, I noticed where her daughter's other hand lay—on her big belly. I glanced back up at Auntie Cha, who still had a huge smile stretching across her face.

That was one lucky baby in there, I had to admit.

I forced a smile on my face. "Your daughter looks nice."

"She is." Auntie Cha grinned at the photo.

"So . . . have you decided what you're going to do yet? About Boba Time?" I asked, heart thumping.

"No, not yet." Auntie Cha shook her head and dropped her phone into the pocket of her apron. "For now, there is no decision to make. Boba Time is still running, and I keep sending the little money I have to her. She needs to relax and rest now before the baby comes."

Whew. I could still help her make a decision about what to do.

I took a deep breath. "Um, Auntie Cha? What would you do if someone gave you the money you needed to fix the fridge?"

Her eyes snapped to mine. "What do you mean?"

I sat a little taller in my seat. "What if I gave you the money you needed?"

"And where would you get that kind of money?"

I held up the robot. "Maybe I could sell my amigurumi dolls. I've done the math. I think I could make enough to help you pay for the fridge." I didn't mention Craftsee or Handmade. "You said before that you love my art and that you could see people buying my dolls at a store. What if you're right?"

Auntie Cha leaned forward and touched my hand. "Oh, Pearl, your dolls are truly wonderful. I have no doubt that people will fall in love with them and buy them up quickly!"

I grinned, blushing slightly.

Then her face turned serious. "But I don't want you to sell your art for Boba Time, or for me. Turning something you love into something you depend on, into something attached to money, changes that love."

She leaned back in her chair. "When I turned my love of tea into this shop, into Boba Time, it was not easy when people did not share the same appreciation for tea as I did. Every time I did not make the money I hoped I would, I would question if I had made the right decision. It made me love tea less, now that my livelihood depended on it. I had to compromise. And maybe I didn't compromise enough, which is why Boba Time's business is not good now."

She sighed, tucking her hands into her apron.

"To sell your art or not is your decision. You must think carefully about why you are doing it. If you decide to sell your creations, do it for reasons that are true to you and what you care about."

I chewed on my bottom lip. Was I being true to myself? What did I care about?

Saving Boba Time was true to me. I cared about it . . . a lot. This was my safe space, and I had to fight for it.

Also, there was that whole "prove the value of my amigurumi to my mom" thing. I cared a lot about that, too.

Both of these things were true to me and why my

amigurumi was so important . . . I think?

Although crocheting had definitely turned into a chore these days. I couldn't go to the movies with my family because of it, I fought with my friends over it, and it was getting to be . . . boring.

I looked at the yarn in my hands. I guess I had been compromising my love of amigurumi a bit, to prove something to Mom.

Suddenly, Auntie Cha looked me straight in the eyes, like she could see my thoughts.

"And what does your mother think about your idea of selling your dolls?"

The metal seat I was perched on got cold and uncomfortable.

Auntie Cha wasn't going to like the fact that this was more than an idea already. And that my mom didn't approve. And that I'd been keeping it all a secret.

If I told Auntie Cha the truth, would she shut it down?

I cleared my throat. "I haven't asked her yet."

"You are smart but young. You need to talk to your parents about selling your dolls. Money matters can get complicated fast. It is for your protection."

I slumped back in my chair. These weren't the words I wanted to hear.

"Promise me you'll talk to them if you decide to do this, Pearl."

I gulped. "But would you take the money if I gave it to you?" I needed to know that all my work was going to be worth it. And that she knew how much I wanted her to stay.

"Let's cross that bridge when we come to it."

Well, it wasn't a no.

"But you must do it right if you move forward with your idea. Promise me," Auntie Cha insisted.

I nodded.

Auntie Cha smiled. "You are a smart girl with many ideas. I'm proud of your initiative and creativity. Sometimes, when I miss my own daughter, it comforts me to know I have an American one here in Sunnydale, in you."

With that, she patted my cheek gently, then stood up and headed back to the counter.

My heart swelled with pride. Auntie Cha thought of me as her American daughter? That made me feel so warm inside . . . and more determined than ever to make Handmade a success and save Boba Time.

Because that's what a daughter would do.

But what Auntie Cha had said about my motivations for deciding to sell my amigurumi made me think. Were they true? Was my decision the right one? Maybe I *should* tell my mom what I was doing.

Then I heard a giggle behind me. Auntie Cha stared

at her phone as she stirred a big pot full of tapioca balls from behind the counter. A silly smile was plastered across her face as she swiped back and forth between the photos of her daughter.

Seeing Auntie Cha beam at the photos, imagining a new life back in Taiwan, made that pit of worry in my stomach grow.

She really did want to leave.

But she hadn't decided yet. She might stay if I got her that money. And when she saw how hard I had worked to keep her shop alive, maybe that'd make her think twice about leaving. Auntie Cha said so before—she could still help her real daughter from Sunnydale.

I could keep Auntie Cha here while her daughter could keep getting money from Boba Time. This arrangement wouldn't be selfish of me—would it?

No, this could work. A win-win for everyone. I had to keep moving forward.

And my fake Code Together plan was the last step.

What I had to do didn't feel good.

But it was my last option.

My only option, actually.

The next morning, Jade drove me to Second Closet to get the decorations I needed for my booth. Luckily, everything Priya, Cindy, and I had picked out was still there.

Going to Second Closet without Cindy and Priya felt worse than I expected. When I grabbed the suitcases Priya had picked out, I could almost hear her calling us from the aisle over, shouting out new ideas for the booth. But I was still angry at how much she had insisted that I tell my mom about the fair. Priya didn't get why that was impossible.

Come to think of it, neither did Cindy. Or Jade.

But maybe I was a little harsh. They were all trying to help. . . .

Then, as the car idled at a stoplight on our way home, Jade pointed at two figures huddled together at a table in front of Sweet Yam Cafe. "Pearl, aren't those your friends over there?"

I'd know that cascade of black hair anywhere. And that backpack with all the key chains.

My heart dropped seeing my two best friends together, giggling at something on a phone that only they could see. Without me.

I thought *I* was the glue that kept our group together. I was the one who met Cindy first earlier this year and invited her to hang out with Priya and me. The rest was history.

"Yeah," I mumbled. "That's them all right."

"Priya's super artsy, too, isn't she? She could probably help you a lot with Handmade," Jade offered up.

"I don't want to talk about it." I crossed my arms around my chest, shutting the topic down.

Jade opened her mouth but then shut it quickly when the light turned green. As she drove the car away, leaving them behind, I fixed my eyes forward and squeezed them tight, holding back the tears threatening to break through. I had to make Handmade happen now.

Or none of this would have been worth it.

After we got home and checked the house to make sure that Mom and Dad were out, Jade helped me lug everything from her Prius's trunk into our basement. We hid the decorations in a corner and put some cardboard boxes around the pile to help it blend in.

Booth decorations, done. I could finally check off one box from the Handmade Craft Fair to-do list.

Now I had to focus on building out my inventory. The more I made, the more I could sell.

So my hands went into factory-mode. I crocheted *all the time*. I even started counting stitches in my sleep. My hands started to ache from the constant, repeated movement. But I had to keep going, tallying up the total number of dolls as I made them.

Working toward my inventory goal also helped me forget how lonely I was starting to feel. Doing this without Priya and Cindy to cheer me on or help me pass the time was the pits. It hurt even more thinking that they still had each other. They were probably bonding over how much they hated me now.

I even stopped browsing Craftsee for new patterns. As much as I wanted to try something new, I needed to stay focused on crocheting things that I could make fast and would sell well.

I was starting to understand what Jade—and Auntie Cha—had said. Now that I turned something I loved into a business, and depended on it to make money, amigurumi did feel like a whole new game.

And not a fun one.

CHAPTER
27

THE WEEKEND BEFORE HANDMADE CRAFT'S opening day, an email with the subject line *Handmade Craft Site Visit* popped up on my laptop screen as I was crocheting in my room.

It was from the fair organizers. They were opening the doors of the venue for a few hours that afternoon so those of us selling could stop by and check out our booth spaces.

How fun!

In my excitement, I picked up my phone and started typing a text to Priya and Cindy, asking if they wanted to come. Then stopped.

Our fight felt like it happened a long time ago, even though it had been only a few weeks. We'd never gone so many days without being in touch.

Well, in touch with me, that is. A few days ago, Priya posted a picture of a pastel sketch she'd done of a building downtown on her social media. I could tell that the backpack on the sidewalk by her feet was Cindy's because of all the key chains on it.

Then, yesterday, Cindy shared a video of them dancing to a popular Chinese pop song together. Priya had commented with a *That was so fun! Next time, I'll teach you an Indi-pop song!* along with two heart emojis. Cindy had even liked the comment back.

Did they not need me anymore? Was I completely out of the picture for my two best friends?

I stared at my phone, finger hovering above the send button.

Was this how Priya felt when Cindy and I did things together, without her?

I didn't mean to leave Priya out. But maybe it's true that I wasn't taking the time or being sensitive about the fact that we were a trio of friends now, after it had been Priya and me for a long time. And to have someone like Cindy join us . . .

It wasn't on purpose. But Cindy said that that didn't matter. Priya still felt left out.

And now they were the ones leaving me out.

Although I *was* the one who started the fight with my outburst.

Well, forget them, I told myself. If they didn't need me, I didn't need them, either.

Then I looked at the words I'd tapped on my phone without thinking—*Hi Team Kawaii! Want to go check out where Kawaii Crochets's Handmade booth is before the big day?*

The big day meant ten thousand customers.

Gulp.

Clearly, my heart was sending me a totally different message.

I took a deep breath and hit delete. What I was about to do was terrifying. But I had to go through with it, and I didn't need anyone doubting my decision. Even if it meant doing this without my friends.

At least I had Jade. But her room was empty and her car was gone.

Guess I was on my own today.

Again.

I hopped onto my bike and cruised down to the convention center where Handmade was going to be held.

A hipster-looking girl with long golden hair tipped in neon pink stood at the door with a clipboard in hand. I locked up my bike in the courtyard and approached her.

"Hi, I'm here to check out my booth for Handmade Craft." I nervously pushed my glasses up my nose. I didn't expect to have to talk to anyone.

"Oh, hi! I need to check you in." She looked me up and down. "Are you a seller in our under-eighteen age group? If so, you need to be accompanied by a guardian to sell."

Uh-oh. I had no idea that was a thing. I was pretty sure I had read all the fine print when I registered, and there was nothing about a guardian.

Great, another setback. Now I needed to figure out how to get someone older to be with me at the booth.

Was Handmade trying to keep kids out of selling their crafts here? For how hard they were making it, it sure felt that way.

But first things first. I needed to get in there to scope out my spot.

My brain whirled. "Um, no, my parents aren't here today. They're busy at their workshop getting things ready for the fair." I tried my best to smile casually. "They were hoping I could take some pictures for them to help them plan the booth decorations, though."

She tapped her pen to her forehead. "Hmm, yeah, I guess that'd be okay. What's the name?"

"Kawaii Crochets," I answered, letting out a breath of air I didn't realize I was holding. Lying was getting easier and easier, although it wasn't feeling any better every time I did it.

"Ah, here you are!" She crossed a name off her list with a flourish. "Head on in. The booth will be in the middle section, spot 18B. The booth numbers are painted on the floor, and the boundaries of each booth are marked with blue masking tape."

"Thanks!" I quickly headed inside to avoid any more questions.

Spot 18B. Another lucky eight. Definitely a good sign.

It took a few seconds for my eyes to adjust from the brightness of the outside to the darkness of the inside. But once they did, my jaw dropped open.

The space was huge. Monstrously huge.

The size of it meant that every whir and bang from the construction echoed off the walls in a way that made the space *sound* huge, too. Workers perched on top of big cranes worked their way from back to front, assembling booths and installing wires and stands. Rows of metal tubing stood like naked skeletons, although some already had black cloth draping down to create separations between each booth.

I'd been to the Handmade Craft Fair before. But never before it was all set up and running.

And never alone. Priya and I always came together, ever since the first time the fair came to Sunnydale three years ago. It was our summer tradition. And this year, we were going to introduce the awesomeness of Handmade Craft to Cindy.

But not anymore.

I swallowed down the ball of guilt and fear curdling inside my stomach. The fair was a lot bigger—and scarier—than I remembered. And it was going to be filled with thousands of shoppers in less than a week.

My heart pounded and my palms got clammy. Maybe Priya and Cindy were right. Standing here in front of this ginormous showroom floor was making me realize that Handmade Craft really *was* a big deal. Maybe I should tell my parents about what I'm about to do.

I forced myself to take one step after another, skimming the floor for 18B.

Then I finally saw it.

My booth wasn't right at the front where people would walk past without seeing it as they took in all the activity. And it wasn't at the very back, where you could easily be missed if customers didn't walk the entire way down. It was right in the middle of the main aisle.

Plus, based on the markings on the floor, Kawaii Crochets was only two booths away from where there was going to be a crossing for people moving from one side of the space to the other. That meant there'd be plenty of foot traffic, which meant plenty of customers.

It was in the perfect spot.

My heart beat like a thousand drums. Because now the chance I could succeed was real. It was right in front of me.

And I was on my own. No Team Kawaii.

But I had to do it.

For my art.

And for Boba Time.

CHAPTER
28

AFTER SNAPPING SOME PHOTOS OF the space, I headed out the door. Blinking against the bright sunlight, I made my way back toward my bike.

"Hey, Pearl!"

Startled, I tripped over my feet and tumbled to the ground. Kendall dashed over and grabbed an arm, helping me up.

"Oh my gosh, are you okay?"

Of course I fell on my face again in front of Kendall Stewart.

"What are you doing here?" I managed to bluster as I picked myself off the hard sidewalk, dusting off my pants.

She waved toward the stationery store across the

street. "I just picked up a bunch of origami paper. Then I'm going to meet my friends."

Looking around, I spotted Kendall's usual crew hanging out on the steps on the other side of the convention center's plaza. Andrea and Nora were there, too, laughing with some boys in hoodies balancing on skateboards.

"That's nice." I smiled weakly and fumbled in my pocket for my bike key. But in my hurry, out popped Oscar, and he tumbled onto the ground.

Again.

Kendall knelt down to pick him up. Cringing, I held my breath. Was she going to make fun of my imperfectly made creation?

But to my surprise, she handled him gently, inspecting him from every angle. "I remember this guy from school." She looked at me with a curious expression on her face. "Why do you carry dolls around all the time, Pearl? And yarn?"

My mind whirled, trying to come up with an excuse to not talk about my amigurumi.

Then the image of Jade's face when I told her how I wished other people approved of my amigurumi flashed into my head.

Did it matter what Kendall, Queen of Tech, thought about my art? As long as I loved it and cared about it . . . wasn't that what was important?

There was a whole convention center behind me that, in just a few days, was going to be full of makers like me. I could practically feel them and their energy.

And their creative confidence.

Like Priya said in our fight: *Just own it, Pearl.*

I took a deep breath.

"I made that," I confessed.

"You made this?" Kendall's eyes snapped to Oscar. "How?"

My face flushed at how direct her question was. But I forced myself to answer. I owed it to Oscar.

"I do amigurumi. It's a way of crocheting that originally came from Japan."

Kendall stroked Oscar's stitches softly. "And you make it all by hand?"

I nodded. "And a crochet hook."

"Cool. It's like origami. I'd never made stuff like that before. It's actually pretty fun."

I cracked a small smile at her observation. "Yeah, I love crocheting. It takes a lot of practice, but it's worth it," I said softly.

Kendall smiled back. "I agree."

She did?

Then I felt my voice get a little stronger. But not because I wanted to confront Kendall. I didn't want a repeat of what had happened with Priya and Cindy.

I didn't want my voice to come out that way again.

But maybe there was a better way to talk about what was really bothering me.

I took another deep breath. "I'm a bit surprised to hear you say that, Kendall. You've said before that handmade stuff wasn't as good as the cool, techy stuff you usually make. But now you're saying making crafts is fun. So . . . what's up with that?"

Kendall's face flushed red, and I could see each little freckle pop from her cheeks. "What do you mean, Pearl?"

I straightened up my shoulders. "At Mama Yang's Kitchen, and then again at Boba Time, you said that doing crafts by hand wasn't cool, that it made things imperfect. Do you think that? If you do, then why are you doing origami?"

Kendall's eyes opened wide. "Origami is the only thing my grandma and I can do together." She looked down at her crisp white sneakers and shifted her weight awkwardly from one side to the other. "I don't speak Mandarin Chinese or Taiwanese, or know much about that side of me. I want to get to know my amah better, but it's hard."

Her face softened. "Turns out, Amah loves to do hand crafts and she was so excited to teach me. So I let her. And now I see how those little imperfections that come with folding paper are what make this handmade stuff so . . . perfect."

I stared back at her. "Really?"

"It's like no piece of origami we fold is the same. I can even tell which folds are Amah's and which ones are mine. Each little thing we make is . . . What's the word I'm looking for?" Kendall chewed on her lower lip.

"Unique," I suggested.

"Yes, exactly." Kendall grinned.

Then her smile faded. "I shouldn't have called your model cute or imperfect or uncool, Pearl. Or said that it wasn't as good as the kind of stuff I was making. I'm sorry about that. It's just . . . everyone expects me to know everything about the latest technology or have the nicest stuff because of my dad. I try so hard to be what other people think I should be. And I guess I project that onto other people sometimes. I shouldn't have done that."

She held Oscar up in front of her. His crooked smile beamed back at her. "Why do you make amigurumi, Pearl? And crafts in general?"

I thought for a moment. "I guess I like using my hands to make stuff. It takes practice, it's rewarding . . ." I shrugged my shoulders. "At the end of the day, doing crafts makes me happy."

Kendall nodded. "That's so great, Pearl, that you do

what you love. And not because anyone expects you to do it. You do it for you. I admire you for that."

I could feel my tongue get all tied up again, although it felt a bit different this time. Kendall Stewart admired *me*??

I managed to get out a soft "Thanks, Kendall. I'd never thought of my art that way."

She smiled sheepishly at me and handed me Oscar. I tucked him safely back into my pocket.

"Maybe I'll see you at Handmade Craft next weekend." Kendall pointed at the big banner stretched across the convention hall entrance. "Who knows, maybe someone will be selling origami there. Or amigurumi."

I stared at Kendall as she turned to join her friends. Her hair swished as she walked away, flowing down her back like a chocolate fountain.

Kendall Stewart thought I was great? For making amigurumi?

I'd never considered that it wasn't that easy for someone like Kendall to be so perfect all the time.

It hadn't occurred to me either that even though my mom pushed me to do tech stuff, I still chose to make my amigurumi. I didn't just do what Mom wanted me to.

Maybe that *was* something to be proud of.

I hopped onto my bike. But before pedaling away, I looked back at Kendall. She sat on the plaza steps, surrounded by friends but intently focused on folding the piece of paper in her hands.

Then the gravity of what I'd just done hit me. I had spoken up for my art in front of someone who didn't appreciate it . . . at least not at first. And I had done it in a way that didn't end in a big fight with hurtful words being thrown around. In fact, Kendall Stewart actually apologized. To me, Pearl Li. And she shared a side of herself that I'm pretty sure she didn't show to anyone.

I suddenly thought of Priya, my knight in shining armor. She'd be so proud of what I just did.

A lump the size of a boulder formed in my throat.

I missed her so much.

As I biked slowly home, the gears in my head kept turning. If telling Kendall Stewart about my art made her see how special crafts were, then maybe telling my mom about my plans for Handmade could make her understand why I loved amigurumi, too. I had promised Jade I'd think about it after all.

Should I try to talk to Mom one last time, before everything went down?

Priya was right. I had to speak up.

At that moment, I made a decision that I'd been putting off for too long.

I'd try to tell Mom about what I was about to do at Handmade Craft one last time. And if I got the feeling that she wasn't cool about it, then I'd stop and put the fake Code Together plan into action.

But maybe she'd be excited about how far I'd come with my art. Maybe, like Kendall, Mom would admire me for how much I was willing to fight for what I cared about, about what was true to me.

Maybe everything would work out after all.

CHAPTER
29

WHEN I GOT HOME, MOM was in the kitchen making tea. I recognized the box from Boba Time. It was one of Auntie Cha's special blends, designed to give you energy in moments of stress. I wondered what stress Mom was feeling—the pilot already launched. That meant her big deadline was over.

But now wasn't the time to wonder about her business. It was time to give mine a real chance. I cleared my throat.

"Hey, Mom. What are you up to? Taking a break from work?"

"Yes, it's been a hard day." Mom rubbed her eyes. "I've been going through hundreds of user feedback comments we've received from the pilot."

"What are they saying?" I asked.

She let out a big sigh. "I'd rather not talk about it right now."

Hmm, what was that all about?

Focus, Pearl.

"So, Mom, remember how I asked you about that Craftsee store a while ago?" I picked at the corner of the countertop where the veneer was starting to peel back.

"Yeah, the one you wanted to do for your dolls."

The timer rang, signaling that her tea was ready. The smell of ginseng and lemon filled the air as she poured some into her mug, and I watched as the steam curled upward before disappearing.

"I think you were right, that the shipping would probably be tricky." My strategy was to start off acknowledging her previous points before challenging others. Hopefully those negotiation tactics I learned for that mock debate in third-period social studies were going to help me out right now.

"But what if it wasn't an online shop? What if it were a real store, a place where I didn't have to handle shipping and things like that?"

Leaning her elbows on the table, she inspected me closely. "Why are you still on this 'selling dolls' idea, Pearl? I told you already. I'm not sure you should be selling them."

"But, Mom, Boba Time needs my help."

"Are you sure Auntie Cha needs you, Pearl? I know how much you love that place, but there's never anyone in there. It's going to be tough to turn a business like that around." She shook her head slowly.

Talking about how I could help Boba Time didn't seem to be working. Luckily, I had another angle I could try.

"Okay, never mind Boba Time, then. What if I could sell my crochet dolls for me? For fun?"

"And how would you do that?"

"It's only an idea right now, Mom," I lied.

"I don't know, Pearl. That stuff is complicated. I don't even know it works. You might want to stick with something I can help you with."

My heart dropped. There she goes again, not trusting me to figure it out myself.

At that moment, Jade appeared at the kitchen doorway. She gave us a quick nod and headed for the fridge.

"Now, Code Together Academy is a business with a solid future." Mom perked up, gesturing at Jade proudly. "That's a company you should throw your weight behind."

Jade emerged from the fridge with a bright yellow can of Apple Sidra soda in her hand. She rolled her eyes at Mom's comment.

"Mom, I said I'd think about it. I'll tell you when I

decide if I want to be in Code Together's brochure or not." She popped open the can, took a sip, and glanced at me. "Am I interrupting something?"

"No, we're just talking," I mumbled back.

"About what?"

"My crochet."

Jade's eyebrows shot up, and her eyes ping-ponged between me and Mom before they landed on my pained face. *Need some help?* I could feel her gaze ask.

Do I? A stamp of approval from Mom's favorite daughter could help my case.

No. I needed to do this alone. I needed Mom to believe in me, not in Jade.

I shook my head at her slightly.

"Okay." Jade turned around and headed upstairs.

"Tell me soon about Code Together!" Mom called out after Jade's retreating back.

Seeing Mom's eyes linger after Jade, the only daughter she was proud of, made my heart ache.

I put my hand in my pocket, feeling for Oscar. I took a deep breath. One more try.

"Mom, I *do* love crocheting. But I could make it more useful if I sold some dolls, don't you think?"

"Useful? In what way?" A wrinkle appeared between her eyes.

I chewed on my bottom lip. "Well, if I made some

money, that's less money that you need to make to spend on me."

"Pearl, that's very sweet." Mom chuckled. "But it's my job to provide for you. You don't need to worry about taking away any financial burden from me and your dad."

"Well, it'd be fun and educational for me to learn how to run a business, like you, right? And making profit is always a good thing, isn't it?" Maybe appealing to Mom's founder side would work.

Mom nodded slowly. "True. Making profit is a good indication that there's market demand for your products. Maybe we can think of something that you could sell that'd be more marketable than your dolls?"

Ouch.

Mom's comment popped the last balloon of hope floating in my stomach. She really didn't think my dolls were worth anything. To anyone.

I knew it. Mom just didn't get it . . . and never would.

I swallowed down the disappointment and blinked quickly to stop the tears that were about to break through.

Abort Mission Amigurumi.

Initiate Fake Code Together Academy plan.

"Okay, fine. No selling." I dropped my shoulders down and hunched over, doing my best to not look too disappointed. "Speaking of selling, I don't think I can make it to the Handmade Craft Fair next weekend."

She turned to me with a confused look on her face. "Why not? I thought you looked forward to that all summer. Priya, too. Come to think of it, I haven't seen her around in a while." Her eyebrows furrowed. "Everything okay with you two?"

"Yeah, everything's fine," I mumbled, then quickly changed the subject. Now wasn't the time to go there.

"I'd been thinking that I should sign up for that class at Code Together. Next weekend is the last weekend they'll offer it this summer."

A huge smile broke across Mom's face. "That's great to hear, Pearl! I'm so glad to hear you're trying something new. But why the change of heart?"

"You've been talking about it for so long, and Jade's probably going to be the spokesperson at some point. Might as well see what the fuss is all about," I said with as much enthusiasm as I could fake.

"Well, that sounds great. Let me know which class it is, and I'll sign you up for it." She beamed. "I'm so glad to hear you're taking an interest in coding! It would have been nice to spend some time with you at the craft fair, but this class will open your eyes to a whole new world that we can share. You'll see, it's going to be so much more useful for your future than crocheting."

I forced as big a smile as I could on my face. But her last comment struck me in the heart so hard, like in those old cartoons, that I almost put my hand up to my chest.

Don't worry, I told myself. She'll see. When I save Boba Time, she'll see how useful amigurumi can be.

Mom flashed me a thumbs-up before heading back into her office. I let out a sigh of relief as the office door squeaked closed behind her.

Plan Fake Code Together had worked. I was in the clear for Handmade next weekend.

Although hiding the truth again was no fun.

Well, as a consolation prize, at least I cheered up Mom for a little while.

Even if it *was* all a lie.

CHAPTER
30

IT WAS FINALLY TWO DAYS before Handmade. And I was ready.

Well, *almost* ready. I still had a few more amigurumi to crochet in order to hit my inventory goals. And that fluttering feeling deep in my stomach, like I was tottering on the edge of a waterfall, about to fall into the churning whitewater below, was getting stronger by the second.

I lay on my bed, arm over my eyes, surrounded by a pile of amigurumi and attempting to "control my breath." Oscar grinned at me from my nightstand.

But meditation wasn't helping. Oscar wasn't, either.

What I really needed was Priya. She'd talk me through this super-scary thing I was about to do. It'd been so long now since our fight that the anger I'd been feeling had melted away.

I knew I was the one who needed to apologize. It was my voice that exploded that day . . . and it was my voice that needed to bring us back together.

But what if it was too late? What if Priya already decided that Cindy was enough, and that she didn't need me to be her art buddy anymore? From the pics they kept posting on their social media, it looked like they were having a blast together.

Without me.

Plus, Kawaii Crochets at Handmade was still a big secret. Would Priya judge me for not having the guts to tell Mom? Would she be disappointed that I didn't do what she thought I should?

What if Team Kawaii wasn't strong enough to survive this fight?

With Handmade only two days away and the fate of Boba Time in my hands, I wasn't ready to find out. What if I didn't make enough at Handmade *and* lost Boba Time *and* found out my friends were done with me? How would I ever recover from all this?

Instead, I pulled both of my arms down by my sides, palms up, and tried to meditate again. But my heart kept fluttering with nerves.

Maybe a pep talk from someone who knew what I

was about to do would help. I peeled myself off my bed-spread and knocked softly on Jade's door.

"Come in," she called out.

I popped my head in. "Wanna do a Boba Time run?"

Jade glanced at her screen, which was, as usual, covered with indecipherable colored text. It suddenly reminded me of a crochet pattern, with letters and abbreviations that probably made no sense to anyone who had never picked up a crochet hook before.

Once you unraveled the code, though, that language would open up a world of creative possibilities.

"Sure, why not?" Jade yawned and stretched out her arms. She spun around in her chair and grabbed the jacket hanging off the back. "Only a few more days to go, huh?"

"Sh!" I put my hands to my lips, throwing her a glare. I pointed downstairs where Mom was working in her study.

"Oh, sorry." Jade sighed. "Yeah, let's have one last investor-investment conversation before it all goes down. I'll drive."

"Great! Let me get my stuff." I headed back to my room and tossed my things into my bag.

This would be my last visit to Boba Time before Handmade Craft started. I'd better make it a good one.

✳ ✳ ✳

Jade ordered her usual taro slush with taro chunks, and I opted for a lychee white tea with àiyù jelly and an extra big scoop of boba. We settled in at the table outside of Boba Time.

"So, are you ready? We can load up the car tomorrow afternoon while Mom and Dad are at their office for their big investor meeting." Jade swirled her straw around in the cup, mixing up the chunks on the bottom with the rest of the slush.

"Yeah, ready as I'll ever be. I just need to make a few more key chains and then I'll be set." I slurped up a rapid volley of boba balls from the big plastic straw. "By the way, thanks so much for agreeing to come with me tomorrow night to set up the booth. And manning it with me this weekend, Jade."

It was such a relief when Jade volunteered to help me out at the booth. As a senior in high school, with her own car and everything, I hoped Jade looked old enough to look like one of my guardians. Or a legitimate seller who didn't need one and happened to have a younger sister tagging around.

Definitely not ideal, but better than the alternative, which was no booth at all.

"Did you make business cards? Those are probably pretty important for an event like this." Jade chewed slowly on her taro chunks.

I shook my head. "No, I didn't. Who knows how long my Craftsee shop will be up? And I sure don't need pieces of paper floating around Sunnydale with my name on it, announcing my amigurumi to the world. It's going to be hard enough, talking to all those booth customers. But having my name on actual business cards that people take home for later . . ." I shuddered. "No, thank you."

Jade shrugged. "Your call. You'll lose out on future sales, though. I read somewhere that online sales often happen after events like these."

Oops. Too late now.

"By the way, Mom didn't ask me again about going to Handmade. Where does she think you're off to?" Jade furrowed her eyebrows at me in concern.

"She thinks I'm taking a weekend class at Code Together."

Jade's eyes widened. "Wow, that's bold. What if Mom asks you what you learned?"

I clasped my hands together and put on my best begging face. "I was hoping you'd teach me a few things. Give me a few phrases about coding that she'd believe. Please, please, pretty puh-lease?"

Jade sighed. "Are you sure this is what you want to do?"

I nodded.

"Okay, okay. I don't like it, but I'll do it. Sister for sister.

And I hope this will be worth it in the end."

I smiled. At the end of the day, although what we cared about was totally different, Jade was becoming more like that big sister I'd always hoped for. Sure, she wasn't teaching me about high school or boys or anything like that. But she was letting me make my own decisions, then sticking by me as they played out.

Jade was all right.

Even if she *was* still the favorite.

At least until Handmade was over. Then I'd finally catch up.

Jade chewed on a taro chunk. "When do we need to be at the fair tomorrow?"

"They'll open the doors for booth setup at six p.m. I'm so glad they're letting us in the night before everything starts so we have enough time to get everything ready," I replied.

"It'll be fun to see all the behind-the-scenes," Jade agreed. "Although I've never seen the 'front-of-scenes,' either. This will be my first-ever Handmade Craft Fair."

"You're going to love it," I assured her. "It's so cool to see all the different things people make. And the creative energy is amazing. Priya talks to a lot of the sellers, too, and they have the most inspiring stories."

Jade's head tilted to one side, and her lips scrunched up. "I still don't get it—why isn't Priya coming with you to this? You two go together every year. So what's up?"

I stared at my boba cup, avoiding her eyes. "Actually, we had a big fight a few weeks ago. And we haven't talked since."

"That sucks. Do you want to talk about it?"

I sighed. "She kept insisting that I talk to Mom and Dad about my amigurumi. And selling at Handmade."

Jade chuckled. "Sounds familiar. She has a point, you know."

I ignored her comment and took a sip of my boba. "Well, she wouldn't let up about it. And she keeps pointing out all the times I'm wrong or when I might not be reacting well to what other people are doing or saying. She even called me selfish."

"Ouch, that sounds harsh. She probably shouldn't have said that. But pointing out times you might be wrong isn't an entirely bad thing." Jade slurped up the last of her taro slush and sat back in her chair, crossing her arms above her head.

"What do you mean?"

"Isn't that what good friends are for? To point out both our good and bad sides? I think it's important to have a little creative tension with the people we care about. Caring means we want each other to be the best versions of ourselves. Otherwise, there's no point. You could just walk away if someone you didn't care about wasn't doing what you thought they should."

My glasses slipped down my nose again, and I slowly pushed them back up. I hadn't thought about friendship that way before.

"Are you saying it was a good thing that Priya and I fought?" I asked.

"No, not necessarily. Fighting is a buildup that can lead to some pretty painful words being said."

"Yeah, tell me about it," I mumbled. My face flushed remembering all the mean things I had said to Priya. To Cindy, too.

Jade continued. "It's another thing to talk about your differences and share them constructively. Relationships are easy when you happen to like the same things or think the same way. It's when there are sides of ourselves that don't overlap that we need to work harder to find the common ground."

"Priya and I do love arts and crafts. That part's easy. And she did help a ton with the booth. Most of the booth decorations were her idea," I admitted. "But she doesn't seem remotely interested in the Taiwanese stuff I've been into these days."

Jade leaned forward in her chair, eyebrows raised. "Is she not interested? Or does she need a little more time to understand them and what they mean to you?"

A pit started to form in my stomach, mixing together

with the boba and àiyù jelly that was already in there. Jade had a point.

"I guess it's true that I haven't talked to her about why I like this Taiwanese stuff," I said, thinking out loud. "And I never told her that it hurt a bit that she didn't seem interested in those things at all."

Or how I was jealous of her and her family. And how much I wished my family was like hers.

"Maybe you should, then," Jade said.

Come to think of it, Priya never said anything about Cindy and me, either, and that she had been feeling left out. Maybe we did need to—as Jade said—work harder to "share our differences constructively."

I *was* being selfish. I *was* scared. And I took it out on my knight, when she was trying to help her damsel be braver. And more considerate.

I was a horrible friend. I needed to fix this.

And ASAP. Then we could be together to see Kawaii Crochets in action at Handmade.

"Jade, can you give me a minute?" I asked.

She nodded her head. "Sure."

I pulled out my phone, took a deep breath, and started to write an SMS.

Team Kawaii, I'm so sorry. I've been a jerk. Can we talk?

My finger hovered over the send button for a quick beat. What if they never responded?

But I tapped it anyway.

Like Jade said, we needed to talk about our differences. So we could be better friends.

Maybe I could be the knight this time in our friendship. I could be the one jumping to the rescue to save Team Kawaii.

I stared at the screen for a few seconds, hoping for a quick response. But nothing.

"Well, I sent Priya and Cindy a text," I said to Jade, putting my phone down slowly. "Hopefully they'll get back to me so we can talk."

"Good." Jade smiled gently. "Friendships aren't easy, but they're so worth it." Then she grabbed her empty cup and stood up from the table. "We better head home. Ready?"

"I think I'm going to stick around for a little while longer." I tried to refocus my energy on the immediate task at hand—saving Boba Time. I held up the crochet hook and yarn I'd brought with me. "I've only got a few more rounds to go before I finish this last one."

"Mind if I go then? I've got a few bugs I need to work through before I push out the latest update this weekend."

"Go for it." I flashed her a thumbs-up. "I can walk home."

Jade grabbed our empty boba cups and popped them

into the bin. It was getting a little chilly, so I headed inside the shop with Jade. She waved goodbye to Auntie Cha, and I sat down at a table in the back to settle into the rhythm of my amigurumi.

Only one day left before I could stop crocheting the same things over and over again. I couldn't wait to start looking for fun new patterns to challenge myself with.

I was so close.

CHAPTER
31

I ONLY HAD A FEW last crochet rounds to finish on this panda before I officially hit my inventory goals for Handmade. I'd already stuffed the doll, and all I'd need to do was stitch it tight and add the last little details, like its eyes and felt ears.

Loop, loop, pull it tight.

Loop, loop, pull it tight.

Jingle.

At the sound of new customers coming into Boba Time, I glanced up from my work. It was Auntie Lin and Uncle Zhang from the Cantonese mahjong circle. Instead of matching blue tracksuits this time, they both wore red checkered shirts and black pants.

We nodded politely at each other.

"Welcome!" Auntie Cha greeted them from behind the counter. "What can I get for you two today? Some tea and a few tea eggs?"

"Yes, that'd be lovely. We'll sit over there." Auntie Lin waved back and shuffled toward her usual table, her bag bumping gently against her side.

I checked my phone quickly to see if either Cindy or Priya had responded. But still nothing.

That's okay, I told myself. Maybe they don't have their phones on them.

I turned my attention back to my amigurumi. After I got my yarn needle out from my bag of supplies, I carefully sewed an ear onto the panda's head.

A few minutes later, the shuffling of slippers passed by my table, and I heard Auntie Cha set down the tray with the clinking of teacups. The smell of pu-erh filled the air, and Uncle Zhang sighed at his first slurp.

"Your tea really is the best," he said to Auntie Cha.

I didn't need to look up to know that Auntie Cha was probably blushing at the compliment and waving it off with a toss of her hand.

But, out of the corner of my eye, I saw her suddenly tilt her head in a strange way.

"I see something different about you today. What's this?" Auntie Cha pointed at something hanging off Auntie Lin's bag.

Auntie Lin laughed proudly. "Ah yes, that's a crochet cat that Cindy helped me buy from a shop on the internet." She pulled it off her bag and handed it to Auntie Cha. "Isn't it precious? It looks like the cat I had when I was a young child back in Hong Kong."

I froze. That wasn't . . . my crochet cat, was it?

Before I could put two and two together, Auntie Cha had the cat in her hands and was inspecting it carefully.

I glanced over, and our eyes met.

I looked away quickly.

I stared at my crochet panda and pretended to be totally engrossed in my task.

"You bought this off the internet?" Auntie Cha asked Auntie Lin.

"Yes, well, from someone selling them off the internet. Cindy ordered them for a bunch of us in the mahjong group. What a sweet girl. She even brought them to us. None of us know how that online shopping works!"

Auntie Cha handed the cat back to its owner. "Yes, it is adorable. Whoever made it is very talented."

I prayed she wouldn't stop by my table on her way back to the counter.

But a shadow loomed over me and I had to look up. Auntie Cha had an expression on her face that I'd never seen before. A stern one.

I cringed.

"Pearl, can you help me with something in the back?"

Uh-oh.

I put down my needle and yarn and followed her to the back room. My head swirled—what was I going to tell her?

Once we were out of earshot, she turned around, hands on her hips. "Pearl, you made that cat, didn't you? What's this about an online store? What have you been up to?"

My heart sank.

Then everything came rushing out. Everything, from starting the Craftsee store at the beginning of the summer to making enough for the booth fee to having everything ready for Handmade Craft.

"And I did it for Boba Time, Auntie Cha. I can make enough money to fix your fridge, and you'll be able to keep sending money to your daughter with what Boba Time will be making. It's a great plan, and it's going to work! The fair is this weekend. Everything is ready."

Auntie Cha slowly lowered herself down until she plopped onto a big, industrial-size box of disposable plastic cups. She put her head in her hands.

"Oh, Pearl." Auntie Cha looked up at me with such tenderness on her face that I felt my heart at the brink of breaking into pieces. "And your parents? They know what you are doing?"

I shook my head.

She sighed.

I pleaded with my eyes. *Let me do this for you.*

The seconds ticked by in the longest minute ever. Then Auntie Cha finally spoke. "Pearl, you are a truly amazing girl. I cannot tell you how much it means to me that you care so much. You are like my daughter, who has a big heart like yours and feels so deeply."

My heart leapt.

She was going to let me do this. . . .

"But I have to tell your parents what you are about to do. They must know. For your safety."

My jaw dropped.

"I can't in good conscience let you go to this fair or to sell things over the internet without adult supervision. As I said before, money matters are complicated."

"But I can do it, Auntie Cha. I'm old enough! I know what I'm doing!" I begged, my face going pale. "Jade's helping me. Nothing will go wrong."

Auntie Cha stood up, wiping her hands on her apron. She reached out and touched me gently on the cheek.

"You shouldn't have done this for Boba Time."

Then she turned away and shuffled out the door.

Alone in the back room, I broke into sobs. I couldn't believe it. The person I was trying to help didn't want it after all.

And she was going to rat me out to my parents?

How could she?

My eye caught a ray of light that shone brightly into the dark room. The back door to Boba Time was ajar. The perfect escape.

I pushed my way through it. Blinking at the harsh sunlight in Boba Time's back parking lot, everything blurred together.

Was it all over?

CHAPTER
32

THE LAST SHADOWS OF THE day stretched over Sunnydale as I turned the corner onto my street. I'd spent the last few hours of daylight wandering around the neighborhood, trying to process what had just happened and avoiding what was waiting for me at home.

But now it was time to face the music.

As our house came into view. I recognized the silver van parked behind Jade's as Auntie Cha's, with its signature Boba Time bumper sticker and upholstery covered in a flowered fabric.

She was here.

I slowly trudged my way up the driveway. Then the front door opened and Auntie Cha appeared. She bent down to put her shoes back on, then waved goodbye to my parents. When the three adults spotted me walking up the driveway, Mom's eyes narrowed and Dad's face dropped.

Auntie Cha's, on the other hand, reflected a sad sympathy.

Feeling numb, I forced myself to walk past them and into the house. I plopped onto the armchair in the living room. My parents each took a spot on the sofa.

"Okay, Pearl." Mom looked at me, crossing her arms. The furrow between her eyebrows practically pulsed. "We want to hear it from you. What have you been up to?"

For a split second, I wondered how much Auntie Cha told them. And if there was any way to save this.

But in my heart, I knew it was time to come clean.

I blinked away tears. "I started an amigurumi business. Online first, to see how I'd do."

Mom's face didn't move. "Even after I told you not to?"

I looked down at my hands to avoid her gaze and nodded.

"Speak up, Pearl."

She wasn't letting me get away with not saying anything this time. I summoned up, as best I could, my inner voice . . .

. . . and then, like water behind the walls of a dam,

pushing and fighting to be released, something inside me broke free.

In a rush of guilt and regret, I spilled everything—from pretending to be eighteen years old to getting the account on Craftsee to signing up to sell at Handmade to lying to the organizers about the booth to how much I wanted Auntie Cha to stay in Sunnydale.

"And the Code Together class?" Mom asked, her voice rising.

"I wasn't going to go. It was my way of making sure you didn't come to the fair with me."

Mom pressed her lips together tightly and stared up at the ceiling.

Dad jumped in. "How did you get all the money you needed to make this happen?"

I gulped. What was I going to say about Jade helping me?

No. I wouldn't tell on her. Not after all she'd done for me.

"I made enough on Craftsee. I sold over two hundred dollars' worth of my—"

"I helped her."

The three of us turned around at the sound of Jade's voice. She stood at the living room doorway, her arms across her chest. "Pearl needed some capital to get her shop off the ground, so I gave it to her. Like you gave me some when I started my mobile app."

"Jade," Mom admonished her. "How could you?"

"She needed it, and she had a good business idea. I saw an opportunity." Jade sat in the armchair opposite of mine. "We know what it's like to take a risk and create something new from nothing. Especially as a girl."

Mom's face softened.

I jumped in. "And I did push myself, Mom, like you always wanted me to. Even though I did it with art, I tried something new, something out of my comfort zone. I learned how to use Craftsee and how it worked . . . and I sold enough to register for Handmade."

Dad spoke up. "Well, that *is* something to be proud of, Pearl. Isn't it?" He looked at Mom pointedly.

Mom's eyes bounced back and forth between the three of us—Dad, Jade, and me. But then they landed on the Code Together pamphlet on the table.

And just like that, her face turned into steel.

"No matter what, lying is unacceptable in this family. Pearl, I can't let you sell on Craftsee anymore. And you're not allowed to go to the Handmade Craft Fair this weekend."

"But Boba Time . . ." I protested.

"Lying is never okay. I don't care for what reason. Now, go to your room." She turned to Jade. "You too, Jade. I'm disappointed in both of you."

I rose from my chair like a robot. Jade followed behind.

As we trudged up the stairs together, she elbowed me gently.

It's okay, she mouthed at me.

I'm sorry, I mouthed back to her.

"Maybe it wasn't the best way. But you tried. That counts for something," Jade whispered right before she slipped into her bedroom.

After my door creaked close behind me, I face-flopped onto my pillow and curled up into a ball. Oscar smiled back at me from the nightstand.

I grabbed him and threw him across the room in a mix of anger and disappointment.

Handmade Craft wasn't going to happen. Saving Boba Time wasn't going to happen. Mom was treating me like a little girl again, and she wasn't taking my art seriously.

And now, without the sales from Handmade, she'd never see how much my amigurumi was worth.

I had failed.

CHAPTER
33

AFTER JADE AND I SHUT ourselves into our rooms, muffled sounds echoed from downstairs as Mom ranted and Dad tried to calm her down. At one point, I heard Jade's steps on the stairs and her voice joined them in the living room. They argued for what felt like forever.

I put my headphones on to drown out the noise. I didn't want to hear a word of what they were saying. Hearing their disappointment and anger said out loud was going to make me even sadder.

Not like I'd get what the three of them talked about anyway.

After a night of tossing and turning, I woke up late the next morning to the sound of the garage door closing. Peeking out my bedroom window, I watched as Dad backed our Subaru out of the driveway. Mom typed away at her laptop in the passenger seat.

Today was their big investor meeting. I guess business was business for them, too, even the day after your daughter terribly disappoints you.

Jade's car wasn't in its normal spot in the street, either. The house was all mine to wander around in lonely self-pity.

And still nothing from Priya or Cindy.

I made my way to the basement, where all my decorations and amigurumi were ready and waiting for the tomorrow that wasn't going to happen.

No Handmade.

No Boba Time.

No friends.

I sank to the cold basement floor, hugging my knees. My head spun with a jumble of unanswered questions.

Couldn't Mom see why I did what I did? To save Boba Time? And help Auntie Cha? Did Jade hate me? Did Priya and Cindy hate me?

And why did Auntie Cha tell on me? I get that I lied, but did she not want to save Boba Time, either? Handmade was her only chance.

I was her only chance.

The basement door creaked open. It was Jade, back

from wherever she'd gone that morning.

She joined me on the floor next to my pile of Handmade Craft supplies, then silently put a Boba Time cup in front of me. It was my favorite—green tea with mango juice, extra boba, and a splash of sparkling water.

I drew my knees up to my chest and buried my head into my arms. "I'm so sorry, Jade, for getting you into all this mess."

"Don't worry, Pearl. I can handle Mom and Dad," Jade replied. "I stand by what I did." Her hand squeezed my shoulder.

At that moment, I wanted to be like her more than anything else. Strong. Confident. The opposite of me.

"Are *you* okay?" she asked.

No, I'm not okay, I wanted to scream. *I'm sobbing in the middle of a basement next to a bunch of supplies you bought for me that I'm never going to get to use. And the one place where I feel like a whole person is going away.*

But all I could do was hide my head deeper into my arms. Like a cowardly ostrich.

Jade sat quietly next to me. After a few long minutes, she cleared her throat and spoke. "So, do you want to know where I was this morning?"

"Where were you?" I mumbled.

"Meeting with Mr. Huang. I'm going to be the Code Together Academy spokesperson."

I looked up at her, my eyes growing big. "Really? Why?"

She shrugged her shoulders. "If what I've done with my mobile app actually inspired my own sister to open a business, then imagine how many other girls might do the same."

I gaped at Jade. *I* was the reason she decided to do it?

"It's not something I'm very comfortable with—promotion and all that. But using my success to show other girls like you what they are capable of is worth me being a bit uncomfortable, I think."

Despite my own misery, I couldn't help but smile. "That's awesome, Jade. Congratulations."

She smiled back. "I thought you might want to know. I know it's not what you wanted, but it's something."

My amigurumi problem was still a huge mess. But I felt my heart lighten a bit at the idea that I'd inspired my older sister to do something so brave and good for the world.

I suddenly felt closer to Jade than I'd ever been before. So I asked her one of the questions that had been churning in my head for a long time.

"Jade, how do I get Mom to be as proud of me as she is of you?"

Jade tilted her head at me with a perplexed look on her face. "What do you mean?"

I squeezed my knees closer to my chest. "I mean . . . you're definitely Mom's favorite. With both of you working on your apps all the time, and you becoming the face of Code Together . . . she just gets you. Way more than she gets me."

Jade stretched her legs out in front of her before tucking her hands underneath her knees. "Hmm. I'd never thought of myself that way."

I rolled my eyes. "Come on."

"No, seriously. I don't think I'm her favorite. But maybe I'm the one who's more familiar. Mom can see where I'm going and the challenges I might encounter. But you, Pearl, with your art . . . you're going in a totally different direction."

"I am?"

"Yeah, you are. And I think that scares Mom, because she doesn't know what the future might look like for you. Dad's more comfortable going with the flow, so you don't push his buttons. But Mom's not like that."

"You think that's it? That I scare Mom?"

"I do. And that's a good thing. That's our job as daughters—to challenge our parents."

I chuckled. "Yeah, I guess you're right."

Jade pointed at the melting boba in front of me that I had totally forgotten she'd brought, and I suddenly noticed how thirsty I was. Wallowing in self-pity really does take it out of you.

I took a big gulp, and its light, floral sweetness reminded me how much I loved Auntie Cha's boba. And why I fought so hard for her.

Jade continued. "For what it's worth, I think you're the cool one in the family, for doing the unexpected. Who else would think to crochet cute animals and sell them at a fair to raise money to save a boba tea shop? So keep doing the things that make you happy and keep fighting for the things you care about. Mom will catch up at some point." She nudged me with her shoulder, grinning. "But maybe without so much lying next time."

I nudged her back. "Ha-ha, yeah, I know. And thanks, sis," I said gratefully.

Even though I wasn't exactly sure how Mom would "catch up," it felt pretty good knowing my older sister thought I was cool for making amigurumi.

Jade stood up, brushing off the basement dust from her jeans. "By the way, you might want to pay Auntie Cha a visit. She's pretty worried about you. She asked me a bunch of questions this morning."

I had questions for Auntie Cha, too.

I peeled myself off the basement floor and followed Jade up the stairs.

"Want a ride?"

I shook my head. "I'd rather go alone."

Jade nodded and headed to her room while I pressed the button to open the garage. As the door creaked open, the length of the shadows on the driveway surprised me. It was later in the afternoon than I expected.

After turning on my headlights and taillights, I clipped my helmet on and headed to Boba Time.

When I got there, Auntie Cha had already closed up for the day. But a faint glow from the back door still shone into the shop. I knocked softly on the darkened window. A shadow appeared in the doorway between the front of the shop and the back room. It approached the door to let me in.

Seeing the mop of hair piled onto Auntie Cha's head and her gentle face, I couldn't hold back and burst into tears.

Again.

CHAPTER
34

THE STORE LOOKED SO DIFFERENT in the evening. The fridge loomed like a giant stretching out of the darkness, and the shadows mixed together to create a jumble of shapes that shifted in weird ways whenever a car's headlights shone through from the parking lot.

Boba Time felt so foreign. The only warmth came from Auntie Cha herself. Her eyes held no judgment, only concern.

She didn't say a word. She just handed me a box of tissues and waited for my sobs to subside. It was like she wanted to give me the chance to speak first.

So I asked the one question I couldn't get out of my head.

"Auntie Cha, do you *want* to keep Boba Time around?"

"Of course I do. Boba Time is my blood, sweat, and tears. It's full of fifteen years of memories, of my love for tea, of my experiences here in America. It's part of me."

"Then why did you tell my parents? I only wanted to help. Why won't you let me help you?" I sniffed.

She looked at me tenderly. "Oh, Pearl, I welcome your help. But it must be done right. And for the right reasons."

"But what other reasons do you mean? I want to help you keep Boba Time here in Sunnydale," I protested.

"And is that it?" Auntie Cha's eyebrows raised in skepticism.

I sucked in my breath. She was right. Handmade wasn't just about saving Boba Time. It was also about me. And my amigurumi.

I swallowed. "I also wanted to prove to my mom that my amigurumi is something special," I confessed.

Auntie Cha leaned forward and put her hand on mine. They were warm and soft, like a blanket wrapped around my cold ones. "I had something to prove, too, when I came to America. I told myself for years that I did it to provide for my daughter in the only way I knew how. Which I did. The money I sent back to my sister gave my daughter opportunities she wouldn't have had if I stayed in Taipei."

She sighed. "But I also came to escape. To leave behind the eyes that judged me for being a single mother. To prove to others that I could do more than take care of a child. Now, when I look back, I know that wasn't the right reason to leave.

"I know that you are scared of your mother's disapproval. And that you are sad she is so busy with her business. But at least she is here," Auntie Cha said quietly. "She's only a door knock away, in the same house, in the same country. I wasn't there for my daughter in the way she needed me to be."

"But my mom's not there for me, either, Auntie Cha. She works all the time."

"And have you ever thought about why your mom works as hard as she does?" Auntie Cha countered.

I stared at her. I always assumed that my mom worked as hard as she did because she liked running her own business more than being a mom.

But I had never asked her.

Like she had never asked me about why I liked amigurumi.

"Auntie Cha, why do you think my mom hates my crocheting so much?"

She thought for a moment. "I don't know, Pearl. Have you two talked about it?"

I shook my head.

"Maybe you should," she said softly.

"Yeah, maybe I should," I echoed.

The flash of a car headlight caught my attention and reminded me how late it was getting. I stood up from the table. "I better go, Auntie Cha."

Auntie Cha patted me on my hand, like she always did. "Good night, Pearl."

But before I headed home, I had one more place to go.

No one stopped me when I walked through the doors and past the big banner that read "Welcome to the Handmade Craft Fair!" As I stepped into the main hall, a flurry of activity and excited chatter greeted me. Sellers milled around the exhibition hall, putting final touches on their displays and getting ready for the customers who'd stream through the doors the next morning.

I walked down the aisles, taking in the amazing variety of crafts on display. Row after row of booths boasted an astonishing array of handmade goods, like scarves, jewelry, hanging mobiles, skateboards, pottery, and home decor like throws and pillows.

There was even a booth that displayed the most intricate origami I'd ever seen. When I paused to examine the pieces, the man behind the table smiled at me and handed me a silver-foiled business card. I tucked it into my pocket for Kendall.

Finally I reached Spot 18B. Kawaii Crochets's spot. My spot.

Instead of an empty booth, though, a charming display of small glass jars etched with beautifully intricate patterns stood proudly in Kawaii Crochets's space. The creator had lined them up on crates that had been placed upright on the table, like shelves. As I got closer, my nose twitched with unfamiliar smells, and I saw that the glass jars were filled with something white . . .

The booth was selling scented candles.

The organizers must have found someone to take my spot last minute. But instead of the envy I thought I'd feel, a sense of relief bowled over me.

A twentysomething girl with a long black braid and a big chunky sweater emerged from underneath the table with more glass candles in her hands. Her bracelets clinked together as she placed her products around her display, turning them so they faced the right way.

A lump suddenly formed in my throat. She looked like an older version of Priya.

I missed her so much in that instant. Having a booth at Handmade was her dream, too.

"Hi there," the girl said. "Are you a Handmade seller, too?"

"Uh, no, just checking things out."

"Ah, cool. I'm Mithali, and this is my booth. Well,

what do you think? How's it looking from your angle?" Mithali walked around the table to join me on the opposite side, tilting her head as she surveyed her display.

"It looks great. The patterns on your candles are amazing. . . . Did you etch them yourself?" I managed to eke out.

"I did, all by hand. The designs are inspired by my South Asian roots. My parents are from Jodhpur in India. And here . . ."

Mithali twisted open a jar and held it up to my nose.

The scent of curry and cardamom wafted into the air. I inhaled deeply—it smelled like Priya's house. I could practically feel the love of art that her family shared with each other wrapping around me like a warm hug.

I exhaled slowly. "This smells amazing."

Mithali laughed. "I'm so glad you like it. Not everyone appreciates these scents. But I love them. . . . They remind me of home."

Exactly, I thought.

She twisted the cap back on. "I'm hoping to introduce people from other cultures to this side of myself and my world through these candles," she continued. "So you're not here to sell. Are you a crafter, then?"

Without a beat of hesitation, I nodded. For some reason, I didn't even have to think about how to answer that question. It just came to me, as naturally as a yarn-over crochet movement.

"What do you make?"

I took Oscar out from my pocket and handed him to her.

"OMG, this is adorable!" Mithali gushed. "This is amigurumi, right?"

I nodded.

"That's Japanese, isn't it?"

"Yes, but I'm Taiwanese American. Taiwan was ruled by Japan for a long time, so a lot of Taiwanese culture has traces of Japanese in it," I explained.

"Well, you should definitely sell here someday. You'd do great!"

If only she knew.

"What's your technique? Do you start with a magic ring, or do you prefer a chain ring?" she asked.

"I like to start with a magic ring. It makes a completely closed circle, which is good for the type of dolls I make," I replied.

Mithali nodded approvingly. "I usually make shawls and so I go with the chain. I don't need it so tight at the beginning."

"You crochet, too?" I asked her, surprised at how much she knew about the craft.

"I sure do."

"Why? You're selling candles. What does crochet have to do with your work?"

She started fussing around with her booth display again. "I don't sell only to make money. I have a day job. But making things makes me happy, especially if they represent who I am. No matter what kind of craft it is."

I smiled ruefully. "Yeah, I get it."

Mithali reached into the fanny pack that hung from her waist and pulled out a business card. "Look me up sometime, crafter to crafter. We need to support each other and our art and our cultures! And maybe I'll see you here one day as a seller," she said with a wink.

I thanked her; then she turned back to her booth.

Mithali had spoken to me in a warm and welcoming way, like we were friends even though we had just met. Like we shared something special . . . but also different.

And she was putting her art into the world, with no apologies for how different or foreign it might be to other people.

Because it was what Mithali cared about. And it was true to her.

Maybe I needed to be as brave as Mithali. I'd been so nervous about showing my amigurumi to the world, like hiding who was behind my Craftsee shop or not telling Kendall about my crocheting. And avoiding Mom for so long. Mitali knew her scent combinations weren't for everyone. But she made them anyway. She was even selling them at Handmade.

Priya was right. I needed to own my amigurumi. For me.

For her, too.

And Cindy. Cindy didn't have the same connection to arts and crafts that Priya and I did. But she still appreciated and supported it.

Standing there in the middle of Handmade, surrounded by the crafts that Priya and I loved and shared, an idea hit me for how I was going to make it up to my two best friends.

I needed to bring Team Kawaii back together.

With my heart feeling a thousand times lighter, I turned around to leave.

As I passed by the rows of booths, empty of paying customers but full of excited crafters, mingling and talking excitedly about what was to come, an unexpected spark of energy tingled inside of me. The air practically buzzed with creativity, with community. It was something that I hadn't felt since—well, since before I booked the booth and got so focused on saving Boba Time.

And on proving something to my mom.

This energy was what I loved about coming to Handmade. It was a celebration of handicraft, of taking one thing and making it into something totally new. It was showing the world who you were and what you believed in . . . and giving them a chance to take a piece of you home. And it was a chance to connect with others who loved and appreciated crafts as much as you did—and then geek out together about the details.

It wasn't about proving anything to anyone. It was just a chance to show the world what you cared about.

Jade and Auntie Cha were right. Turning something you loved into a money-making business wasn't easy. My goal of selling at Handmade did change how I felt about amigurumi and the joy that I used to get from it.

I wanted it back.

And I knew what it'd take.

CHAPTER
35

WHEN I GOT HOME, I found Mom sitting alone in an armchair in the living room, staring off into the distance with a mug of tea in her hands. A pot sat steaming on the coffee table.

I knocked on the doorframe to get her attention.

Seeing me, she sighed. "Pearl."

I took a deep breath to calm myself. That meditation app sure was coming in handy these days.

"Mom, can we talk?"

She waved me forward.

"Yes, of course. I need to talk to you, too." Mom pointed to an empty teacup. "Want some tea?"

"Yeah." I poured myself some. Then, heart thumping, I settled onto the couch and conjured up the nerve to look Mom straight in the eyes.

"I'm sorry I lied about the Craftsee store. And Handmade." Tears sprung to my eyes, and I swallowed hard, trying to keep them back.

Mom put her mug on the table and leaned forward, hands clasped. "Why did you do it, Pearl? I don't understand. We could have brainstormed other ways to help Auntie Cha."

"All the things I did—it wasn't only about Boba Time."

Mom waited patiently. "What was it about, then?"

My body tightened, and my throat went dry. Then Priya's and Jade's faces popped into my head. *Just tell her.*

I took a deep, shaky breath.

"I wanted to sell my amigurumi to prove to you that what I made was good. Good enough that people would buy them. A lot of them."

A cloud of silence hung in the air. Mom's eyebrows slowly pinched together.

"Why would you need to do that?"

"Because you hate that I crochet." I couldn't hold back a sob.

"Oh, Pearl." Mom's face fell. She got up to sit next to me on the couch. "Why do you think I hate your crocheting?"

"Your face. It looks so disappointed every time you

see me doing it." I sniffed and pulled off my glasses to wipe the wetness away with the back of my hand. "Then you bring up programming or something technology related. And that crocheting isn't an appropriate activity for a modern girl and that I should do better than make cute stuff all day."

"I said that?" Mom looked surprised.

"Yes, in front of Kendall Stewart that time at Mama Yang's." I tried to put my glasses back on, but they kept slipping off my wet nose. "You're obviously prouder of her and what she can do than of me and what I can do."

Mom covered her face with her hands, then shook her head slowly.

"Pearl, I'm so sorry that I made you feel that way. I don't hate your crocheting. Not at all."

I stared at her, shocked.

She reached out and gently tucked a strand of my hair behind my ear. "You've loved doing crafts since you were little, and you've gotten really good at it. When you started crocheting, I was worried that you weren't trying new things and stretching yourself. That you were staying in your comfort zone."

"But I did push myself. Opening up the Craftsee shop was something I'd never done before," I insisted. "And I had to learn things like how to use product tags and how to ship things. I even turned bad reviews into good ones with my customer service."

Mom's eyebrows popped up in surprise. "Wow, I'm impressed. Is that how you know about SEO?"

"Jade taught me that. Although she didn't know she was teaching me at the time."

A small smile spread across Mom's face. "I'm so happy to hear that you've been learning all these new things. I had no idea." Mom picked up her mug of tea and blew at it gently before taking a sip.

"But, Mom," I pushed, my voice rising, "I learned all these things *because* I ran the Craftsee store. Even though I wasn't supposed to. Why are you so against me selling amigurumi? Why don't you want me to push myself that way?"

"I should have been more honest about that." Mom rubbed her eyes in that tired way she did. "When you asked me about the Craftsee store, I didn't say no because I didn't think your dolls were good. They *are* really cute. That hot dog you showed me . . . I've never seen anything like that before."

I pulled Oscar out of my pocket and handed him to her. "His name is Oscar."

Mom chuckled. "Nice branding. Giving your product a memorable name is really important. And that's not easy to do."

A small flicker of pride warmed my insides.

Then she got serious again. "I was nervous about the logistics of running a business that involved physical products. My whole world has been the opposite, where people only need to download something and that's it. I wasn't sure how I could help you. I realize now that I should have trusted you and given you the freedom to figure it out yourself."

Mom looked at Oscar, who was still sitting in her hands. "There's another reason, Pearl. I also wanted to protect you from the criticism that can come when you put your work in front of strangers. It's hard when someone criticizes something you've made from your own brain, from your own heart. For every hundred compliments I get on our software, there's one piece of bad feedback. And that bad comment feels like it wipes away all the good ones."

I grasped her hand. "Mom, I feel the same way when someone leaves a bad review on my Craftsee store!"

She stroked Oscar gently. "And sometimes, it can get worse than someone criticizing your work. Sometimes, people can get personal."

"What do you mean?"

Mom let out a deep breath. "Some people question my position as a woman founder. They think I can't do as good a job running a company as a man could."

"What?" I whispered. "That's so unfair."

"Yes, it is. And if this business doesn't work, if we don't have a good product, then that'll mean they're right." Mom's eyes turned glassy, and she blinked a few times.

My heart ached, while my insides felt . . . rattled. This was a side of Mom that I'd never seen before. She was always so strong, so sure of herself.

Unlike me.

"But thanks to you, I'm feeling more confident about our product."

"Thanks to me?" My mouth dropped open. "What did I do?"

"You gave me the idea to talk to professional artists, like Mr. Gupta. I actually interviewed him the other day about how he runs his business to get ideas on how to make our product better. And I'm going to add some new features to help people like him. Or like you, if you become a professional artist one day and decide to sell your art."

Hearing my mom call me a professional artist made me feel like I was floating on air. And that I had helped her make her product better?

"Wow, that's amazing, Mom," I managed to say.

"At the end of the day, I wanted to protect you, and the only way I knew how to do that was to say no. But you're right. That was your decision to make, not mine.

I should have told you about what might happen, what people might say, and the challenges you might encounter. Then I should have let you decide for yourself if you wanted to put your work out there or not."

"Yeah. Like you always say, I'm twelve now," I said softly.

Then Mom put down her mug and looked me in the eyes. "Pearl, you've reminded me what being a modern girl really means. It's not about what path you decide to take. It doesn't matter if it's the arts, or tech, or anything else. Being a modern girl is about being brave. It's about pushing yourself. It's about challenging what other people tell you you should—or shouldn't—be doing." Mom gave me a big hug and tousled my hair.

"Even if that person is your mom."

It felt like two huge, heavy bags of rice were being lifted up off my shoulders. Mom approved of my amigurumi, and of my art. I didn't have to hide what I loved doing anymore.

I thought about the conversation Auntie Cha and I just had. And how I could do more to understand my mom a little better.

"Why do you do the work you do, Mom?" I asked.

She paused and seemed to think for a moment.

"I enjoy the challenge," she finally replied. "It makes me feel like I'm doing something good for the world.

I also work so you and your sister can have a better future."

I put my hand on her arm. "I think you're brave, too, Mom. To do what you do."

Mom put Oscar gently back into my hands. "Why do you love amigurumi so much, Pearl?"

I took a sip of tea, letting the warm liquid coarse down my throat. Kendall had asked me the exact same question a few days ago, and I had said that I loved making amigurumi because it made me happy.

That was definitely true. But I felt like I owed Mom—and myself—a more thoughtful answer, one that got to *why* crocheting dolls in particular was so special to me.

"I like making something out of nothing, using materials as simple as a strand of yarn and a crochet hook," I said, thinking out loud. "I like the precision it requires, and that every little stitch you make counts. I like that you can make things in parts, then put them all together to create a complete, cute thing."

Then I thought about Priya and her pastels, Auntie Cha and her special tea blends, and Handmade Craft sellers like Mithali, who used different techniques but still shared the same love of craft. I thought about Kendall and her grandma, bonding with each other over the simple act of folding paper. It didn't matter that they didn't speak the same language. They had art.

"I also really like how being creative is something that connects people, that it's something we can share with each other, no matter what materials or techniques we use," I said.

A grin spread across Mom's face. "The way you describe crocheting almost sounds a bit like coding. I remember how much fun I had learning how to code when I got my first computer. Figuring how to make every character, every line I typed count pushed me to be creative. Coding comes down to ones and zeroes, which is as simple as yarn for you. And then, when all the pieces fit together to make something new and useful . . . it felt so satisfying. The people I've met and gotten to work with over the years is something special, too."

I remembered how Jade's computer screen covered in text reminded me of a crochet pattern. They also looked like gibberish if you didn't know how to read it. But if you did know, then you'd see how every line was important and added up to something really creative.

I guess coding was like that, too.

"I have to admit, I didn't realize how precise you had to be with crocheting." Mom peered at Oscar's even, tight stitches. "I'm sorry for saying that you could do better than cute. Your dolls are both cute *and* extremely well-made, Pearl."

I grinned. "Thanks, Mom."

"No, thank you, Pearl. You've reminded me that running my own business is also fun. Sometimes, it's easy to forget that."

"You and Dad *have* worked a lot this year." I stared at my empty teacup. "I wish you were both around more."

Mom put her hand on mine. "I know, Pearl. That's why I was hoping to go to Handmade with you. I want to do fun things with you and Jade, too, and not work all the time."

I remembered how hard it was that night to stay home and work on my amigurumi instead of going out with Mom and Dad and Jade.

"I understand," I said softly.

"But maybe it doesn't have to be so hard. Maybe we can figure out together how to balance the things we love to do with the people we love to be with." Mom put her arm around my shoulders, pulling me close. "Thank you for telling me more about your amigurumi. I'm glad you have fun doing it. I don't know where you get all your amazing creativity."

I nestled into her chest, like I did when I was younger and got scared during a movie. "I do, Mom," I whispered.

Priya's dad was right. Mom—and Jade, too—made something new whenever they entered code into a computer, letter by letter. I made new things by tying yarn together, stitch by stitch.

The things we loved—programming software and crocheting amigurumi—weren't all that different. We just needed to stop for a minute to see that.

And to share why we loved doing what we did with each other. I didn't know before how much her work meant to her. And how hard it could be. But now I did.

And she knew how much my amigurumi meant to me.

Because I told her.

Even though there was nothing from Handmade to prove how much my dolls, or my amigurumi skills, were worth, Mom finally getting why I loved it was enough.

In fact, it was priceless.

CHAPTER
36

AFTER MY TALK WITH MOM, I stayed up late crocheting in my room. And for the first time in a while, I had a lot of fun doing it.

Because this time, I was making something that mattered. Not something I needed to sell to a random stranger.

The next morning, I texted Cindy and Priya again. It was scary to do it, because it was clear they weren't interested in being friends again.

But like Jade said, if I didn't care, I could walk away. And I did care . . . a lot. I had to fight for them.

Please forgive me, Team Kawaii. I need you two.

I felt tears spring to my eyes as I hit send. Then I put my phone facedown on my bedspread, like it'd hide the truth. The truth that I'd messed up so badly that my friends weren't my friends anymore.

But to my surprise, my phone pinged almost right away. I quickly flipped it over.

It was Cindy. *Pearl, I've missed you! I didn't see your first message. . . . I'm so sorry! My mom had to borrow my phone and didn't tell me you texted. Are you ok??*

When I read what Cindy had sent me, I felt like flying. She wasn't ignoring my messages . . . and she didn't hate me!

I noticed, though, that she sent the text to only me, without Priya in the thread.

Not a good sign.

I typed back: *Yes, I'm ok. I'm sorry for hanging up on you. I know you were trying to help. And you were right about me leaving Priya out. I shouldn't have done that.*

It's ok. I've been wanting to text you but have been afraid to! Apology accepted.

Yay. I'm so relieved. How's Priya?

I bit my lip as I stared at the three dots blinking on my screen while Cindy tapped her response.

Priya's still mad. :(

My heart sank. But I deserved it.

I know, I was so terrible. Can you get her to talk to me?

I'll try.

A few minutes later, Cindy texted back.

I'm meeting Priya at her place in a half hour. She doesn't know you're coming.

Whew. There was a chance I could make things right.

But I still had my work cut out for me.

Mr. Gupta answered the door with a mug of chai in his hands. The gentle look on his face told me that he knew about our fight.

"Pearl, welcome. It's been a while. How have you been?"

I nodded politely. "I've been okay, Mr. Gupta."

Then I paused. Being polite didn't necessarily mean I should lie.

"Actually, I've been better," I admitted. "I miss Priya."

He smiled at me. "She won't admit it, but I know she misses you, too. The girls are downstairs." He waved me in and winked.

At the top of the basement stairs, I took a deep breath. I had rehearsed what I wanted to say on the bike ride over, but my heart still pounded. Would Priya ever forgive me?

Cindy and Priya were lounging on the beanbags on the floor when I showed up, chatting with each other. They stopped the minute I walked in. Cindy looked at me with a hopeful expression on her face. But at the sight of me, Priya's face hardened.

"What are you doing here, Pearl?" she said, folding her arms over her chest.

I reached into my bag and took out one of the dolls I'd worked on all night. Channeling as much of Priya's dramatic energy as I could, I knelt on one knee before her, the doll in my hands, like I was presenting her with a sword.

"Oh, knight in shining armor," I began. "This damsel regrets the pain she's put you through. Will you protect her once again with the acceptance of this gift?"

Priya slowly took the doll from me.

I had made her an amigurumi knight, complete with a crocheted outfit of gray armor, a red cape, and a bright yellow shield. But instead of short brown hair like in the original pattern, I sewed on strands of long black yarn to make it look more like Priya. And rather than a sword, I knit a little paintbrush and stitched it onto its hands.

I wasn't done with my apology, though.

"I'm sorry that I reacted the way I did whenever you suggested I talk to my mom about my amigurumi and about Handmade. You were right—I was scared and selfish and I should have been more open to hear what you had to say." I sat back on my heels and took a deep breath.

"The truth is, I've always been jealous of you and how

artsy your family is. And sometimes I'm not sure if you get how I feel. But at the end of the day, me being jealous wasn't about you. It was about me not being strong enough to stand up for my art." I reached out and gently stroked the hair on Priya's knight.

"I also shouldn't have pushed you so hard to accept all the new things I'd been exploring. It wasn't fair of me to expect you to . . . and I should have told you why those things were important to me, instead of assuming you'd just know." I pulled my hands back onto my lap, sniffing, face flushing.

Priya's face softened, and she looked down at the doll. She stroked its hair gently. "I'm sorry, too, Pearl. I should have been more supportive and not pushed you so hard about your mom. I got so caught up in what I thought was right that I didn't think about your feelings as much as I should have. Or tried to understand where you were coming from."

"You were being my knight in shining armor. Sometimes your damsel needs a reality check. That's what best friends are for, right? The hard conversations," I assured her.

"The hard conversations, huh?" Priya puckered her lips. "I need some practice with those, too. I should have told you that I was feeling left out, instead of holding it in. I think that's why I've been a bit hard on you, and why I was rejecting the things you were trying to get me to like. I think I was trying to hurt you, like how you were hurting me." She picked at the nubs on her rug, avoiding my eyes.

I scooted in a little closer to Priya and nudged her shoulder with mine. "It's okay. We need to be more open with each other and figure out how to tell each other when things are bothering us. I don't want to joust with you that way ever again, my knight in shining armor."

A small smile crept onto Priya's face. Then she grabbed me into a big bear hug and laughed out loud.

I couldn't see a thing through her curtain of hair. It didn't matter, though.

"Oh, Pearl," she hooted. "You're not a damsel in distress, anymore." She let me go and grabbed her new doll, cradling it in her arms. "Not one that needs a knight, that is."

"Well, maybe I just need a different kind of knight now. And you're perfect for the job." I beamed back at her.

For Cindy, I had crocheted a new sloth using purple yarn, her favorite color, and added a pair of dangling, jingly earrings with little bells on them. It looked super silly, which I knew Cindy would love.

She accepted it without a beat of hesitation. "Āiya!" she laughed. "It wasn't the same without you around, Pearl!"

"Āiya is right," Priya joked, nudging me and wiggling her eyebrows at me. "See, I can understand and speak some Chinese, too!"

I joined my two best friends in laughter, pushing up the glasses that had slipped down my nose. Too bad I didn't have my red pair with me to celebrate the moment.

Team Kawaii, reunited at long last.

Whew.

"I really am so sorry," I insisted. "I was such a jerk and shouldn't have yelled like that. And Cindy, I know you were only trying to help. I've missed you two."

"We missed you, too," Priya said. "I've been worried about how you've been doing with your art. And your mom."

"Yeah, catch us up on what has been happening, Pearl." Cindy leaned forward, the sloth in her arms. "What's going on with Handmade? We've been dying to know! Isn't it this weekend . . . like *now*?"

I got up from where I was kneeling and settled into my usual spot on the beanbag chair. I pulled Oscar out from my pocket and started tossing him back and forth in my hands as I told them about all that had happened in the past few days. About Auntie Cha discovering my plans, about Mom taking my Craftsee store away, and about not being allowed to sell at Handmade anymore.

Priya bit her lip. "Ugh, that sucks."

"Yeah, it's a bummer that Handmade's not going to happen . . . and after so much work," I agreed. "I don't know what I'm going to do with all this amigurumi! But, Priya, I did it. I did what you said I should have done since the beginning."

Priya tossed me a confused look. "What do you mean?"

"Auntie Cha made me tell my parents about Kawaii Crochets. But more important than that, I finally told Mom why I loved amigurumi so much. And why I wanted to save Boba Time," I said proudly.

"That's amazing! How did she react?"

I smiled. "Actually, she was pretty great. I talked, and she listened. That made a big difference. After I explained to her why I loved crocheting, she explained why she loves to code. Turns out, creativity runs in the Li family, just in different ways."

"I'm so happy for you! And I won't say I told you so." She winked mischievously.

"That's so great that you finally talked to your mom! That must have been really hard. But . . . what does this mean for Boba Time?" Cindy asked.

I looked at Oscar's happy smile. "I think Boba Time's done. Once that fridge breaks, Auntie Cha won't have the money to replace it. Then she'll lose Boba Time and go back to Taiwan for sure."

A silence filled the air.

"That's terrible. And you had to go through all of it without us." Priya looked down at her hands. "What a bummer about Handmade, especially after you had sold so much on Craftsee and had the booth ready and everything." She waved at the walls of her studio. "One day, when we have enough money, we'll sell at Handmade together. And on our own terms, without adults around to tell us what we can or can't do."

"Yeah," I agreed. "That booth fee was huge. On top of that, I needed an investment from Jade to be able to pay for booth decorations. The Handmade rules around being a kid seller weren't clear, either. It's not fair that kids like us have to go through so many hoops for a chance to show off what we've made and earn a little money."

Priya nodded. "And look at how much you learned about business, Pearl! Wouldn't it be so cool if more kids like us could experience something like Handmade?"

Suddenly, a flash of inspiration hit me. Maybe there *was* a way to make that happen.

And on our own terms.

I jumped up from the beanbag chair, catapulting Oscar into the air.

"Priya, you're brilliant!"

She and Cindy stared at me. "What are you talking

about, Pearl?" Priya furrowed her eyebrows.

"You said it when I first had the Craftsee idea! A craft fair for kids! What if we organized one ourselves? Kids could sell whatever they wanted to make a little extra money, and any money I make could still help Boba Time!"

Cindy's jaw dropped open, and Priya's eyes grew as big as two rice bowls.

"Organize one ourselves?" Cindy sputtered.

Priya flipped her hair back. "Do we know other kids who make handmade stuff and might want to sell something? We'd need a lot of booths, don't you think?"

I thought about Kendall Stewart. She did more than hand-crafted origami; she also made some pretty cool stuff with her 3D printer, like those bracelet charms. The photos Andrea took with her fancy phone were always amazing, and even Nora seemed to know a lot about food and how different dishes were made and how healthy they were. Did the things being offered by kids at this fair have to be handmade?

What mattered was that they sold something that showed off their creativity and their passions. It didn't matter if they used their hands or a machine to make it.

Like Mom and Jade with their coding. Programming apps was creative, too.

"I don't know about handmade stuff," I replied. "But

I bet kids could come up with ideas for something special or creative they could sell. They could even offer a service, like doing something for someone." I tapped my foot, thinking. "Maybe instead of calling it a craft fair where everything has to be made by hand, we open it up and call it a . . . creativity fair!"

Priya leapt up from her spot on the rug, joining me on her feet. "Oh, how fun! A kids' creativity fair—what a fantastic idea, Pearl!"

Cindy stood up, too. "Pearl, you had to pay a fee to get a booth at Handmade. Maybe you could ask each kid who wants a table to pay for one. That money can also help the shop."

"Cindy, you're brilliant, too!" I threw my arms around both of them and squeezed them in the biggest best-friend hug I could manage.

Team Kawaii was back up and running!

And this time, with an awesome set of business partners.

"We need to find a place to do it." I put my finger against my lips in thought. "Like . . . the parking lot behind Boba Time. Yes, that'd be perfect. It's off to the side, away from the main lot. Plus, hosting it there could mean more customers for the shop."

"How would we get the word out? How do we find those kids who would have something creative to offer at our fair?" Priya wondered.

I smiled. I had a feeling that Kendall could convince a lot of kids to book a table or come to the fair. She could also contribute an origami fox or two to the cause. "I'll make a call," I replied, grinning mysteriously.

Putting together a kids' creativity fair was the perfect plan.

Now we just needed to sell the idea to Auntie Cha.

And to my mom. But this time, I'd do it right. No more sneaking around, no more lying. And not because Oscar deserved it.

Because I did.

CHAPTER
37

THE SECOND I GOT HOME, I ran to find Mom. She and Dad were watching TV in the living room while Jade was flipping through a book. I breathlessly explained my idea to them.

"Hmm, that's interesting." Mom turned down the TV. "Do you think there are enough kids like you who would have something to sell?"

"Absolutely. We're all creative in our own ways, and it'd be nice to share that side of us with others," I said. "That's what this fair will do."

Mom smiled. "That's true, Pearl! I like your entrepreneurial spirit. And I bet kids your age could learn a lot from this experience. It also sounds like a lot of fun."

Jade put her book down. "Do it, Pearl. You're ready for it."

Mom stood up and grabbed the keys off the hook by the garage. "Let's go talk to Auntie Cha together. I'll drive you."

But when we pulled up to Eastridge Mall's parking lot, I could tell right away that something wasn't right. As I swung open the car door, I saw it.

A "Closed" sign hung on Boba Time's shopwindow.

But it was three o'clock in the afternoon. Why was Boba Time closed already?

Mom and I peered through the darkened windows. Auntie Cha sat at a table, her head in her hands and a stack of papers scattered about.

Mom knocked on the door. Auntie Cha looked up, then walked over and unlocked it to let us in.

The minute I stepped inside, it struck me how quiet the shop was. It was never this silent in the store, even when there weren't any customers. Auntie Cha always had Chinese music playing, and the fridge hummed day in and day out, filling every corner of the shop with white noise.

The fridge.

I glanced over at it.

It was dark and silent. Broken.

"Yes, it finally happened. The fridge took its last

breath this morning." Auntie Cha sighed.

"I'm so sorry. What does this mean?" Mom asked.

Auntie Cha sat back down and motioned for us to join her. "This is the moment where I need to decide what to do. Stay here and keep Boba Time going, somehow, or go back to Taiwan. I was just going through my records to see where I could find some extra money to fix the fridge. But there's nothing."

"Tell her, Pearl." Mom nudged me with her shoulder.

Auntie Cha turned to me with a curious look on her face. "What do you have to tell me, Pearl?"

I took a deep breath. "I want to organize a kids' fair in Boba Time's parking lot."

"A what?"

"A kids' fair. For kids to sell things they make or offer services for things they're good at. All we'd need is a few folding tables and a way to mark a space where no cars can go. We could charge kids who want to sell anything a small table fee, and that money, and anything I make selling my amigurumi, will go to you for Boba Time. I have a lot of dolls that I made for Handmade Craft that I can sell."

I glanced at Mom, afraid to see her disapproving look from my mention of Handmade.

But Mom just smiled and nodded at me. "I think this is a good idea, Auntie Cha. Pearl is showing real initiative, and you'd be supporting the creativity of kids throughout Sunnydale. And entrepreneurship."

"Yes, we'd all learn about business by doing this," I said, echoing Mom's words. "Maybe it'll even get the word out about Boba Time. Having it in the parking lot would introduce the kids and their parents to the shop."

Auntie Cha stared at her lap. "But I wouldn't be able to sell anything at the fair. And how can I take money for you, Pearl? This is your hard work. You should keep the money you make."

I straightened my shoulders. "Auntie Cha, you've always told me that it's important for kids to make their own decisions. It'd be my money, and I can decide what I want to do with it."

Auntie Cha laughed. "You listen well, Pearl."

I grinned back. "Well, it's good advice."

Auntie Cha paused, her eyes darting back and forth between my eager face and Mom's serious one. She took a deep breath.

"Okay, let's do it. Let's give this new idea a chance. Boba Time deserves it." Then she looked at me with stern eyes. "But only if, Pearl, you understand that what you make at this fair is not a reflection of your talent. Talent isn't about how much money you make. It's about how much you love and care."

I smiled. I knew now that what made my dolls special

were the attention and thought I put into them, like Oscar's mustard strand or designing the knight doll to look like Priya. I hoped I'd make enough money at the fair to save Boba Time.

But I knew that putting my art out there into the open was going to feel amazing, too.

"Yes, Auntie Cha." I nodded. "I understand."

"Then it's on!"

I sighed a big breath of relief. The Kids' Creativity Fair was going to happen.

I still had a chance to save the shop.

CHAPTER
38

IT WAS FINALLY AUGUST 18, the day of the Kids' Creativity Fair! Or 8/18, to look at the date another way.

You'd think someone picked such a lucky date on purpose.

The summer sun shone brightly that morning, and the weather was perfect for a day of selling. The parking lot behind Boba Time bustled with activity, and kids milled around, busily setting up tables.

After I called Kendall and pitched her the Kids' Creativity Fair idea, she jumped at the chance to both sell her and her grandma's origami and to use her popularity (and widely followed social media accounts!) to get other kids to sell, too.

"You can sell 3D-printed stuff, too, if you want," I had

suggested. "Those charms on the bracelet you always wear—you made those, right?"

"I did." Kendall's voice sounded surprised on the other end. "How funny that you noticed! But I made those with my dad, so they're kind of special. My grandma's origami will be perfect for the fair. Plus, it's a great way for her to meet more people here in Sunnydale."

"That works!" I exclaimed. "By the way, the next time Cindy and I watch a Taiwanese or Chinese movie together . . . do you want to join us? Priya will come, too, and we'll have subtitles on for everyone."

Kendall's side of the phone got quiet for a second.

"That'd be great," she finally said. "Thanks, Pearl."

Even though she couldn't see, I had a huge grin on my face. The Queen of Tech would make a pretty awesome addition to Team Kawaii.

As kids started showing up to set up their tables, I was amazed to see how many of my classmates were into making stuff. One group of kids designed and screen-printed funny slogans onto T-shirts, while another group was offering bookings for babysitting and pet-sitting services. Enamel pins, hand-drawn greeting cards, and ceramic mugs adorned a cluster of tables by the parking lot entrance, each run by another Lynbrook Middle School student.

Even Nora Thomas and Andrea Vasquez signed up for

booths. When Nora checked in for hers, she handed me a mason jar filled with what looked like layers of flour, brown sugar, chocolate chips, and other baking ingredients. "Gluten-free is good for your body. So I made these gluten-free cookies-in-a-jar. It's got all the ingredients you'd need and the recipe is taped here," Nora said, pointing at the label.

I had to admit that her idea was pretty ingenious.

Meanwhile, Andrea covered her table with prints of photos she'd taken with her fancy phone and add-on lens. She was offering kids quick and inexpensive photo shoots for their social media profile pics—or photo shoots for their favorite furry pet friends.

I had so much fun seeing what great business ideas my fellow Lynbrook Middle School students had. Even though I passed these kids in the hallways or sat next to them every day at school, I'd never seen them for their passions and interests. They were just kids I happened to go to school with.

Turns out we all had something we cared about and enjoyed making or doing. And could offer to each other.

Scanning the crowd, I spotted Kendall a few tables over and waved hello. She waved back, then continued placing delicate origami pieces on her display. Her grandma sat on a folding chair, fanning herself with a Boba Time flyer.

Next to Kendall's table stood Jade, who was balancing precariously on a chair and attaching a banner to the front of a blue tent. It read, "Sign up at Code Together Academy." Mr. Huang was placing brochures and clipboards around their booth while Mom and Dad milled around, chatting away.

When I announced to my family that I was planning this fair with Priya and Cindy, Jade asked me if Code Together could have a table. "I get it if you didn't want to include us, though. Programming isn't something all that creative," she had said hesitantly.

"Oh, yes, it is," I had replied.

I even gave them an especially big spot.

Mom caught my eye and walked over to Kawaii Crochets's booth. Priya joined her.

"Pearl, your table looks amazing! The nicest one here by far." Mom motioned me to join her on the customer side of my booth.

My stand was pretty amazing, if I do say so myself. A mint-green-and-cotton-candy-pink pastel tablecloth with a pattern of clouds and suns with kawaii-style smiles covered the folding table. Strands of pom-pom garlands hung like an upside-down rainbow across the bottom, and I had stretched a banner with letters spelling out "Kawaii Crochets" between two wooden ladders that doubled as freestanding shelves for some of my dolls.

On the table itself, the vintage suitcases Priya picked out weeks ago sat proudly as the stand's centerpieces. I had propped them open, with the back upright, and I put my animal and people dolls inside. They grinned happily at customers, with the suitcases' red-and-white lining a bright contrast to the dolls' soft colors.

Scattered across the remaining table space were small baskets that held my smaller dolls. The dessert ones were in pink cardboard bakery boxes that I had gotten from Sheng Kee, and the vegetable ones sat in plastic shopping baskets. I even borrowed a bamboo steamer from home to put my amigurumi buns inside. I finally made them after getting the idea at Mama Yang's Kitchen.

This wasn't a booth at the Handmade Craft Fair. But having my closest friends and family see Kawaii Crochets come to life was more rewarding than showing it off in front of the ten thousand strangers who would have walked by it at Handmade Craft.

"Pearl, before the fair starts, I wanted to give you a little something to wish you good luck. Priya helped me with it." Mom handed me a long, thin box. Inside was a row of small pieces of paper, all standing upright. I picked one up to see what was printed on it.

On one side was an illustration of a bunch of my amigurumi dolls, including Oscar. I could see Priya's touch in each sketched line.

I flipped the card over. Printed on the other side, in big bold letters, was:

Pearl Li
Maker of Amigurumi
Owner of Kawaii Crochets

At the bottom was my email address and a link to my Craftsee store.

I gasped.

Mom had made me business cards.

I swallowed down the rush of feeling that surged up my throat. I tried to say thank you, but I couldn't muster up my voice.

Although for a very different reason than usual this time.

Mom pointed at the Craftsee link printed on the card. "Dad and I discussed it, and we'd like to help you with your Craftsee shop. But with our supervision this time. We trust you, but not all the people who are online. You need to follow the rules, too. They're for your protection."

"Yes, Mom," I managed to say. I stroked the business card in my hand. "Thank you."

She touched my cheek gently. "No matter how much

you sell today, I'm proud of you, Pearl." I beamed back at her.

"And don't forget to have fun with your amigurumi," Mom added, smiling. She checked her watch. "It's time to open the fair doors, Pearl. You have customers waiting." She pointed to the crowd of people standing behind the banner stretched across the parking lot's entrance to keep them out until the booths were ready.

I glanced back at Boba Time's dark storefront. With the fridge busted, Auntie Cha couldn't serve drinks anymore. She was only keeping the doors open so people could use the bathroom or buy boxes of tea. We couldn't count on new Boba Time customers to help make the money Auntie Cha needed for a new fridge.

It was up to me and Kids' Creativity Fair now.

I took a deep breath. "Will you do the honors, Priya?"

She bounced over to the entrance. With a flourish of her hair, Priya pulled the banner off and shouted, "Welcome to the Kids' Creativity Fair!"

With that, business was open.

The rest of the day flew by in a blur. A never-ending line of customers kept coming by Kawaii Crochets. The stream of comments and questions was almost overwhelming:

"Aw, look at this smiling donut! It's so cute I could just eat it up!"

"I never thought you could make such adorable things with yarn. All my grandma makes for me is itchy sweaters and scarves."

"Could I make something like this, too? Will you teach me?"

Andrea Vasquez showed up at my booth, too. She snapped a few photos of me and my dolls with her fancy phone and promised to send them to me later. Even Mom, who planned to help Jade answer questions about coding at the Code Together Academy booth, saw the crowd at my table and came over to help me process sales.

All of a sudden, I was the expert in all things amigurumi in Sunnydale.

I won't lie. It felt pretty amazing to talk about my crocheting out in the open like that.

Some took dolls home, while others took business cards and promised to buy something online later. By the time the last customer left, I had sold an entire box of my amigurumi dolls. It wasn't all my inventory and probably not as much as if I had sold at Handmade. But it was enough to feel pretty good.

Tired but happy, Priya, Cindy, Kendall, and our families all gathered inside Boba Time after the other kids had left. The air-conditioning and cold tap water felt so good after a whole day on our feet talking with customers.

I had all the cash I'd collected from the day spread out on the table. I slowly sorted through it all, making sure not to miss a single penny.

"Girls, that was a great turnout!" Mr. Gupta patted Priya proudly on her back.

"Thanks, Dad!" she chirped. "Can you believe it? So many cool things kids were selling! The mayor even bought my pastel drawing of downtown Sunnydale."

Kendall chimed in. "I had no idea that many people liked origami. The blow-up balloons Grandma and I made sold pretty well, especially to parents with little kids." She giggled. "Did you see them around my table? They'd stomp on the ball and then whine at their parents to blow them up again. We probably sold more because the kids kept poking holes in the balloons by accident, which made the parents buy more to keep them happy."

"And your amigurumi!" Cindy hooted. "I saw so many people walking around with them! You were a hit!"

I grinned. "Yeah, they did sell pretty well. Especially all the food ones." I put the last ten-dollar bill on a stack with a flourish.

"Okay, finally finished sorting!" I pulled out my phone and counted up the stack of bills and coins. Then I punched the numbers into the calculator app on my phone.

"Drumroll, everyone!" My friends quieted down and

turned to me with hopeful eyes. I tapped the = sign.

"In total, Kawaii Crochets made . . . eight hundred and forty-five dollars." Mom's eyebrows shot up from the other table, and Dad flashed me a double thumbs-up.

I turned to Priya. "How much did we make from the table fees?"

She checked her phone. "Five hundred and fifty."

I did the math quickly.

That was a total of $1,395. But Auntie Cha needed $2,000 to fix her fridge.

My voice trembled. "We're short about six hundred dollars."

It wasn't enough.

At least this made Auntie Cha's decision to keep Boba Time going or to move back to Taiwan easy. There was no reason for her to stay.

Boba Time was done.

CHAPTER
39

I SHOVED THE LAST BOX of Kids' Creativity Day supplies into the trunk of our family's Subaru and slammed the door shut. The now-empty parking lot looked so strange in the long, early evening shadows. A few hours ago, it was packed full of kids, crafts, and eager shoppers. I had been on top of the world.

But it wasn't enough. Now I wasn't sure what to think about everything we'd accomplished. Or what to feel.

We said our goodbyes after Auntie Cha closed up Boba Time for the night. Priya and Cindy gave me huge hugs and promised to check in with me later. Kendall thanked me for letting her be a part of the fair before leaving with her grandma and dad.

Auntie Cha had given me an especially firm hug as

she locked up the door.

"Don't worry, Pearl," she whispered in my ear. "You did the best you could. I am so grateful for all your hope and work for Boba Time. I am not disappointed. I'm extremely proud."

Her words made my heart ache even more. I had to turn away so she couldn't see the tears that sprang to my eyes.

Then, as Dad started up the car to head home, Mom suggested we have dinner at A&J's that night.

The only thing I wanted to do was crawl into bed and cry my eyes out. But a bowl of warm soup did seem like an appropriate way to mourn my failure.

And it *was* helping a tiny bit. With every savory spoonful, I could feel the disappointment from the day melt slowly away. As my stomach got fuller with each tender beef chunk and thick, hand-rolled noodle I inhaled, my head felt lighter and lighter.

I resigned myself to accepting yet another consolation prize. And this time for failing Boba Time.

And Auntie Cha.

Dad blew at a tangled knot of noodle dangling from his chopsticks. "I know you're disappointed, Pearl. But you still did really well today. Eight hundred and forty-five dollars! That's a lot of money."

"Absolutely! I'm very impressed." Mom chuckled.

"You proved me wrong, Pearl."

It was true. Even though I didn't need a dollar amount anymore to prove what I could do, it still felt pretty good to see so many people excited about my amigurumi.

Jade tapped on the table by her empty cup, and Dad poured it full of tea. "Well, the Li family is all together now. Maybe we can brainstorm other ways we can make up the money Auntie Cha needs for the fridge?"

"You're right, Jade. The Li family is together now." I smiled at her gratefully and lifted up my teacup in a mini toast. "Thank you for helping throughout the day. Even though we didn't save Boba Time, Kawaii Crochets still did pretty well."

"Code Together also got a good number of new student sign-ups." Jade raised up her teacup, too. "I'd say we all did pretty well today."

Seeing my family gathered around the table and grinning proudly at each other lifted more of my disappointment off my shoulders. Everyone had helped me make the Kids' Creativity Fair happen. We were in it together. I wasn't the odd one out anymore.

The image of Auntie Cha flipping through her phone at photos of her daughter flashed into my head. I thought about the tenderness and pride on Auntie Cha's face every time she talked about her daughter and grandchild, and the wistfulness in her voice whenever she talked about the idea of spending more time with them.

Auntie Cha deserved to be as happy as I was with my family.

For the second time in my life, my voice spoke faster than my brain could think.

"I don't want to give the money to Boba Time anymore," I declared.

Jade's mouth dropped open, and Mom choked on the soup she'd just scooped into her mouth. Dad patted Mom on her back and handed her a napkin.

She wiped her mouth and took a big gulp of tea. "What do you mean, Pearl? Saving Boba Time is what you've wanted this entire time. Isn't that what you've done all of this for?"

I took a deep breath. "Yes, that's what I've wanted. But I don't think that's what Auntie Cha wants. I think what she needs is to be with her daughter right now."

I continued. "I want to give Auntie Cha the money so she can buy a plane ticket and go back to Taiwan."

Mom's eyes filled with tears. She reached out and put her hand on mine. "Pearl, that's so beautiful. She'll be so grateful."

"If Boba Time needs to close so Auntie Cha can be with the people who are most important to her, then that's the way it should be," I said. "Auntie Cha's happiness is the most important thing."

Dad smiled at me. "That is so generous of you, Pearl. Yes, I suppose this means Boba Time will close. That's too bad. Didn't Auntie Cha send money back to her family every month?"

I nodded.

He shook his head. "I guess we can't have it all."

I sat back in my chair. It did make me sad that despite everything that has happened, Auntie Cha was still forced to make a decision between one thing she loved, her family, over another thing she loved, her business.

Then I thought about how Priya and Cindy had helped me make both my Craftsee shop and Kids' Creativity Day a success. Jade had called herself my business partner when she helped me buy the booth decorations. Kendall was also a huge help in getting lots of kids to sell and come to the fair.

Although I had tried to save Boba Time on my own, I couldn't.

Even Mom and Dad had each other.

An idea started to crystallize.

"Maybe she doesn't have to give up Boba Time to go back to Taiwan. What if Auntie Cha had someone she could run Boba Time with?" I said. "Like a business partner who could help her watch the shop while she was away?"

Mom arched one of her eyebrows. "Hmm, that's an

interesting thought." She tapped her chopsticks against her plate. "A partner is usually expected to invest some money in the business they're joining. That's the way they show their commitment to making the partnership work."

Dad joined in. "Yes, that's exactly right! Auntie Cha could bring in someone to contribute enough for a new fridge, maybe even some upgrades to the space. Then they'd split whatever revenue the shop made."

"Pearl, that's a fantastic idea!" Mom squeezed my shoulder tightly. "Look at you, my crochet-loving daughter. Caring and creativity together in one package. You've become a true businesswoman."

I felt like I grew a hundred feet tall at her words.

"Shall we share this idea with Auntie Cha?"

I nodded my head. She fished her phone out of her bag and dialed Auntie Cha's number.

"Auntie Cha, can we meet you at Boba Time in a half hour? Pearl has another idea she'd like to share with you—and you're going to want to hear this one." Mom met my eyes and grinned. "Okay, we'll see you there soon." She hung up and gave me a big thumbs-up.

"We're on, Pearl."

On the drive back to Boba Time, I stared at the twinkling lights that bounced off the never-ending chain of strip malls that whizzed by. I wondered which ones hid special shops like Boba Time inside, run by special people like Auntie Cha.

Her energy, her strength, and her support made me feel so safe, especially when I couldn't find my voice anywhere else. She was also what made me fight so hard for what I cared about and to take risks that led me to find the strength inside I didn't know I had.

But she always knew it was in me.

No matter what Auntie Cha decided to do or where she ended up, here in Sunnydale or in Taipei with her daughter, she'd always hold a special place in my heart. She always wanted me to be proud of myself.

And now I finally was.

I reached into my pocket and pulled out Oscar. He'd been my lucky charm this whole time. But as I stroked his soft stitches and knowing smile, I couldn't help but think that maybe I didn't need him that much anymore.

It wasn't luck that was going to make me happy.

Just myself.

EPILOGUE

THE BELL RANG, SIGNALING THE end of the school day. Seventh grade had started a few weeks ago, and I already had a ton of homework to do this weekend. But Fridays are Fridays, and I couldn't wait for some free time to work on new amigurumi projects and process my latest Craftsee orders.

I grabbed my bag out of my locker. But I'd accidentally left a zipper open, and a crocheted cactus tumbled out into a sea of moving pant legs and scuffed sneakers. I scrambled after it.

"What is this?" A pair of fluffy boots stopped in front of the doll, and a tall girl with slicked-back hair in a high ponytail and a string of bracelets on her wrist picked it up. She inspected it. "A crochet doll?"

I held out my hands and motioned at her to toss it back to me. "It's an amigurumi cactus. Her name is Spike." I handed the girl a business card before grabbing Priya's hand as she bounded up behind me. "If you want to see more dolls, or make a custom order, check out Kawaii Crochets on Craftsee!" I called over my shoulder.

Kendall was the one who gave me the idea to offer custom amigurumi through my Craftsee store. Customers could send me a picture of what they wanted, like a pet or their favorite food, and then I'd try to make it. It was the perfect way to challenge myself with new designs and techniques, instead of making the same dolls I'd made before, like I had to do for Handmade. Customers loved getting custom dolls, too, because they were so personal.

In between custom orders, I'd find new patterns and practice by making a few versions, which I'd also put up for sale on Craftsee.

It was a perfect balance of craft and commerce. Challenging and fun, without feeling like an amigurumi factory. And making extra money to spend on yarn and boba was the delicious icing on the cake.

I'm only twelve after all. My future could come later, whatever it might be.

Priya slung her arm around me as we headed outside. "Ha, some damsel! Like I said, you don't need your knight anymore."

"I always need my knight. But not to save me. I can do that myself." I grinned back. "Come on. Let's go find Cindy and Kendall and head to the party!"

By the time we arrived at Boba Time, Mom and Dad were already there, chatting with Kendall's grandma in rapid-fire Taiwanese. Jade was showing something on her phone to Mr. and Mrs. Gupta, and the entire mah-jong group sat in a corner around a small square table, a game already underway. Cindy's dad passed out cups while her mom carried a bowl filled to the brim with a pile of Auntie Cha's tea eggs.

Behind the counter, Mr. Huang, the owner of Code Together Academy, stirred a bubbling pot of boba while Auntie Cha gave him instructions on the right ratio of agave syrup to tea. A brand-new fridge hummed quietly behind them.

Actually, Mr. Huang wasn't just the owner of Code Together Academy anymore. He was also the proud new co-owner of Boba Time. After we shared our idea with Auntie Cha the night of the Kids' Creativity Fair, she agreed to give finding a business partner a try. News of the opportunity traveled fast throughout the Sunnydale Chinese community.

Mr. Huang jumped on the chance to invest in Boba Time. Not only that, he made arrangements with the owner of the barbershop next door to take over their lease when it ran out in a few months. He wanted to turn it into the next Code Together location.

Having the boba shop and academy right next to each other was going to be great business for both. Parents waiting for their kids to finish classes at the academy could enjoy tea at the tea shop. Then, when classes were over, the students could come to Boba Time to enjoy boba and other drinks, too.

Because of the new customers they were expecting, Mr. Huang and Auntie Cha had already started to make some changes to Boba Time. They took my idea of advertising the all-natural ingredients and made big posters of tantalizing food that now hung on the walls. They also made new menus with a ton of pictures to make it easier for kids and adults who weren't so familiar with boba to get a better sense of all the things they could add to their drinks.

The tea eggs and other Chinese snacks were here to stay, though. Auntie Cha had set up a weekly Sunday morning mahjong corner with real, green-felted mahjong tables to accommodate Auntie Lin and Uncle Zhang's mahjong group. They devoured the eggs and kept asking for more Chinese snacks and desserts like boiled peanuts and egg puffs.

The party today was for Auntie Cha. She was getting

on a plane tomorrow to go back to Taipei. Her daughter was going to have her baby in about a month, and Auntie Cha had decided to spend the next six months there to help her and be with her new grandchild. Then Auntie Cha would come back to Sunnydale for six months to run Boba Time.

Back and forth between the two things that she loved the most. The best of both worlds.

"Let's have a toast!" Mr. Huang called out over our chatter. "Does everyone have a cup of tea?"

Priya, Kendall, Cindy, and I grabbed the drinks that were waiting for us on the counter. I lifted up my sparkling mango green tea boba high in the air.

"To a new beginning for both Boba Time and Auntie Cha. We wish you the best of luck in Taiwan and thank you for everything you've done for us here in Sunnydale." Mr. Huang bowed to Auntie Cha. "Gānbēi!"

"Gānbēi!" we shouted, then lowered our heads and hands, too, before taking a sip of our drinks. She blushed and put her hands together in a return bow of gratitude.

Then we each approached her, one family at a time, to say our last goodbyes.

I could hear Auntie Cha thanking Mr. and Mrs. Gupta for teaching her how to make masala chai. Auntie Cha added it to the menu a week ago, and it was selling really well. While it was an easy starter drink for some of Boba

Time's newer South Asian customers, customers of all sorts started ordering it. The blend of warm, comforting spices was perfect for the upcoming fall, and the addition of boba made it a little different and fun to chew.

Kendall's grandma handed Auntie Cha a list of the best tea places in Taipei, and Kendall gave her a small origami lotus flower in a white box.

As they headed out the door, Kendall called out to Priya, Cindy, and me, "Don't forget that we're watching that new Chinese movie at my place tomorrow night!"

"For sure!" I waved back.

After the Kids' Creativity Fair, the four of us started getting together once a week to watch something fun on Netflix together. Turns out although Kendall didn't know much about the latest Chinese or Taiwanese shows or movies, she knew a ton about Korean ones. Priya even found some shows and movies from India that she had heard were good.

We'd switch off who got to pick what we'd watch, and we agreed to turn our phones off so we could enjoy being in the moment. I also managed to train myself to not read the English subtitles whenever we watched something in Chinese. It turned out to be much easier than I thought it'd be.

And it was worth it, because with all of us so focused on the shows or movies, Priya and Kendall started picking up on some Chinese words and phrases! It was adorable. Plus, we each got little windows into different worlds, which was super fun.

It was a win-win for everyone, as Mom would say.

After my parents said their goodbyes, I approached Auntie Cha, just her and me. She wrapped me up in that huge hug of hers, and her usual scent of tea, honey, and herbs surrounded me like a soft, fluffy cloud. I tucked the feeling of her into my memory as tightly as I could.

I sure was going to miss her.

And Auntie Cha deserved to hear me say it. My voice was stronger than ever now. Because of her.

I took a deep breath and looked into her soft eyes. "Auntie Cha," I began. "From the first time I stepped into Boba Time, you made me feel so safe, so warm. You helped me make my first amigurumi, and you helped me turn my art into what it is today. And I've realized that what's true to me is the freedom to do the things I love, and to share them with the people I love. For all this, I wanted to say thank you."

Auntie Cha's eyes filled with tears, and she dabbed at them softly with the sleeves of her blouse. "Oh, Pearl. You're the one I should thank, for what you've done for Boba Time. You will always be my American daughter . . . and I'm grateful that you chose to walk through Boba Time's doors that day."

We smiled tearfully back at each other. Then I remembered.

"One last thing, Auntie Cha." I handed her two bags. "I have some presents for you. One is for your daughter, and one is for you."

She reached into the first bag and pulled out a yellow amigurumi rabbit rattle.

"Oh, Pearl, it's precious. The baby will love it." Auntie Cha shook it to hear the delicate clinking sound.

Then she reached into the other bag . . .

And pulled out Oscar. She gasped.

"Oh, Pearl, I can't take him to Taiwan! He's your favorite!" Auntie Cha tried to shove him into my hands. Laughing, I hid them behind my back and shook my head.

"He was my good-luck charm when I needed it," I explained. "He'll bring you good luck, too, in your new life."

Auntie Cha wiped a tear from her eye. "Xièxie, Pearl, for this special gift. I hope you never forget how caring and talented you are, no matter what anyone tells you."

Deep in my heart, I didn't need anyone to tell me that anymore.

I already knew it.

I smiled back at her, and then at Oscar, one last time.

"Take care of yourself and of Oscar. He deserves to

see Taiwan. And to get to know the Taiwanese side of himself better."

I winked at Auntie Cha.

And Oscar winked back.

ACKNOWLEDGMENTS

When I first decided I wanted to write for kids, I was laser-focused on picture books. The idea of a whole novel, with no visuals and thousands and thousands of words, never crossed my mind as something I could ever write, let alone get onto bookshelves. Then my agent, the wonderful Jamie Weiss Chilton, dared to suggest I consider writing long-form so I could tackle some of the more complicated and nuanced themes that my early writing veered toward.

For planting that seed and helping me discover the joy of writing middle grade, I owe the biggest thanks to you, Jamie. I'm so fortunate that I happened to pass you on the way out of the Big Sur workshop that year and you said those hopeful words to me, "Please keep in touch." Your patience, encouragement, and critical eye continue to push me to become a stronger writer and bolder thinker, and I couldn't have done any of this without you and the ABLA family.

To my editor, Jennifer Ung, wow, oh wow. Every interaction we have shines with your love of this story, of Pearl and of our shared identities as proud Asian Americans. Your guidance has made Pearl Li and her world pop brighter than I could have imagined. Celina Sun, thank you for all your thoughtful feedback and for your help with the pinyin! Kat Tsai, you've captured the essence of Pearl and the energy and heart of this story so beautifully in your cover, and thank you to Kathy Lam for your meticulous attention to craft and detail in designing this book.

To the Quill Tree and HarperCollins teams, I'm so lucky to have your support and passion. Thank you for doing so much to get this book into the hands of real readers!

Behind every writer is the support and camaraderie of their writing communities. Laura Lee, you were the first flesh-and-blood person I knew who actually wrote a book and got it onto bookshelves. It wouldn't have occurred to me to dream of doing the same if you hadn't done it first, so thank you for showing me what's possible. Arree Chung, you were the second person I met in my kidlit journey, and it was your guidance on the craft and business of writing stories for kids that took me and my writing to the next level.

You also introduced me to Belen Medina, who's been my tireless advocate, critique partner, and friend as we both navigate this world of kidlit publishing. The world is going to absolutely fall in love with your beautiful stories, and I can't wait to keep building our long, productive careers as creatives together.

When I first put pen and paper on Pearl's story, Carrie Jones's encouragement gave me the energy, joy, and confidence I needed to actually finish the whole thing! You were the best writing coach I could have asked for. Bethany Hegedus, without the Writing Barn's WSS program, this book might never have come to life. To Sana, Claire, Kirsten, Susan, Marzieh, Adaela, Gen, Deb, Linda, and JoAnn—thank you for your thoughtful critiques on my first attempts to craft this story.

The intersection of the arts, technology, and business have always fascinated me, and it's funny to look back and see how all the dots in my professional career eventually connected and led me to anchor on those three themes in my first novel. To all the amazing creatives I've had the pleasure of working with over the years, you inspire me.

To my family . . . Lisa, thank you for being the first

Chen to read this story! Mom and Dad, you encouraged me since I was a young child to draw, paint, and make crafts. For that, I'm eternally grateful. Ironically, it was that freedom that led me to the emerging design and tech world as a young adult, which then pushed me to want to understand business as well.

Alex, you never doubted that I could do this. Thank you for putting up with my random meanderings as I geek out about the creative journey I've embarked on. I feel your love and support in every fiber of my being. And to my amazingly creative, smart, and cuddly grinch—I write my stories for you, so that you can see yourself in the books you'll be able to read on your own one day.

Twenty years ago, I'd go to a tea shop in Cupertino Village with my college friends and we'd chat with the owner as she prepared our drinks. Her hair up in a messy bun, she'd bustle about her shop, taking shots of tea to make sure your drink was just right. Your dedication to your craft struck me and has stayed with me over the years. I hope this story somehow makes it into your hands.

And finally, to every young reader who picks up this novel and sees a piece of themselves in it, I hope, with all my heart, that you dare to dream big and pursue your passions. There's a place for you and your layered selves in this world, I promise.

GLOSSARY OF BUSINESS TERMS

Best Practices: methods to run a business that have been generally accepted as best-to-follow

Business Partner: someone with whom a business is shared, usually through co-ownership

Capital: money needed or used to start a business

Expenses: money that is spent by a business in order to make money, or revenue (common expenses include the cost of materials and labor if people are hired and paid to help run the business)

Inventory: all the items, goods, merchandise, and materials held by a business for selling to earn a profit

Investor: a person or company that contributes money to another business in hopes of making more money

Pilot Test: a type of software testing where a group of

users are invited to use a software before it is widely available to the public to gather feedback and identify bugs

Profit: the difference between the money that flows into a business (revenue) and the money the business spends (expenses); profit is how much money your business actually earns

Revenue: the amount of money that flows into a business, usually in the form of sales

Revenue Projection: an estimate of how much revenue a business is expected to make over a certain period of time

Search Engine Optimization (SEO): the practice of getting a webpage to come up higher on the results page of an online search

Sole Proprietor: a person who owns and runs a business by themselves

HOW PEARL CALCULATES PROFITS FOR KAWAII CROCHETS

Kawaii Crochets Sales

	Item	Revenue	Expenses		Sent?	Profit	Total Profit
			Shipping Fee	Craftsee Transaction Fee (5% of Revenue)			
1	Robot	$10	$3.00	$0.50	✓	$6.50	$6.50
2	Cow	$15	$2.00	$0.75	✓	$12.25	$18.75
3	Donut	$15	$2.50	$0.75	✓	$11.75	$30.50
4	Avocado	$15	$3.00	$0.75	✓	$11.25	$41.75
5	Octopus	$15	$2.50	$0.75	✓	$11.75	$53.50
6	Unicorn	$15	$3.00	$0.75	✓	$11.25	$67.75
7	Honeybee	$15	$3.00	$0.75	✓	$11.25	$76.00

The formula to calculate profits is revenue minus expenses:

Profit of Individual Item = Revenue - Expenses

= Revenue – (Shipping Fee + Craftsee Transaction Fee)

= Revenue – (Shipping Fee + (5% × Revenue))

Example—Robot:

Profit = [$10.00 – ($3.00 + (0.05 × $10.00)) = $6.50]

To keep calculations simple in this story, material expenses were not deducted from Pearl's sales chart. For Kawaii Crochets, the cost of yarn, felt, crochet hooks, and stuffing could be subtracted from revenues to calculate profit.

AUNTIE CHA'S SPARKLING MANGO GREEN TEA BOBA RECIPE

Below are instructions to make Pearl's favorite Boba Time drink. One of the great things about boba, however, is that you can adjust the recipe to be just right for you! So feel free to experiment with different flavors and combinations.

Please be sure to ask for help from a trusted adult when preparing this recipe. Have fun!

This makes a single, 16-ounce serving of boba tea.

INGREDIENTS

Green tea (Auntie Cha uses loose tea, but a tea bag is perfectly acceptable)

1 cup of diced, ripe mango (fresh or frozen, but if frozen, thaw it first)

1/3 cup of uncooked tapioca pearls

agave syrup or honey

sparkling water

INSTRUCTIONS

1. Steep the tea:

Follow the steeping instructions of the tea you've chosen, but use half the amount of water (you'll be adding sparkling water later).

Put the tea in the fridge to cool it down while you prepare the other ingredients.

2. Prepare the mango puree:

Put the diced mango into a blender and blend until smooth. Set aside.

3. Make the boba:

Boil four cups of water on high heat in a small pot or saucepan.

Add the uncooked tapioca balls and stir them a bit so they don't cook in a big lump. Be careful when you stir, though—the water is hot!

When the boba floats to the top, turn the heat to medium and cook for another twenty minutes.

Turn off the fire, cover, and let the boba cook for another fifteen minutes (you can cook it for longer or shorter depending on how QQ, or chewy, you would like the boba to be. Cooking longer makes it softer and less chewy.)

Strain the boba and toss gently with cold water.

Dribble some agave syrup or honey onto the boba and toss. This will coat the boba so the balls don't stick together.

4. Assemble the drink:

Pour the mango puree into a serving glass. Add the cooled green tea and mix.

Spoon the boba inside and stir.

Fill the rest of the glass with sparkling water.

Sweeten to taste with agave syrup or honey. Stir gently, though, so the water stays bubbly.

Enjoy!

Some other fun things to try: add a splash of milk, puree other fruits with the mango (Pearl likes coconut or strawberries!), or use flavored sparkling water.